# KILLING TIME

## RUSSELL C. CONNOR

"Weak Will" originally published in *Sanitarium* Issue 2
"That Old Rugged Cross" originally published by *Burial Day
Books* at www.burialday.com

# DarkFilament.com

Contact the author at
facebook.com/russellcconnor
Or follow on Twitter @russellcconnor

Cover Art by SaberCore23 Artwork Studio
For commissions, visit sabercore23art.com

ISBN:
978-1-7331133-6-6

Second Edition: 2019

# Praise for Russell C. Connor's Work:

## Good Neighbors

"Connor's ability to richly develop each character and plot thread is fascinating even when the horror is reserved... the constricting pressure as the dread piles on makes this book hard to put down and even harder to go to sleep after reading. This is a great novel..."
-David J. Sharp, *Horror Underground*

## Second Unit

"Intricately plotted and vividly layered with suspense, emotional intensity and strategic violence."
-Michael Price, *Fort Worth Business Press*

"Drips with eeriness...an enjoyable book by a promising author."
-Kyle White, *The Harrow Fantasy and Horror Journal*

## Finding Misery

"Major-league action, car chases, subterfuge, plot twists, with a smear of rough sex on top. Sublime."
-Arianne "Tex" Thompson, author of *Medicine for the Dead* and *One Night in Sixes*

## The Jackal Man

"Connor delivers a brisk, action-packed tale that explores the dark forests of the human--and inhuman--heart. Sure to thrill creature fans everywhere."
-Scott Nicholson, author of *They Hunger* and *The Red Church*

Also by Russell C. Connor

*Novels*
Race the Night*
The Jackal Man
Whitney
Finding Misery*
Sargasso*
Good Neighbors
Between
Predator

*Collections*
Howling Days*
Killing Time*

*The Box Office of Terror Trilogy*
Second Unit*
Director's Cut

*The Dark Filament Ephemeris*
Volume I: Through the Deep Forest
Volume II: On the Shores of Tay-ho
Volume III: Sands of the Prophet
Volume IV: The Halls of Moambati

*eBook Format Novellas and Shorts*
Outside the Lines*
Dark World
Talent Scout
Endless
Mr. Buggins
The Playground

*Indicates Dark Filament Ephemeris supplementary connection

# Table of Contents

# Outside the Lines

# I. The Chase

The kid with the gun shoved Andrew out of the way in front of the bank teller's window.

Of course, he didn't *know* the kid had a gun, not then. He was in the act of putting the final flourish of his signature on a check when a hand fell on his shoulder. The world tilted violently, and he had to move fast just to keep from sprawling across the slick tile.

He swung around, ready to let loose a tirade, but, when he registered the weapon, the words evaporated on his tongue. A steely cold slipped over him, and he moved Joey behind him, shielding the boy with his body.

With his free hand, the kid tossed a balled up plastic bag over the desk at the teller, a small man with square glasses and an epic comb-over. It smacked him right in the face, but he didn't even flinch. Instead, the teller's mouth swung open like the gaping maw of an airplane hangar as he looked down the barrel of the revolver pointed at his forehead.

"What're you waitin for?" the kid yelled. His voice was shrieky with urgency. "Put the money in it before I give you a closed casket funeral! And if you hit the alarm, you're fuckin dead!"

The teller jumped and nodded quickly, his jaw so loose it waggled independently from the rest of his head. He reached into his cash drawer and drew out fistfuls of money.

The First Regions Bank was a tiny, independent unit off the access road to 280, just before the Steinman exit. Andrew opened his account at the sleepy location a couple of months ago, after he moved into the city, and had never seen more than one teller assisting customers at any given time. If there was anyone else in the bank beyond the open doorway behind the counter, he didn't know.

While the teller finished dumping bills into the plastic bag, Andrew took the opportunity to examine the punk, committing details to memory.

He was young, but only a 'kid' in comparison to Andrew himself. Probably no more than twenty, slightly acne-scarred face, three-day-old scruff along his angular chin and cheeks, stud earring, shoulder-length blond hair. Wearing a ripped Anarchy Club t-shirt, jeans and sneakers, with a gun bigger than he was. The moron hadn't even worn a mask. Even in a small bank like this, the cameras would record every pixel of his face for playback in front of a jury. Then again, Andrew marveled at the fact that anyone tried to rob banks at all anymore; the technology was just too severe, the police response too quick, and only one in twenty actually got away with it.

And the police response today was going to be *lightning* fast. Record time, in fact.

The kid noticed his scrutiny. He fixed Andrew with the pair of bloodshot marbles in his skull. "What are you lookin at, Jap?"

"Nothing," Andrew said, wanting to say more, or at least correct the little shit stain on his nationality. But now, with his eight-year-old son hidden behind him, was not the time to piss this guy off.

"Daddy, what's goin on?" Joey asked, trying to peer around his father's waist.

"Stay back, son." Andrew pushed his head away so the boy couldn't see the tableau in front of them.

"Cute kid," the bank robber quipped. "Keep him that way and just…mind your own business."

*Go for your piece*, Andrew's head screeched, but he ground his heel into that impulse like he would a discarded cigarette. The threat, no matter how carelessly tossed out, put him on such a strong defense he was close to losing control. But he could not—*would* not—make a move, not with Joey anywhere close to danger. With only the three of them in sight, the punk might decide his chances at escape would be better if he just killed them all, or he might want a lightweight and easily manageable hostage. Andrew didn't want to put the idea in his head.

But once he left…it was open season.


The goddamn teller was taking so *long*.

Ronnie Pearson had discovered that people underwent a metamorphosis to rival Kafka when you stuck a gun in their face, and one of two personalities emerged: those that kept their cool, gave you what you wanted, and got you out of their lives, and those that locked up tight with fear, suddenly had trouble thinking about anything other than their pathetic existence and how they never saw Venice, and generally had to be slapped around a few times before they came out of their trance.

The teller was looking to be one of the second variety.

"C'mon, move it, or you're not gonna have to worry about that gaping bald spot anymore." He felt antsy. He wished he'd smoked some pot before walking in here, but there had been little time for anything but a few tears.

The clock in his head was doing laps at warp speed. Every second he spent in here only increased his chances of getting caught. He'd wanted to find a convenience store, a Mickey D's, a Walmart, something where the collective IQ of the employees was close to that of farm animals, but funds from those kinds of establishments were next to nothing. He'd be forced to hit every cash register between here and his brother's place in Tijuana just to get there. Better to make one big score and *drive*.

He felt eyes crawling on him again.

That was what worried him, the damn muscle-bound Jap beside him. Hard to tell age since all these Asians looked the same, but Ronnie thought he must be in his late-thirties with a kid that old. The guy was thick across the shoulders, beefy arms, mocha skin, black hair shaved practically bald, wearing khakis and a dark blue polo. Big enough to use him as a toothpick, if circumstances were different.

The thing was, he acted too calm for Ronnie's comfort, like he was used to this sort of situation. Or having notions of being a big American action hero, with his name in the paper and the key to the fucking city.

Maybe Ronnie had the gun on the wrong person. Sometimes it took a little pressure before one of those two reliable personalities surfaced. *Might even be fun to see if you can make the guy cry in front of his son.*

He opened his mouth to issue another threat, but the teller cut him off by squeaking, "H-here." The man held the bag of cash out for him.

Ronnie grinned. Easy as pumpkin pie with a side of whipped cream.

He snatched the sack and backed away from them, waving the gun from teller to customer. The teller put his hands in the air as soon as he freed them of the cash, his eyes as big around as dime bags. That was good, that was comforting, that was just the way things should be in the world.

The Jap though…he didn't look scared in the least.

Ronnie didn't like it.

His back was against the glass entrance door, and freedom was on the other side. He said, "Don't hit any alarms, don't call any cops, and I won't have to come back in here, okay?"

After this last mandate, he pushed through the door and fled to his ride.

Though it seemed interminably longer, the whole ordeal lasted less than two minutes.

The tension whooshed out of the room like a gale force wind as soon as the crook exited, leaving the poor teller as limp as a marionette with no puppeteer. Andrew knelt, pulled his nine-millimeter from the ankle holster he wore when he was off duty, and stood back up.

The teller gave a miniature shriek of terror when he saw it, and shot his hands back up in the air.

"Relax, I'm a cop," Andrew told him. He pulled his wallet and flipped it open, displaying his shield in a flash of silver. "You already hit the alarm?"

The teller took a full five seconds to digest this question and then his hands worked beneath the counter. He nodded so hard, drops of fear sweat flew from his sparse hair. "I d-did it now! I should call the security company also!"

"When you talk to them, tell them Andrew Horner, officer number 1705 from Glendale PD precinct 15 is in pursuit in plainclothes. I'm driving a black 2004 Ford F-150 pickup. You got all that?" The teller nodded again, but Andrew knew he would be lucky if half the message got relayed with the shock the man was in. It didn't matter; Andrew would call himself once he got to the cell phone charging in his glove compartment. From the hallway door behind them, a scared female voice asked if everything was okay, but both Andrew and the teller ignored it. "I'm leaving my son here with you. I need you to watch him until the police arrive and then turn him over to them."

"Daddy, where are you goin?" Joey demanded, pulling on the pocket of his jeans.

Andrew turned and hunkered in front of the boy. This was all happening so fast, events spinning out of control on what was supposed to be a simple trip to the San Diego Zoo with his son on his day off, but that old sense of civic responsibility—what Michelle called his, 'incessant need to balance the world' just before she'd left him—screamed at him not to let this punk get away, to show him he had picked the wrong bank on the wrong day.

"It's gonna be okay," he told Joey, holding the boy by the shoulders at arm's length. No one would ever mistake them for blood relatives; the boy had more of his mother's soft American features than Andrew's rugged mongrel looks.

But this was his son, clutching the latest coloring book he'd been working at for over a week now, carefully filling in each page and getting upset when he made the slightest error. The boy would be an artist someday, but for now he just didn't have the dexterity needed to keep from going outside the lines.

Joey's face fell, already reading everything he needed to know from the avoidant nature of his answer. "We're not goin to the zoo?"

"No, we will, I *swear* we will. Daddy just has to do one thing real quick. Right now I need you to stay here and go with the policemen that show up until I come to get you.  I need you to be brave for me, big man. Can you do that?"

Joey nodded seriously. "Are you gonna get that bad man?"

"Yeah," Andrew said with a grin. "That's exactly what I'm gonna do." He hugged the boy to him, overcome with sudden love. "I love you kiddo, you remember that. And… and you tell Mom that too, okay?" That last part had been blurted, and he had no idea why it slipped from his mouth.

Joey wrapped thin arms around his neck, and Andrew patted him on the back between the shoulder blades.

He released the boy and ran out of the bank with his pistol pointed skyward.


The damn car wouldn't start.

It was a 1987 Mustang, the boxy body style that most people hated. One of Ronnie's few legitimate possessions. She looked like a dream, but the cherry red paint job was the best thing about her. He did most of the work on it himself, treated it better than he had any woman in his life. Most of the dollars he'd managed to get his hands on in this miserable world had been poured right into this vehicle, for him to roam the highways of the U.S. of A.

And during her first bank robbery, she decides to crap out on him.

"C'mon baby, c'mon," he muttered through clenched teeth and turned the key again, listening to the inexplicable sputtering beneath the hood. The money and revolver lay in the leather passenger seat where he'd tossed them.

He sensed movement through the passenger window, and looked up to see the doors of the bank flying open and the muscle-bound Jap come running through. There was something different about him this time, and it took his dumbfounded senses—still soaring high on adrenaline—a full three seconds to figure out what it was.

The man had a fucking gun.

He spotted Ronnie, twenty yards away, leveled the pistol in his hand, and shouted something so unmistakable, that even though Ronnie couldn't hear it through the glass, the guy's shooting stance—legs in a perfect vee, free hand supporting the base of the pistol's handle—provided flawless interpretation.

*"Freeze, police!"*

Suddenly his cool-as-ice demeanor in the bank made perfect sense.

He wasn't just a muscle-bound Jap.

He was a muscle-bound Jap *pig*.

*That's fuckin perfect Ronnie-o. You robbed a bank with a cop already in it. A real time saver, you know? You'll be eating your first shitty meal of many behind bars by lunch.*

His eyes rolled in their sockets, and landed on the revolver in the seat next to him. Sunlight winked off the burnished silver barrel.

He'd had the thing longer than the car and never had to fire it; brandishing was always sufficient. He'd never even fired it for practice.

*You kill him, and that ten-to-twenty is gonna be life. Or death.*

"Only if I'm caught." He picked up the gun and opened fire right through the rolled-up passenger window.

~ ~ ~

Andrew had never shot at a single person in the line of duty; he certainly had never been shot *at*. The experience—practiced a hundred times but never undergone for real—did not inspire the terror he was afraid it would. He had more care for Joey's safety than his own.

He'd expected a getaway driver and for the kid to be long gone, but he was alone. He did freeze for a moment in his blindingly red Mustang (*congrats, genius, let's see you elude the cops in* that *thing*), but only to debate if he wanted to risk that Andrew wouldn't just blow him away before he could get his gun up. Andrew considered doing just that, but either his training or his moral compass kept him from squeezing the trigger.

He was already diving to the blacktop when the first shot blew out the passenger window. A microsecond later, one of the doors of the bank shattered as well, dropping shards of tinted glass across the parking lot. Andrew knew a lot of armed robbers used unloaded weapons so they could plea bargain in the event of their capture, but not this guy though; oh no, the punk was packing grade A heat.

No cover anywhere. Andrew kissed sun-heated concrete while a second and third shot rang out. He hit his shoulder hard enough to rattle teeth when he landed, and tore the knee out of his khakis along with a layer of skin, but he ignored the pain. He had to keep moving, keep the guy focused on him and not let any more stray shots go through the bank building's all glass exterior. He rolled toward the vehicle, intending to stay out of the line of fire beneath the level of the window. He came to rest with his sore shoulder against the guy's rear tire.

Silence stretched into infinity.

He gripped his pistol and waited to see what the kid would do.

The engine throttled to life, there was a burst of raucous music, and then the Mustang peeled out of the lot, laying down an inch of rubber beside Andrew's prone body.


Ronnie wasn't prepared for the weapon's massive recoil, but the shots gave the pig something to think about. He twisted the key frantically in the ignition until he was sure it would break.

Instead, the engine screamed to throaty life, and the car was filled with the raging voice of the god of metal himself, Mr. James Hetfield, growling about how someone needed to give him fuel, give him fire, and right now the words of the man Ronnie had worshipped since he was old enough to steal CD's had never seemed wiser or more applicable.

He threw the car into gear. The cop got to his feet in the rearview mirror, aimed the pistol again, but the dumb fuck never fired a shot.

Ronnie laughed aloud, and even above the blessed shrieks of Metallica, he could hear a crazed note in it that made him uncomfortable, as if a stranger had borrowed his vocal chords.


Andrew's truck was parked in the space closest to the door. He sprinted to the driver's side, jumped behind the wheel, and set his pistol on the passenger seat as he started the engine.

The bank's parking lot opened directly onto the access road for 280 Southbound. Traffic wasn't too heavy for a Saturday, but deep enough that pursuit would be dangerous without sirens and lights. The nearest onramp was a good distance down however; if he could delay the kid long enough, backup should be available to take over within minutes.

But as soon as he jumped the curb, slewing sideways onto the road and pushing his V6 as hard as it would go, he understood what a fantasy this was. The Mustang was a blur, tearing up the pavement as it sped away in a spurt of exhaust. The best he could hope for was to keep the guy in sight.

Andrew reached across the seat, leaning so far that his head slipped below the level of the dashboard, and opened his glove box. His silver Nokia was right on top, nestled among insurance paperwork, receipts for auto repair, and a spare pair of handcuffs. He snagged it with one finger and straightened up, already flipping open the phone so he could dial.

His eyes landed back on the road, and he felt something in his bowels loosen.

The Mustang crawled along right in front of him. He was seconds away from ramming it at sixty miles per hour.

He yelped and yanked the wheel to the left while standing on the brake. The cell phone dropped from his hand, bounced off the seat, and disappeared into the passenger floorboard.

He heard a demonic screech. Sparks flew up beside his window as the front end of the truck grinded against the side rail. Andrew cursed. He felt the rear end start to slide around as the vehicle tried to go into a spin. It came to a stop at an angle with his passenger door just short of the Mustang's rear bumper.

Andrew looked out the passenger side window—now facing the suspect—and saw the kid lean out of the car with the revolver.

~ ~ ~

Ronnie smirked as the truck bounced onto the onramp after him. There was no way the pig could catch him in that thing, and, as of yet, there were no sirens, no flashing lights, and no helicopters.

Which meant if he lost this lone Jap pig, this John-Mc-Clane-wannabe, he was free.

This is when the Mustang decided to tell him what it thought about the whole shebang, in the voice of an asthmatic old man. Ronnie's mouth flapped in an endless string of obscenities. The steering wheel shook in his hands, all the way down the base of the column. Thin wisps of smoke curled out from under the hood, and Hetfield's chorus on "Memory Remains" cut out between every other syllable.

He felt the power go out of the gas pedal. The engine fell silent. He was coasting along at a mere thirty miles per hour and dropping fast.

"Start, you piece of shit!" he yelled, turning the key. Nothing. He glanced in the rearview mirror and saw the Ford pickup coming fast.

Too fast. And it didn't even look like there was a driver behind the wheel.

For a split second, Ronnie entertained the action-movie notion that the pig actually dove out of the truck in order to ram him, but then the fucker sat back up. Surprise passed over his slanty face as he braked and turned to avoid collision, scraping his front driver's side against the metal guardrail hard enough to shower sparks.

The Mustang was almost at a dead standstill. It inched out of the way as the behemoth bore down on him, ultimately stopping short by mere feet.

Ronnie looked over at the revolver lying on the seat beside the cash. That bag looked pretty pathetic now, compared with the trouble he was going through to get it. He felt manic, crazed and out of control.

He picked up the revolver again, rolled down his window this time, twisted in his seat to track the stopped pickup as the Mustang rolled away, and opened fire.

Andrew threw himself full length upon the bench seat as his own passenger side window exploded inward. If he'd had his seat belt on, he would've been dead. He heard the weapon report twice more, hitting the hood somewhere and then putting a large bullet hole in his front windshield before thumping into his seatback. He fumbled for his own pistol under him, waited to make sure the ceasefire would hold, and then sat up and thrust his gun through the missing window, prepared, at last, to return fire.

There was nothing to shoot. The Mustang was picking up speed again, and the onramp was just ahead.

But instead of going for it, the guy turned left onto an overpass that spanned the freeway beside them. On the other side was the entrance to a suburban housing development.

"Uh uh, no way," he muttered as he sat back up and brushed Saf-T glass out of his hair. "You're not getting away, motherfucker."

Andrew straightened the truck out, hit the gas, and took off after him.

After three shots, it became painfully obvious he wasn't going to hit the cop. Ronnie swiveled back in his seat and tried the key again, got a sickly surge of acknowledgement from the Mustang, and started to pull away from the damaged truck behind him before it could change its mind. The damn engine was probably going to explode any second.

The onramp to the freeway was just ahead, a scant half mile, but it looked a million. He'd lost confidence in his getaway vehicle, and therefore lost confidence in his escape plan. Now the freeway seemed too open, too hard to hide in. He could imagine this happening on the road, with a platoon of cops on his ass (which were surely coming any minute). He'd be a joke on the next "World's Scariest Police Chases."

Besides the dead-end strip mall parking lots along the onramp to his left, there was only one turn between him and the freeway, one chance to deviate from his present course, and Ronnie took it on impulse. It led to a bridge over the freeway and toward a large sign which read, in stylized, cursive, gold letters on a faded black background, 'Strangewood Homes.'

His only hope.

An incredibly vivid red brick wall flanked the road ahead, one with ornate columns at the ends. It stretched out both ways along the far side of the northbound onramp, encompassing the entire housing addition as far as he could see. He roared through, and then Ronnie found himself in the middle of one and two level modest tract housing, with lawns so green they probably glowed in the dark. If the cars in the driveways had been a little older, it could be the neighborhood where he grew up.

"Suburban hell," he said aloud. The quaint little pastel house fronts made him want to gag.

The cop's truck was visible in the rearview, but Ronnie was scared to push the Mustang's engine much past forty.

He took a left and then a right, weaving into the maze of narrow streets. Trees, sidewalks, and curbside automobiles pressed in on each side, and he knew if the cop had been in a regular, sirened vehicle, people would be wandering out of homes to gander at the excitement.

He checked the mirror. He hadn't lost the cop. The black truck turned onto the street a mere hundred yards back. He needed to face it: the Mustang wasn't going to make it. He had to ditch his pursuer somehow, so he could try and plan his next move.

Ronnie braked, turning the wheel sharply left. He came to a stop blocking the middle of the street.

The truck halted at the other end, its right side a mangled wreck, California sunshine gleaming off the hood. Ronnie could imagine its driver considering this turn of events.

*"That's right, I'm drawin the line,"* he shouted.

The truck surged forward suddenly, picking up speed, and Ronnie stuck the gun through his window, taking careful aim at the figure approaching behind the wheel.

"Come and get it, piggy."

He pulled the trigger.


Andrew followed the Mustang through the residential streets, gaining ground on each straightaway. He turned a corner next to a one-story yellow stucco house to find the punk waiting for him sideways across the road ahead. He braked and sat with his engine idling.

"Where the hell is my backup?" he wondered aloud. Even if the dispatcher had stopped to have lunch before calling them out, *someone* should've responded by now. Maybe they really had lost them before they could arrive on scene.

If that was the case, he needed to end the chase now, with as little risk to the residents of this community as possible.

The kid was waiting for him to make a move.

He buckled his seat belt and tromped on the gas.

The punk's arm snaked out the window with the revolver, and Andrew felt anger at this kid's homicidal brazenness, the rash way he was willing to extinguish a human life over a few thousand bucks, and he got so lost in that righteous fury that he barely registered the fact that the asshole was jerking the trigger and nothing was happening. He saw the look of surprise on that thin, angular face as he realized he'd used up all six rounds in the gun's cylinder; three at the bank and three more back on the access road.

Andrew was laughing as his front end connected with the Mustang's driver's side at forty miles an hour with a sound like percussion drums in hell, and in the short flash before the airbag exploded in his face and stole his consciousness, he saw the other vehicle shoved away and go up on two wheels from the impact, then roll over onto its top, flinging the guy inside like a rag doll.

## II. THE NEIGHBORHOOD

Joey was in Andrew's head even before he awoke, caught in the too-bright dream of a memory.

He sat at the big glass table in the kitchen of Andrew's cramped apartment (the 'born-again bachelor's pad'), one of his coloring books open in front of him, holding a crayon as delicately as a feather. Sun streamed in through the window beside him in impossible amounts, a fiery flood that got caught in his son's hair and lay across his work in one great swatch. The boy's body was hunched in concentration, his hand directing the drawing utensil right up to the stark black outline of Diego or Barney or Bugs or whoever he was coloring this week, and crying out as the tip missed its mark and slid over into the vast, uncharted wilderness beyond.

Andrew's eyes fluttered open. Something felt wrong.

He had no idea what that meant. The first explanation that popped into his brain was that he wasn't in the same place anymore, but that was ludicrous. When he could focus his vision, all he had to do is look past the airbag upon which he rested and see the same houses beyond his broken side window, brightly exposed with spring sunlight, to put that to rest.

Andrew tried to move and had to bite down from the agony that ripped through him. Every inch of muscle felt like broken glass, his head sick and heavy. He moved one hand up and gingerly probed the right side of his forehead. He found a knot there the size of half an egg.

He forced himself to lean over and search the cab for his gun. He had no idea how long he'd been out, and if the kid had beat him to consciousness, bullets might start flying any second. He saw the handle sticking out from under the passenger seat, close to where the cell phone ended up.

First things first; neutralize the suspect.

He retrieved the pistol, found his door handle in the folds of the deflating airbag, and stumbled out onto the street on legs that felt like wobbly stilts. His truck sat squarely in the middle of the residential avenue, in a roughly circular cloud of debris across the pavement. The vehicle looked like a giant polka musician had mistaken it for an accordion. Every window was broken besides the rear cab. The engine compartment was about half the length it had been when it started this day, the hood buckled and bent up enough to give him a generous view of the pulverized engine within. It would have to be towed out of here, and go straight to the junkyard.

He still owed twenty-something payments on it. The city might be good for some of it, but he wouldn't hold his breath. God, he wished he'd thought this maneuver through a little better. This was sure to go down in history as a prime example of *It-Seemed-Like-A-Good-Idea-At-The-Time*.

The Mustang rested on its top and hood twenty feet in front of the truck, and it was to this that he turned his full attention now. The vehicle looked in better condition than his own, but the damage would be on the driver's side anyway, which now faced away from him after its 180 degree flip. Streams of thin but steady smoke drifted from the engine.

He looked around for help, but the street was utterly deserted. He couldn't have been out too long if no one from the surrounding houses had emerged to gawk at the accident site. The noise of the collision must've been heard for blocks. He hoped someone would call 911 before coming out to rubberneck.

Andrew pointed his pistol at the passenger window of the Mustang with one hand, then added the other after observing how badly it shook. The world was still a little swimmy from the bump on his noggin, but he blinked it back into focus.

"Police," he croaked. "Can you hear me in there?"

No reply except the tick of the cooling engine. He circled around the front of the vehicle, keeping his pistol trained downward with each wary step. He peeked around the edge of the car's exposed undercarriage at the driver's side.

If the giant had played the accordion with his truck, it used the Mustang as a punching bag. The entire driver's door was crushed inward in a rough crescent shape where the truck had broadsided it, bending the framework and doors entirely out of shape. A pale, limp hand was flopped out of the side window, resting on gummy pieces of window glass.

Andrew moved faster now, keeping the gun aimed at the window and circling out wider from the vehicle so he could get a better line of sight. He could see the slumped form in there now, legs and arms in a tangle.

"Police," he repeated. "Sir, are you conscious?"

Still no reply. Jesus, what if he'd killed the guy?

Andrew glanced back at the engine. The smoke seeping from the edges of the hood and up through the undercarriage hadn't slackened.

He put away his gun, sticking it in the back of his waistband this time rather than his ankle holster. He moved forward and tried the door handle without much hope. His expectations were met; the handle creaked upward but the door didn't budge.

"Goddamn it, kid," he muttered. "You better appreciate this."

He swept glass out of the way with the side of his hand and lay down on his belly on the concrete, scooting his head and shoulders through the bent window frame to get a better idea of the situation. It was obvious the guy hadn't been wearing his seat belt. Even Joey was trained better than that, but Andrew figured when you were in the middle of a bank robbery some of the little amenities had to go by the wayside. The kid was on his side facing away from Andrew, one leg stuck straight up in the air and propped against the console, the other twisted forward and disappearing over the other side of the dashboard, arms flung above his head and between the bucket seats. Andrew reached over his torso, found his mouth, and held his fingers there.

Warm air met his palm, but when Andrew drew his hand back, the fingers were covered in tacky blood.

*Look for the bleeding, try to stop it. No, can't move him, could have spinal injuries.* A thousand fragments of half-remembered first aid classes argued in his head. Ironic, considering that he was agonizing over the way to save the life of a person who'd been trying to kill him minutes before. All just so he could be arrested, get some sleaze attorney, and be back on the street in two days.

In the end, it was the strengthening smell of smoke that decided him.

He worked one arm under the unconscious body and wrapped his other over it. The weight was more than he expected. He had to readjust his effort, but the body finally slid sideways. Once Andrew could get to his feet outside and pull by the underarms, the kid popped right out of the crushed window as neatly as though the car had given birth. He dragged him several more yards away from the vehicle before laying him against the curb.

In the light, he saw the source of the blood. The guy's nose was a wreck. Maroon spilled down his lips, chin, and neck to stain his black t-shirt even darker. Other than that, he appeared to be in good shape, no obviously broken bones or severe bleeding. Andrew's father always insisted God favored drunks and idiots, and he was sure this punk fell somewhere in between.

The kid moaned and tossed his head once, flinging his long hair.

Andrew stood and started back to his truck for his hand-cuffs.

Ronnie hadn't been in this much pain since his father broke his arm when he was twelve.

And in fact, that's what Ronnie was dreaming of before consciousness returned, his father standing over him like a pissed-off Roman god after the cops brought him home that first time. Petty larceny that had been, complete with a court appearance and hefty fine. He'd grabbed Ronnie's left arm and twisted, twisted, *twisted*, until there was a brittle crack. Ronnie dropped to the ground and stayed there until his mother was given permission to take him to the hospital an hour later.

He thought those arms around him were his mother's at first, as they dragged him over some rough surface before gently laying him down.

Ronnie opened his eyes and stared up at the clear, blue sky.

The injury from his dream relocated to the middle of his face: his nose radiated pain like electrical pulses from a generator. He touched it with one hand and came away with a generous amount of fresh blood on his fingertips. The rest of his body felt bruised and battered, hurting in places he couldn't even identify yet.

He tried to sit up.

"No, you don't," someone said, and strong hands forced him back down and then eased him over onto his stomach. He was too weak to protest. Something heavy pushed into the small of his back, and then his arms were wrenched behind him. A second later came the unmistakable click of handcuffs, a noise he knew intimately.

He turned his head, wincing as his shattered nose brushed the pavement beneath him, and saw the cop looking down at him from his perch on Ronnie's back.

"Oh, you goddamned *pig*," he groaned, and was amazed at the cartoonish sound of his voice. He paused to spit out blood collecting in the back of his throat. "You broke my fuckin nose, you gook!"

"Shut up," the cop told him coolly.

"You can't tell me that!" Ronnie snapped.

"No, you misunderstood me. That's your first right, you see, to shut the *fuck* up. It's an invitation, not a command. Right number two..." He went through the perfunctory list while he finished with the handcuffs, making them too tight on Ronnie's aching wrists, and then patted him down for weapons. He had nothing on him except his wallet. He felt better, his head clearing, but he was still in too much pain to struggle.

When he finished, the cop stood up and took the weight off his back. Ronnie pushed through the pain, determined not to show weakness to this bacon-wrapped chink. He flipped over, and caught sight of the upside-down Mustang.

"Oh shit, my CAR! Look what you did to my ride!"

"Yeah, it's a cryin shame."

"It's gonna be when you have to pay for it! I rebuilt that car with my own two hands!"

"Then next time don't use it in an attempted bank robbery. Last I heard, insurance doesn't pay for vehicles used in the perpetration of a crime." The cop squatted down and looked him in the face. "Besides, I'd say we're about even in the ride department." He jerked a thumb over his shoulder at the crushed remains of the truck.

"You did all that yourself. You're the dumb shit who rammed me. And it looks like you're growin a second head." He gave a vicious grin.

The cop fingered the lump on his forehead and winced in pain. "And I'm sure you'll get a lot of boyfriends in prison with that crooked nose of yours." He smiled in return and started back toward his truck, leaving Ronnie to fume.


Where was the cavalry to take this thug off his hands?

He glanced at his watch. Just hitting 10:30. The kid had shoved him away from the teller window nearly thirty minutes ago. By now, the local PD was swarming all over that bank, and spreading out to search for them. He strained his ears, listening for the distant sound of sirens.

Nothing. He and the genius had fallen off the radar. Which meant the little shit had been dangerously close to getting away with it.

"One in twenty," he muttered. "Yeah, right."

Something else bothered him. That same feeling of something being…*off*. He kept glancing around, hoping whatever it was would jump out at him. It was like looking at one of those pictures in *Highlights* magazine, another favorite of Joey's, where they gave a pleasant picture of a farm or a city street, and challenged you to find as many things wrong as you could. Usually it was blatant stuff, like spoons in the clouds or cows with arms, but it wasn't so easy here.

He went first to the driver's side of his truck and tried turning the key. The engine gave a sickly bark but wasn't even close to turning over. He walked around to the passenger side and pulled open the door—it creaked loudly as some warped part rubbed against the frame—leaned into the cab, and fished the cell phone out of the floorboard. Miraculously, there was no apparent damage. The phone turned on when he opened it, but the display informed him he was out of service range.

There were more relay towers in this state than there were trees. He tried dialing 911 anyway and got a continual beeping signal. He tried again and got the same.

"Perfect. Just perfect." Must be damaged after all. He tried once more and got the same beeps, but only for a moment. Then there was a pause…followed by the hiss of an open line…and then…

Andrew took the phone from his ear and stared at the display blankly.

He put it back to his ear and heard only the electronic beeps again.

It had to be his imagination. Or worse yet, a byproduct of that pulsing lump on his forehead. But he could've sworn that, for just a second, there had been the distant sound of…

"Hey pig!" the kid honked from the ground, breaking into his thoughts. "You can't leave me here, it's a violation of my constitutional rights!"

"So what, you're a lawyer now? And here I thought you were just a two-bit thief."

"Take these cuffs off and I'll show you two-bit, you Jappy pork rind!"

Andrew didn't take the bait. He'd been called—and threatened with—much worse. Guys like this never ran out of insults. He gave the phone a final look, shook his head, and slipped it into his pocket.

The smoke from the Mustang had slowed after all, so at least he didn't have to worry about a fire or explosion. He turned in a slow circle, looking at the rows of houses on both sides of him, the kind of middle class, bedroom community Michelle wanted them to move to when she found out she was pregnant, and instead he'd kept them in the dirty little starter house on the east side of L.A.

Yeah, Strangewood Homes was a nice neighborhood.

But where the hell were all the people in this quaint little Norman Rockwell suburbia?

He still could see no one. There should've been people wandering out in robes and sweats by now. It happened at every residential call he ever responded to, be it burglary, domestic violence, or otherwise.

Instead it was just him, Lex Luthor in the handcuffs, and a severely deserted street.

A single cold finger slid from the nape of his neck down to his waist.

He strolled back over to his prone villain. "You have a cell phone in the car somewhere?"

"Fuck you."

"That's what I figured. I have to find someone to call for backup to haul your sorry ass in. I don't want to see you so much as lift your head from the pavement, got it?"

"Whatever," the kid snorted through the remains of his nose and hissed in pain. Fresh blood was still running down his lips and cheeks.

Andrew rubbed at his own injury as he approached the house closest to them, a white with blue trim one-story on the left side of the street, with a manicured lawn, a tiny garden in the front beside the door, and a blue Suburban in the driveway. For just a moment he imagined a life where this was his home, where Michelle was tending the garden in flip-flops and a sunhat when he came home, and Joey was somewhere inside, coloring frantically. The fantasy was surprising not only for its sudden, gripping poignancy, but its realism as well, as if it were so close he could cross an invisible barrier and enter into it.  Maybe the accident scrambled his brain a bit. He had to work to shake off the illusion as he walked up the concrete path that led to the door.

He glanced over his shoulder to make sure the kid was obeying and then rang the doorbell. The tone echoed through the house.

Andrew waited a full minute and tried again.

He banged on the fresh, white paint of the wooden door. Shouted, "Police, I need assistance."

"I don't think anyone's home, you stupid bitch! That's what it means when no one answers the door! That, or they can't stand to look at your slanty face!"

Andrew turned around. The kid sneered up at him from the street, leaning just above the curb, his lower face a ghoulish grimace of blood. He walked back out to the edge of the street and looked at the houses on either side, considering which to try next.

*Doesn't matter. There's no one in any of them.*

The voice wasn't his own, but it was a ridiculous idea. There was no one home at this one, but there had to be someone here. *Had* to be. But when he looked up and down the street, he only got an impression of vast loneliness. If not for the cars in the driveways, he might've convinced himself that this was just some kind of model neighborhood.

He ran to the houses on either side of this one and the one across the street, like a berserk trick-or-treater, and got the same results. This was creeping him out. That feeling of wrongness was like water filling up a closed room, with him in it. He considered breaking into one of the houses to find a phone, but the idea felt too drastic. God, if only his thoughts weren't so muddled…

He had a responsibility to get his suspect into custody. They couldn't have driven more than a few blocks into this neighborhood, and the bank was just up the onramp.

"We're gonna have to take a stroll," he told the kid as he crossed the street again, trying not to show how rattled he was.

"Fuck you pig, I ain't goin nowhere."

It was about the response he expected, so Andrew ignored him for now. There was one other problem that needed his attention before they could leave the scene.

He searched through his truck, and finally found a pair of leather gloves behind the seat, a large plastic bag that Joey had eaten cereal from when they started out this morning, and a broken kite with Spider-man on it that he and the boy had flown two weeks ago in the park.

Andrew knelt beside the driver's window of the Mustang again and peered around the interior.

"Hey, what are you doin in my car?" the kid bellowed.

"Collecting enough evidence to make sure your ass stays

in prison," he answered without turning around. The kid continued to yell at him, but Andrew stopped listening as he pulled on the gloves and wormed back into the car's interior.

He saw the plastic sack full of cash on the ceiling above—now below—the passenger seat. Using the plastic from the kite, he wrapped the entire sack up to preserve threads or fingerprints and tied a knot at the top. Spider-man's face stretched out of proportion and stared up at him with blank, white pupils. It wasn't top forensic methods, but it would have to do.

Andrew had to search a bit harder for the gun. The crash had thrown it in the back seat, where he found it under fast food wrappers. It was a big bore .357, black grip and burnished silver cylinder big enough to roll dough with. He used the cereal bag to preserve the grip, where most of the prints would be, and dropped it in with the money.

"You got any spare ammo for this piece?" he called out. If so, he couldn't leave it here for some kid to find. Or, if the Mustang decided to explode after all, the fire would trigger the bullets in random directions.

"Fuck you."

"You know, that's getting a little repetitive."

"Fuck your mother."

A smile stole across Andrew's face as he opened up the glove compartment, spilling a heap of crap and, sure enough, a box of revolver ammo. He took this, put it in with the rest of the evidence, and slid back out of the car.

When he approached the kid, he made sure his face was set back in a scowl. "Let's go, get up."

"I told you, I'm not goin anywhere with you." His nose was so swollen it looked like a cucumber glued right between his eyes. "How do I even know you're a real cop and not some pervert tryin to kidnap me?"

"Trust me, you're not my type. Now get up."

"I'm hurt here, man! I was just in a car accident!"

"At this point, I don't give a shit. The quicker we get back to civilization, the sooner you get some medical attention." He realized how stupid it was to say that in the middle of an American street, but something about this place felt (*outside the lines*) desolate. He slipped a hand through the handcuff chain and hauled the kid to his feet. His legs wobbled but held him up. Andrew gave him a shove in the direction of the sidewalk, back the way they'd come, resisting the temptation to pull his pistol. He didn't want to force the kid along at gunpoint like a death march unless given no other choice.

He thought at first the punk would continue to be stubborn, but then he stepped over the curb and started walking.

They took only a few steps up the street before he had a new complaint. "You can't just leave my ride here! Somebody might steal it!"

"Nobody's gonna steal it while it's upside down. We'll send a truck back for it. By this afternoon it will be nice and snug in a police impound lot."

"If anybody takes anything from it, I'm holdin you responsible!"

Andrew looked around at the silent houses around them. "I don't think you have anything to worry about. Now, let's get you to jail."


Trust was a weakness to be exploited.

Lull people into a sense of security, and it just about took a baseball bat to wake them up. They would look the other way while you stole their grandmother. And most people didn't even require too much to make it happen, because trust is not-worrying and not-worrying is comfort and what was the human race except a bunch of over-developed tadpoles looking for a place to get comfortable?

So no matter how much it looked like he was cooperating with Jackie Chan back there, he wasn't. No way on earth would he ever go to jail this quietly; he'd rather die before going back in a cell. The rap for this wouldn't be the standard in-and-out he was accustomed to.

But maybe if he played nice until the oinker let his guard down…

Because, let's face it, this wasn't a typical arrest situation. As long as it was just him and the pig in street clothes, he could get out of this, maybe not with the money (which the cop was carrying in some weird cartoon evidence bag… man, was there anywhere they *wouldn't* put an ad these days?), but that was okay, because the highest priority right now was staying free. When he heard sirens or saw flashing lights…that was all over.

He tried to glance over his shoulder to see if the cop had his gun out, but the fucker was directly behind him, out of sight. The movement rekindled various pains all over his body.

"Don't suppose you got any aspirin, do ya chink? My nose feels like someone took a blowtorch to it."

"Nope, but I'm sure they'll have some at the station." The cop paused for a moment and then said, "For the record, my father was just as white as you are."

"*What?*"

"My father. He was white. I'm half-Korean."

Ronnie laughed. He couldn't help it. It made his whole body hurt, from his big toe all the way up to his goddamn hair, however that was possible, but he let it spill out.

"What's so funny?" the cop asked in a defensive, hard-edged voice.

"Just that you think I give a shit how many branches your fucked-up family tree has."

"I'm only trying to show you that some people's parents aren't cousins."

"Oh hardy hardy har." Ronnie started to say more, but they'd reached the first intersection at the end of the street. He noticed a curious thing. There was no street sign, no means of marking one road from the other. He couldn't remember ever having seen a street in a neighborhood like this that wasn't marked. How did they give directions, or even find their own way home after a hard day at the paper clip factory?

He didn't comment on this, but wondered if the cop noticed it too.

They turned left, in the direction of the freeway and the front of the neighborhood. He thought. Everything looked the same, a rainbow row of houses marching all the way to the horizon, some of them originals, but every third one the exact same design, just shat out by a machine like cookie dough on a conveyor belt. The cop directed him right at the next turn, crossing the empty street to reach the far sidewalk. Again, no marker. No one outside either, no cars moving, no sprinklers turned on, so eerily silent it hurt his eardrums.

*Not even any freeway traffic, eh kemosabe?*

Ronnie faltered a step, jingling his cuffed hands behind him. He hadn't driven more than a few blocks into this subdivision. Even if the place was deserted, like one of those towns they used for nuclear bomb tests, they should've been able to hear the sounds of cars shooting by on the freeway.

"Turn," the cop said, giving him a tap on the shoulder,

the way you'd direct a carthorse or a mule. They turned left onto another nameless street and then right once more. Whether they could hear it or not, soon they would turn a corner and see that blood-red brick wall at the front of the housing division, and then those sirens and flashing lights would almost be upon them.

*Will you?* a little voice—a strangely frightened voice—whispered in his head. *Will you* really?

Of course they would.

So he had to think of something soon.

He stopped abruptly in the middle of the sidewalk and knelt, sliding his cuffed hands over the shelf of his butt and down until he could massage the back of his left calf.

The cop nearly ran into him, and then hurriedly circled around to the left, out of Ronnie's blind spot. "What are you doing?"

"My leg, man. I think it got twisted in that crash. I don't know how much longer I can walk on it."

"If you don't walk, I drag you. Simple as that."

"At least take the cuffs off," he pleaded, injecting as much innocence and misery into each word as he could.

The cop shook his head. "Not on your life."

"Then at least cuff them in front of me so I can walk comfortably."

He considered this. "If you can do it yourself, then do it, but I'm *not* taking those cuffs off."

Ronnie fell on his back on the hot sidewalk, trying not to let his wicked smile show. Concessions were the first sign of trust. He brought his knees up to his chest, tucked them up under his chin as far as they would go, and then swung the handcuff chains under his legs and past his feet, so his hands were now resting on his belly.

The cop watched him. "Nice trick. Looks like you've had practice."

"Long arms," Ronnie said. He climbed back to his feet and brushed hair out of his eyes.

"Great. Now keep walking."

They continued on, the pig behind him again, and Ronnie weighed his options. The best thing to do was just attack the guy, try to wrestle the gun away. He would do it at the next corner, when the cop would be to his right for just a moment.

The houses cleared, and the next street stood just ahead. Ronnie Pearson's last stand.

They turned the corner in front of a one-story house with plastic ducks waddling across the lawn. He tensed to leap.

What he saw caused all those thoughts to fade. He drifted to a halt.

In front of them was an upside-down Mustang, a crushed Ford truck, and more streets.


"That's impossible," Andrew whispered, as he looked over the kid's shoulder at the wrecked vehicles. They'd left this street by the far end, the one on the truck's side; now they were coming back onto it from the opposite direction, closer to the overturned car.

They'd come in a huge, full circle.

The faraway sound he'd heard (*imagined* he'd heard) on the cell phone flitted through his mind like a tiny bird, bringing with it a shudder.

"Great detective work, Cochise," the kid muttered. "You got us lost in Pleasantville."

Andrew moved around him in a daze, walking further up the street to get a better look at the truck and make sure it was actually his. As if there was going to be another set of wrecked vehicles. He knew that was silly…but so was the idea that they somehow ended up back here.

He sensed motion behind him and rounded on his prisoner, suddenly aware of how vulnerable he was. The kid wasn't paying him any attention. He seemed just as transfixed by the cars. "I didn't get us lost anywhere!"

"Well, this sure don't look like the way out."

Andrew sighed and put a hand to his sore forehead, brushing against the knot there. "No, but listen! If we're here, we went in a circle, but to go in a circle we would have to make three rights in a row. But we were going left and then right, left and then right. The same way we came in!"

The kid shrugged and looked away…but not before Andrew caught a glimmer of something in his squinty blue eyes. "Hey, *you* were leading. I wasn't payin attention. For all I know you were jackin off back there." No confidence in the words; they were just autopilot insults.

"What's your name?" Andrew asked.

The punk hesitated, probably trying to think what racial slur to use next, and then finally settled on a classic. "First name's Eat. Last name's Shit."

Andrew walked over to him. The kid flinched when he stuck out the hand not holding the makeshift evidence bag. "I'm Andrew Horner."

The kid looked at the hand for several seconds as if trying to determine where the poison stingers would come from if he touched it, and then finally lifted his cuffed hands and shook it curtly. "Ronnie, okay man?"

"Listen Ronnie, as you probably noticed, we're in kind of a strange situation here. But I just think, whatever happens, it would go a lot smoother if we could ease off one another and get through this civilly, all right?"

"*Civilly?*" The kid—now Ronnie—smirked, cracking the mask of dried blood on his cheeks. His puffy nose reminded Andrew of those gargantuan schnozzes sported by puppets of Jim Henson pedigree, another favorite of that young Picasso-in-the-making Joseph Horner, but the worst of the bleeding had stopped. "I'm not your friend. I'm not even the guy sitting at the next table in a restaurant passing you my salt shaker." His eyes blazed with sudden hatred. "There is no 'civilly' between the two of us. I'm the crook and you're the cop and you're trying to take me to jail."

"Yeah, and you tried to kill me an hour ago."

Ronnie stepped up to him, put his red-smeared face inches away. Andrew forced himself to meet that burning glare pound for pound. The kid had so much anger in him, but they all did these days. He prayed Joey wouldn't grow up a member of this lost generation. "Get this straight, you piggy little Jap. I wouldn't piss on you if you were on fire, unless there was something in it for me. Take these cuffs off, and then we'll talk cooperation. Until then…watch your back."

They stood frozen like that, nose to bloody nose, for a handful of seconds. Then Andrew nodded and looked away, letting his eyes roam the street…

And did a double take at the house on the corner they just turned.

"What?" Ronnie asked, spinning in the same direction.

"I saw someone. In the window, on the second floor. He was watching us." No one there now, just quaint blue curtains over the glass, but when he scanned past he'd seen a staunch figure, with the fleeting impression that it was wearing a full three-piece suit. Like one of those jobs you saw in the faded photographs from the turn of the century, taken by one of those cameras with humongous flashbulbs.

*Are you sure Andrew?* The question had a patient, probing tone, like a psychiatrist, complete with the condescension. *Because you also thought the phone…*

"Yeah, so what?" Ronnie said. "No law against that, is there?"

"We're never gonna be best buddies, Ronnie, I get that, but haven't you noticed anything about this neighborhood? Besides the fact there are no street signs and apparently all roads lead here?"

"No." Again, an automatic response. He paused, considering, and then said, "I'll tell you what *is* weird-o-rama though. Take a look at your watch."

Andrew did and was shocked to see it still said 10:30. He shook it and put it next to his ear. "It stopped. How did you know that?"

"I didn't." Ronnie frowned and raised an eyebrow. "That…wasn't my point. I was just gonna ask you what time it was."

"I don't know. Couldn't be later than 11."

Ronnie nodded. "Right. Basically still morning. So why's it gettin dark, dude?"

Andrew digested the inquiry and snapped his head up.

It was barely noticeable, but Ronnie was right; the clear blue California sky was darkening. The sun was still there, high overhead, but the light from it looked weaker, sort of filtered. He could almost see it happening in gradual degrees as he watched, like an eclipse or a cloud shadow.

"We have stumbled into the Twilight Zone," Ronnie said.

"I've got to find a phone." He would be a laughingstock when the other officers from his district found out he'd gotten lost in the suburbs, but he didn't care. He would welcome the laughter, jokes, and nicknames if it meant he was back in the sane, rational world again.

That icy finger on his back was becoming a whole hand.

"Go ahead man. Find a phone, I'll stay right here. I *promise*." Ronnie sneered.

"Move. Back to the truck."

"Why?"

Andrew put a hand on the pistol in his waistband. "I said *move*. I'm all out of patience."

"So much for being civil." Ronnie headed past Andrew, back toward the crippled truck.

Andrew steered him to the passenger side, and opened the door with its blown out window. He tossed the bag with the money across to the driver's seat. "I'm going to undo one of your cuffs. You make any move to run or fight, I'll be forced to shoot you."

Ronnie shook his head and said nothing.

Carefully, Andrew pulled his key ring from his pocket, found the cuff key, and undid Ronnie's left bracelet. "Put your arm through the window," he commanded.

The kid stared at the shattered window until the idea got through. "Oh, give me a fuckin break! You're gonna leash me up?"

"No, I'm gonna handcuff you to this truck so you don't escape. I'm the cop and you're the crook, remember?"

Ronnie's eyes rolled in panic. "C'mon man, there's a few grand at least in that bag! It's yours if you just let me go, I won't tell nobody!"

"Let me say this again for the hearing impaired," Andrew growled through clenched teeth. "*I'm* the cop and *you're* the crook. Now do it."

Another split second passed where Andrew thought he might fight anyway, gun or no gun, and he wondered if he would be able to pull the trigger if that happened, but then Ronnie raised his uncuffed arm and put it through the broken window. Andrew resnapped the cuff, binding him to the door frame.

"There now, you look great. Very fashionable."

"This is humiliating. I'm tellin my lawyer."

"You do that," Andrew said, and trotted away from the truck, back toward the house up the street. If they ever got out of this neighborhood, he would find the kid a lawyer himself.

## III. THE PEOPLE

The house where Andrew thought he'd seen the figure was a two-story ranch-style with a wide porch, overhanging eaves, and shutters painted in shades of off-white and green. The front loomed over him in funhouse fashion, threatening for all its hominess. Even the lifeless eyes of the plastic ducks marching across the lawn sized him up. Andrew figured this was how members of the bomb squad felt when opening a package that might contain a life-ending explosion, wondering if they would have time to see and comprehend the horror before it consumed them. He searched each window facing the street for any sign of the half-glimpsed man in the old-fashioned suit.

By the time he reached the yard and crossed to the porch steps, the darkness in the sky was actually noticeable, and showed no sign of slowing. The sun was still high in the sky, but its light no longer reached the earth. It felt like mid-afternoon out here now, and on a short, autumn day.

*You're jumping at shadows. Literally. You'll feel stupid when you find a phone and all of this is explained.*

That sounded good, sounded cozy, sounded *sane*, but what the hell kind of explanation could there be for an abandoned neighborhood with no end and darkness falling before lunchtime? Perhaps the bigger danger here would be not getting scared *enough*, of coddling himself with assurances that everything was hunky-dory. As Ronnie suggested, they were in the Twilight Zone, and the sooner he stopped denying it, the sooner he could figure out the punchline of this episode.

He checked over his shoulder and saw the kid watching him intently over the hood of the truck.

Andrew approached the door. The mat in front was plain brown with 'CHILDRESS' written across it in white capitals. He rang the doorbell.

Once again he heard the chimes ring on the other side; once again there was no response. He peered through the frosted glass set into the door, but could see nothing.

"All right, here we go." Technically, in an emergency situation, he was given authority to commandeer or break-and-enter. He just didn't know if this qualified as an emergency situation.

Oh well. He would just have to answer to charges later, if they came. Daylight was actually wasting, and he didn't want to still be here when it got dark.

Andrew stood back a few paces and made ready to kick the lock, when it suddenly occurred to him to try the handle.

The door swung open.

Mean-spirited laughter drifted up the street behind him. Andrew ignored it and stepped inside.


As soon as the cop (oh wait, 'Andrew,' wasn't it? Jappy little Officer Andrew, as if introductions would turn them into the very bosomest of buddies) disappeared into the house, Ronnie strained against the cuffs. As soon as he saw that wasn't going anywhere, he turned his attention to the door instead.

Most of the devastation to the truck was localized at the front end and driver's side. Besides the window he shot out, there was no damage over here. Therefore, no hope of ripping the door off its hinges and carrying it with him either.

He caught sight of his sweaty, blood-covered face in the side mirror. He tucked his hair back and used the bottom of his t-shirt to gently clean the blood away from his nose and out of the cracks of his face. When he was mostly clean, he stared at the unfamiliar topography. His entire nose was crooked to the right now and grossly swollen. It would shrink again, but never properly set.

And all because of that cop, all because of his good friend 'Andrew.' The sooner he left this guy in the dust, the better. He looked over at the driver's seat, where the bag of cash sat tantalizingly within reach, if only his hands weren't bound. The idea of being arrested and then escaping *with* the stolen dough was enough to make him drool.

*Ronnie-o, you're like a goddamned retard. Look around you, and get it through your blunt skull that something's going on here, something bigger than cops and crooks. And you may just need him to get out of it.*

Ronnie straightened and did as the voice suggested, looking around at the silent houses, at the weirdly darkening sky. "I don't need anybody," he growled, pulling and straining against the cuffs and the door anyway.

He was still trying when he heard the shuffling footsteps behind him.

The interior of the house was decorated in an overpowering Southwest motif. A large Mexican mural of a lonely *vaquero* covered the far wall facing the door, just before one had to turn right to head upstairs or left to go deeper into the house, flanked on both sides by paintings of desolate western landscapes. The living room had matching black leather furniture, an end table with a cowboy boot lamp, and a 50-inch widescreen. The fireplace was on the wall to the left, and on the mantel above it he could see pictures—presumably the Childress family—in various frames themed with things like chili peppers and barbed wire.

Everything looked neat and tidy and normal.

Save for the large puddle of blood across the entryway, which Andrew would be forced to step in or over to reach the rest of the living room. He knelt to stare, ripping his pants a little more. His own red-tinged reflection stared back. He reached a hand out and touched the edge of the puddle.

It was still wet.

It was still *warm*.

Andrew wiped the blood unconsciously on the hem of his khaki pant leg and pulled the pistol from his waistband. He crouched perfectly still, listening to the noises of the house. He wanted to yell out, identify himself as a cop, but was afraid of who might be listening to receive that information. Everything in him, all the instinct he was born with and those that he'd developed since, told him to march back out the door and try a different house.

*And what if they* all *have blood puddles? Or worse? What then?*

Deal with that if it happened.

*Then what if someone needs help right here? This blood didn't get here by osmosis.*

Andrew stood and hopped over the stain, one leg in front of the other. He moved across the living room, walking by the fireplace and mantel as he did. He paused to take in a family portrait in the middle: middle-aged white father, mother aging but still attractive, two girls, the oldest probably close to seventeen, and one boy that could be Joey given another year of growth spurt, all gathered together in their Sunday best in front of one of those blue smudged backgrounds that professional photographers loved. He memorized those faces, both as practicality and motivator, and kept moving. The logical place to look for someone would be upstairs, where the man in the suit had been, but he wanted to clear the ground floor first and try to find a phone. He glanced up the stairs once and then headed toward the opposite hallway.

He poked his head into the kitchen, found nothing amiss and saw no phone. The shadows in here were deep, the light from the two windows above the sink dwindling in the unnatural eclipse. He turned to the hall behind him.

It was short, a door on the left and a door on the right, an end table in the nook at the end with more cowboy and Mexican crap. He reached out to the door on the right, pulled it open without hesitation, and almost opened fire at the shape that came leaping out.

He managed to hold off, but emitted a strangled bark of a scream before realizing it was a fold-out ironing board. The interior was nothing more than a utility closet, sandwiched in the wall space between kitchen and hall. After his heart slid back down out of his throat, he closed the door.

Andrew turned to the door on the left and, with a hand that felt like a lump of congealed grease at the end of his arm, gave it a shove. He gripped the pistol as it swung open.

The master bedroom lay within. The door opened from a corner and he leaned in, sweeping the weapon from side-to-side. In the waning light from the large, curtained window, he could see a desk against the wall to the left of the door, and a king-size bed with side tables at the head, the one on the left with an actual cradled phone, not a cordless. But Andrew could only let his eyes linger greedily on it for a second before they rolled to the figure slumped across that desk beside him.

"Sir?" he asked. His words were swallowed by the infected silence of the house. The profiled figure didn't stir.

He moved across the threshold and gasped at the change in temperature that washed over him with the brutality of an avalanche. The interior of this room was as hot and arid as the afternoon Sahara. He paused, almost breathless, and then stepped back into the living room.

The delightful coolness of central air-conditioning soothed his assaulted nerves.

He knew certain rooms in houses could be hotter than others, but the difference in temperature was too extreme for it to be a mere fluke of the house's construction. And the barrier between the two was so defined it could be cut with a razor.

Andrew stepped back in and didn't stop this time, pushing through the uncomfortably warm air. The first trickles of sweat coursed down his face by the time he crossed half the distance to the small desk. He held the gun up, not quite covering the person at the desk but ready to do so. It was hard for that icy hand on his back to get a hold on him in this kind of heat, but it was still there, clinging as tenaciously as fungal rot.

The figure sat in a leather writing chair pushed all the way up to the desk's edge, upper half slumped across the wooden surface so that he rested face down with hands at each ear. Andrew didn't think it was the figure from the window. Judging from the size and the haircut, it was most likely Mr.

Childress, the man of the house himself, wearing jeans and a brown shirt, ready to go out and mow the lawn on Saturday morning.

The desk was clear around him except for one plain, un-lined sheet of white paper above where his head rested. There was writing on it, and something told him it wasn't the grocery list for the day. Andrew leaned far enough over his shoulder—careful not to touch the prone form—to read it.

The sheet contained only one word in an all capital, blocky script, written over and over again in *Shining* fashion. They were large enough that he didn't have to squint in the dimming light to read them.

STRANGER, it said, in nice, neat, even rows, crammed together from edge to edge. Andrew stared at it blankly.

"Sir?" he asked again. His mouth was so dry; the single word rasped over sandpaper lips and croaked out. The heat in this wilting room seemed to be increasing just as the light from the windows was fading. His hands involuntarily tightened their grip on his piece, squelching out sweat against the gun's grip. "Sir, are you all right?"

He put one hand on the man's shoulder.

The body leapt into the floor as if it was spring loaded, and Andrew jumped away, again almost unloading his clip. It landed on its side and rolled onto its back. Andrew's eyes bulged in horror.

Mr. Childress had no *face*.

From his forehead to his chin was a gaping, blood-crusted hole, as though someone had taken an industrial size ice cream scoop and run it through skin, bone, and brain alike, coring the center of the head like an apple. Andrew could see all the way to the red stained flesh at the back of his head, because all of the gore and brain matter that should have been occupying the space was missing. Not just gone, but removed with such surgical precision that there wasn't so much as a drop of blood on the carpet or the writing desk. It looked more like he'd been born that way, and somehow made it through life this far without two-thirds of his head.

Andrew's thoughts went dizzy. This was a murder, murder most foul, murder in quaint Strangewood Homes, which meant there was someone else here, someone worse than his current captive, and why was *Andrew* here, if he hadn't chased that damn kid he'd be at the fucking zoo right now, and once again that image of Joey at the kitchen table occurred to him, coloring with the attention and focus of Michelangelo...

He could feel his breath increasing, lungs choking in the searing heat, and knew if he didn't calm down he was going to pass out.

Andrew forced himself to look away from the gruesome discovery and turned to the phone. He hurried across the room to it, put his pistol on the nightstand and snatched the handset off the cradle. He dialed 911 on the base without checking for a dial tone. Put the phone to his ear.

No connection, no tones, just the droning hiss of an open line. But it was heavy with potential, like the silence of an open canyon, and he moved to put his finger down on the cutoff button when he heard something in that void.

It was oh-so-faint, but growing louder. Even so, he knew it was the same sound he thought he heard when he tried his cell phone.

The giggle of a child.

It kept growing in volume until it would be impossible to write off as imagination, high and lilting, the pitch and timber making it hard to place as male or female.

"H-hello?" he rasped. He was shaking now, his hand stuttering the phone across the surface of his ear, and he pressed the plastic hard to his flesh to make it stop. He was terrified suddenly, his heart pounding in his chest and blood roaring in his ears and the heat in this room was making him so sick...

"Hi," the child said, in a voice whose innocence did its best to belie the malice stuck to the bottom of each word like gum under a table. "Would you like to hear a song?"

"Who are you?" Andrew asked. He had the surest thought he was dreaming, that this whole surreal experience would fragment any moment when he was jolted awake by the electronic wail of his alarm clock. "What is this, what's going on?"

"*Little Andrew Horner, sat in the corner, looking at aaaaall the blood,*" the voice began.

"I...How do you...?" he choked out. The air in here had warmed past the breathable threshold, and he couldn't afford to waste the dribble he pulled into his lungs.

"*He picked up his gun, said 'Let's have some fun,' and went out to join the flood!*"

"No," Andrew said, and his own voice was the one that sounded distant now. His eyes rolled back in his head, lids fluttering.

The voice was snarling now, malicious and deep. "*Little Joey Horner, dead in the corner, a feast to feed The One; when He arrives, the Sedoc and Nod, will amount to nothing and none!*"

"STOP IT!" Andrew screamed, and flung the phone away. It bounced against the carpet and landed earpiece up, and the sound of that awful giggling drifted out.

And, God help him, he wanted to put it back to his ear.

He raised a foot and stomped on the plastic, again and again until the housing cracked under his foot and the electronics shredded and that laughter was still coming out…

Ultimately, it was a shout outside that snapped him back to reality.

He blinked and looked around. The phone lay in jagged shards on the carpet, and for the smallest of seconds he honestly couldn't remember why he was bashing it to pieces. The room was no longer sweltering, and that feeling that he was in a dream world was gone.

Another shout came from outside, followed by the honking of the horn in his truck.

Andrew snatched his gun from the nightstand, jumped over the body in the floor, and ran for the front door.


Ronnie spun when he heard movement behind him, the motion too violent for the leeway he was given by the handcuff chains. His arms jerked in their sockets. He tried a different approach, sliding his right arm through the window of the truck and turning his entire body.

A man staggered up the gutter toward Ronnie with dogged determination, several yards beyond the truck's bed. He was old, late sixties, and looked like somebody's grandfather ready for retirement in Florida, wearing slip-on corduroy shoes, white pants belted nearly up to his nipples, and a button-up Hawaiian print. A crown of thinning white hair stood up in listless tufts on top of his gaunt skull. So the neighborhood wasn't deserted after all.

"Goddamn, old man," he said. "You scared the shit out of me."

The guy didn't answer. His face was nothing but slack, no

expression whatsoever, his mouth swinging open and eyes rolling like marbles. Even so, there was something anguished in his face, in the barely drawn corners of his wrinkled lips.

He took another halting step forward, almost losing his balance, and then another, reaching the truck's bed. His shambling movements set Ronnie's hair on end, but he wasn't about to waste this opportunity.

"Listen, you gotta help me!" he cried, putting as much desperation in his voice as he could muster. "This guy hit my car and…and he's crazy! He pulled out a pair of handcuffs and locked me to his truck! Can you run and, like, get a hacksaw or something?"

The geezer's rolling eyes looked everywhere but at him. He lurched forward, just a few steps from Ronnie now, and stood there, swaying slightly as the late afternoon sunlight faded toward dusk.

"Hey! Hey man, did you hear me? I said I needed help!"

Those roaming eyes stopped bouncing and fastened onto him like an eagle's talon. His lips peeled back from age-yellowed teeth. He snarled. Before Ronnie could respond, the old guy leapt at him, hands encircling Ronnie's head and neck, open mouth moving toward his face.

"What the *fuck?*" Ronnie yelped. With one arm through the truck's window and the other shackled to it, he couldn't bring them up enough to defend himself. As it was, he twisted in the old man's grip, turning his head away. A smell like rancid pickles filled his nostrils. One of the hands clawed at his broken nose, setting his face on fire, but then he felt teeth sink into the cartilage of his ear, just above his earring. His attacker reared back, taking a hunk of flesh and the metal stud with him. Ronnie bellowed in pain as the man leaned in for another bite.

This time he thrashed, throwing his whole body back against the crumpled front side panel of the truck. He managed to get a knee up between him and the old man and shoved to break contact. Once there was room, he kicked out and caught the guy in the stomach with his boot heel.

The old man tumbled backward, sprawling across the curb, but sat up again almost immediately. Ronnie's blood was smeared across his lips and dripping down his liver-spotted neck. He gnashed his teeth, a dumb, feral expression.

"*COP!*" he screamed at the top of his lungs. "*CO*-uh, *ANDREW!*"

Even if the chow-mein motherfucker heard him, there was no way he could make it in time. The old man was almost on his feet. Ronnie circled the edge of the doorframe, swinging around to the inside and avoiding a swipe of the old man's hand at the same time. He hopped up into the passenger seat backward, positioned his hands so the chain was in the gap between door and frame, and jerked with all his might. The door slammed closed with a crash, but couldn't latch with the chain blocking it. He held it closed anyway.

Of course, it didn't prevent the old man from just leaning in the shattered window to grab at him.

Ronnie yelled again. His wrists and hands were vulnerable trapped so close to the door and with such little room to move, and that's what the bastard went for, bending his neck to snap at them. He pushed the door open again, flinging him away, and then pulled it back closed. Before the old man could get at him, he lay down on his stomach on the seat, stretched his legs out, and used his foot to press down on the horn in the middle of the deflated air bag flowing out of the steering wheel. The high-pitched blat rolled up and down the street.

The old man lunged back through the window, squirming inside almost on top of him, and Ronnie could only thrash as merciless teeth snapped at his exposed back and neck.

Andrew almost slipped in the blood in the entryway, but then he was hurdling the threshold (the mat on the stoop now said 'CHILDRENS,' he noticed, bright and bold, and how could it ever have said anything different?) and running across the darkening lawn toward his truck. He came around the far end with the gun at his side.

At first he thought his prisoner had gotten himself stuck through the window of the truck trying to get free. Then he saw the handcuff chain and flailing hands and realized the legs sticking out the open window weren't Ronnie's.

"Hey, what's going on!" he shouted.

The legs stopped their kicking. The body slid in reverse out of the window and wobbled to face him.

It was a blood-stained old man, his eyes rolled up to the whites.

"Jesus Christ kid, what did you do to him?"

Ronnie's head popped up below the level of the window in the cab. *"It wasn't me, man, he's fuckin crazy! He bit my ear off!"*

Andrew looked back to the newcomer. The old man staggered forward, arms out like a silver screen mummy, a look halfway between crazed and mentally challenged caught on his face.

"Sir, I need you to stand back," he said authoritatively.

*"Shoot him! Shoot the son of a bitch!"*

The old man didn't stop. He was just a few yards away, gnashing his teeth and wheezing. As Andrew watched, he gave a shiver, and then a dark stain spread across the front of his groin and down his pants leg.

Andrew raised the gun. "Stand back, or I will open fire!"

*"Quit givin him warnings and SHOOT HIM!"*

The old man broke into a sudden burst of speed, his hooked fingers reaching.

Andrew pulled the trigger.

The pistol discharged directly into the middle of his chest. He staggered back, drool and blood running from his mouth, then charged again. Andrew fired once more, the report rolling across the street. The old man fell full out backward on the pavement—his head made a brittle crunch against the concrete that set Andrew's hair on end—and lay still.

"Thank Christ," Ronnie panted from the truck. "He woulda killed you and come back to finish me!"

"What the hell happened out here, Ronnie?" Andrew demanded.

"I don't know, I'm sittin here, handcuffed to your truck, and he just walks up and starts attackin me!"

"Where did he come from?"

"I didn't see, man, he was behind me! He bit my ear off, I'm bleedin all over the place again! Fucker prob'ly had rabies or AIDS or some shit!"

Andrew took a few steps forward with the gun trained on the old man's prone form. He knelt slowly, extended two fingers, and placed them against his throat. "Ah God. No pulse. He's dead. Shit!" That opened up a whole new can of worms. Jesus, this was probably someone's medicated grandfather that had wandered off, and now he'd ended the man's life. For a dizzy moment, nothing else mattered, none of what he'd seen in that house, just the fact that he'd killed another human being, that they were going to take his badge if he didn't end up in jail himself.

"What happened in the house?" Ronnie asked, breaking his panic. "Did you find a phone?

"No," he lied. "I mean, yeah, but…it was out."

"Well then what are we gonna do? You can't leave me tied to this thing forever!"

He opened his mouth to answer, but a new noise cut him off. There was no wind here, not the slightest flutter of breeze, and sound carried far. This one was unmistakably human, a distant, lamentable moan.

"Hey. Hey, man. Uncuff me," Ronnie said quietly, opening the truck door and hopping out.

"Hold on. Be quiet a sec." Andrew stepped around the truck. That moaning continued, drifting to them, getting steadily louder. He stared up the street in the direction they'd walked the first time. It was now dark enough for the lamps lining the sidewalk to begin kicking on one at a time. The sun was gone above them, lost in the starless black that was slipping over the world.

"C'mon man, set me loose."

"I said, shut up!"

He saw the first few as they careened around the corner of the next intersection: hunched, deformed figures that stopped to goggle at their surroundings like cavemen dropped into the modern world. By the time these early arrivals had caught sight of the two smashed vehicles half a football field away, they were joined by more shufflers with the same broken gait as the old man; first five, then ten, then a crowd too big to count. Most had something wrong with them; shriveled arms, backward legs, kinked spines. He saw a lady that appeared to have the stump of a head growing out of her abdomen and a wriggling hand on the end of her neck. The few that spotted him pointed and roared, capering like monkeys to get the other's attention. The entire group broke into a shambling run en masse, jogging toward them, a marathon from hell.

"GET ME THE FUCK OFF THIS TRUCK!" Ronnie roared.

Andrew tore his gaze away from the ravening, twisted horde of suburbanites descending upon them and ran to his prisoner. He jammed his hand in his pocket to get the keys while Ronnie yelled and the pounding footfalls and gibberish of the mob got closer. He spared only one glance back before he leaned over the lock and saw there were dozens of them coming, and the first would be upon them in seconds. He found the key he wanted and slid it into the lock on the cuff around the kid's left wrist.

As soon as it fell away, the kid jerked his arm back through the window, turned and ran.


Ronnie watched those things coming while the cop tried to unlock him. All of them had the same vacant, rattled expression on their faces (wherever those faces happened to be on their mutated bodies) as the old man. As strong as that fucker had been, there were more than enough of them now to tear the two of them apart barehanded.

So when he was finally free, he didn't waste breath or seconds. He pounded pavement, with the handcuffs still dangling from one wrist.

He looked back to find Andrew hot on his heels. Those freaks reached the truck and swarmed around it. Andrew pulled his pistol, shouted a warning, and opened fire into their midst. Ronnie saw a couple go down from well-placed torso or limb shots, but the rest kept lurching after them without hesitation.

Nothing around except more houses. The next intersection was far ahead, but if they couldn't gain any ground, then turning corners wouldn't help them lose their pursuers. They needed to put obstacles between them, and fast.

From the corner of his eye, he caught a flash of movement. He looked in time to see a figure in an old-timey suit step back into the growing shadows of a narrow gap between a lime green Colonial and a blue one-story next door. No way to be sure, but he thought the movement he'd seen was a beckoning wave.

Moving on nothing but instinct, Ronnie veered sharply in that direction. The cop continued a few paces along the street before realizing he was alone, and then changed his course to follow. The mindless crowd curved its path like a flock of birds, coming up onto the curb and cutting across the lawn to head them off.

Ronnie reached the side of the house. It was fully night now. There was no moon in the sky (not even any stars, some back part of his brain noted), yet somehow there was still enough light for him to see the tall picket fence that ran between these houses. The wooden gate into the backyard of the Colonial hung wide open. He rushed through and halted, reached to pull it shut. Andrew slid inside just before it banged closed. Something hit the other side of the wood a split second later, hard enough to shake the whole length of the fence. Ronnie held the inside of the lever in place. There was no lock of any kind, but after a few seconds it become obvious the things were too stupid to just lift the latch.

Andrew had sprinted forward, crossing the backyard and heading toward the fence that bounded the opposite side.

Ronnie went after him as the gate cracked down the middle from dozens of misshapen fists pounding at the other side. He moved down the alley between fence and house, out into the open part of the backyard. The figure that had brought them here was nowhere in sight.

The cop reached the back fence that separated this yard from the house that backed up to it. He snagged the top, pulled himself up, swung a leg over, and disappeared on the far side. Ronnie never had the upper body strength for chin-ups, but he sprinted after him.

Wood splintered with a rough sound. Ronnie looked back as he reached the fence. Two or three of their brainless pursuers tried to slither through the small hole they'd created at the same time, and ended up getting stuck. Ronnie saw one little kid with cloven hands get his torso punctured by a jagged board, and still he clawed and reached after them, making a snarling, squealing noise. The others went back to pounding and tearing, widening the entrance.

Ronnie jumped and grabbed the top of the fence. He kicked and struggled, tried to find purchase for his knees or feet against the boards, but just couldn't pull himself over. He was fucking trapped.

A hand lowered in front of his face. Andrew clung to the fence top, leaning over precariously, sweat dripping from his forehead. Ronnie took the offered assistance, and together they manhandled him up and over the top just as the entire gate came down with a crash.

They ran. Around the pool in this backyard, out through the gate along the side, closing it behind them. They were on another dark street now, and they ran a block, turned one corner, ran three more, and made another turn. Finally, after both were panting and exhausted, Andrew waved him over to a large, brick house with a "WE SUPPORT STRANGE-WOOD HIGH GIRL'S VOLLEYBALL" sign in the lawn. The front door was secured, but the cop busted a small window next to it with the butt of his pistol, reached through, and unlocked it.

In the gloomy entrance hallway, they passed a side table with an elegant centerpiece and brass candlestick holders. Ronnie snatched one of these.

When they reached the living room, Andrew turned to him. "I think we're okay for now," he panted.

"Good," Ronnie answered, and hit him right between the eyes with the heavy base of the candlestick.

# IV. THE PROFESSOR

Andrew's second trip from the land of unconsciousness was even more unpleasant than the first. The knot on his head was a throbbing Vesuvius ready to erupt. This pain was coupled with the almost immediate realization that his hands were bound behind him.

He opened his eyes. It was pitch black, but he was already as adjusted to it as he could get. He lay on an unfamiliar couch in what he thought was the living room of the house he'd dashed into. He could see only the lumpy silhouettes of furniture, and the banister of a staircase rising up from the far side of the room. His last few minutes of memory were hazy, but he could recall that prick bashing him.

A tiny flame flared across the room in the darkness, startling him. It floated up and lit the tip of a cigarette. A curl of smoke drifted up. In the glow, he could see his former prisoner's face watching him from a recliner. The blood was off his face now, but his nose was still ruined.

The kid waggled Andrew's gun. "Hope you don't mind."

"Let me go," Andrew said.

"I don't think so."

"I'm a cop. You know how much trouble you could get in for this?"

"Probably about as much as I could for robbin a bank." The kid grinned toothily, but it only lasted a second. "Besides, I'm a little more concerned with what just happened than I am with how bad my wrist is gonna get slapped when this is over."

"If that's true, why bother knocking me out at all?"

"Well...gotta take those opportunities when they come, Officer Andrew."

Andrew sat up on the couch and leaned over in case the vomit in the back of his throat decided to go for the gold. His head was woefully sore, but it was just a miracle he didn't have a concussion. "How long was I out?"

"Just long enough for me to cuff you, throw you on the couch, clean up what's left of my ear and nose, and find some smokes in the kitchen. Course, you gotta ask yourself, how long is long in a place where night fuckin *falls before noon?*" He jabbed a finger at the blinded window. "How is that possible out there, man? What was wrong with those people?"

Andrew recalled the mob of freakish residents. Those re-arranged bodies...they looked like something from a B-grade horror movie, monsters you would laugh at unless they were chasing you down the street to tear you apart. "Maybe there was...some kind of accident, like a toxic spill or a disease."

"Do you realize you're quoting, like, every zombie movie ever? Besides, that theory don't explain all the other weirdness. I mean, is it just this neighborhood or has something happened to the entire *world?*"

"Oh God, I hope not." The idea had yet to occur to him. The thought of Joey involved in this mess was sickening. Jesus, *why* had he left the boy to get involved?

They were silent, during which Andrew had time to think about what he'd found at the only other house he'd entered. "Did you...did you see anything in *here?* Anything unusual happen?"

"Again, the word 'unusual' has been redefined for me. You gotta be more specific than that."

Andrew shrugged and leaned back against the couch cushions. "Okay, so…you've got me fair and square. You're in control now. What happens next?"

Ronnie stood up, the cigarette bobbing from his lips as he spoke. "What happens next is, I find the keys to the car that's in the garage, and get the fuck outta this nuthouse."

"What about me?"

He stuck one index finger in the barrel of Andrew's gun and mimed pulling the trigger with the other.

"Don't do that. Please."

"One less witness. And, like you said, I could get in a lot more trouble for everything I did to you."

"I saved your life earlier! Twice!"

"Maybe, maybe not. Either way, that's your problem."

Panic suffocated him. He didn't want to die at all, but certainly not like this. He latched on to the last straw in mental reach. "Ronnie…I have a son. Joey. He's eight-years-old. You saw him at the bank. Don't take away his father."

"I grew up *with* a father, and look at me." The kid shrugged and snuffled blood through his crooked nose. "Trust me, sometimes you're better off without 'em."

Ronnie pointed the gun at him. Andrew closed his eyes and pressed back into the couch cushions. The silence in the house deepened until they could be at the bottom of a forgotten chasm.

"I ain't gonna kill you," Ronnie said finally. "I just want you to remember that I *coulda*, in case we're ever facin one another across the courtroom. What I *am* gonna do, is chain you to somethin while I make my getaway."

"Okay. All right, fine." Andrew was too thankful and breathless to ask for anything more.

Ronnie stubbed his cigarette out on the arm of the couch. "C'mon, get up."

Andrew wiggled down on the couch until he could stand.

From outside, a blast of noise hit the house, hard enough to rattle the windows in their frames.

"What the hell was *that?*" Ronnie whispered.

Dull thuds came from the street. They looked at one another a second longer, and then leapt for the window. Ronnie pulled the blinds far enough apart for them to see outside.

A monstrous shadow, cast by the still blazing streetlights, moved up the street away from them. The side of the house next door blocked the source, but judging from its silhouette, it looked big enough to be a dinosaur. That roar came again, more distant this time.

"Jesus," Ronnie whispered.

"Maybe we could see it better from another window."

They pelted down the hallway that ran beneath the staircase and into a room on the far end of the house. Ronnie threw open a door to reveal a bedroom the owners had converted to a hobby and display area. One of the streetlights shone almost directly through the room's only window, revealing shelves upon shelves of antique baby dolls lining the walls, some of them fancy Chinas with frilly dresses, others no more than plastic babies with wisps of hair and only diapers for clothing. Their dull eyes stared, unblinking.

The window had a workbench table beneath it, so anyone sitting at it could look out. The remains of several dolls rested on top, in the process of cleaning and refinishing. They looked out, Andrew having to lean awkwardly over the table with his hands still behind him.

This view had a better angle on the street, but whatever had unspooled that deformed shadow was too far gone to see. Andrew caught one last glimpse of chitinous legs and an elongated spine, the shape more foreign even than those prehistoric lizards Joey got so excited about.

"That ain't real," Ronnie whispered. "It *can't* be."

Andrew started to answer, but one of the baby dolls on the table in front of him caught his eye. It lay on its back, a foot long from hairless head to plastic toe, with cherubic cheeks and those weighted eyes that closed when laid prone. It wore nothing but a diaper; impossible to tell if its creators had intended it to be male or female. Its arm was detached next to it, its head partially turned away on the neck joint.

As he watched, the face swiveled toward him.

Its eyes slid open.

Andrew jumped away from the table.


At first Ronnie thought the cop was trying to run, but then he heard the yelp and turned in time to see the man skipping backward halfway across the room, his handcuff chain jingling behind him. He wore a look of surprised disgust.

"What?" Ronnie demanded. He was already keyed up about that thing outside, as jumpy as a two-day clean heroine addict. "What is it?"

"That doll! It *moved!*"

Ronnie looked down at the table. The three dolls in pieces on it stared back at him, but none of them so much as twitched. He finally managed to get enough of a breath to ease his tense lungs. "What, you think that's funny? Cause I gotta tell ya—"

He trailed. On the shelves behind Andrew, there was movement. The other dolls stirred. They stood and raised their glass and plastic arms above their heads. Andrew spun.

The menagerie of dolls lining both walls hopped up and down like excited kindergarteners, bending at joints they shouldn't have. Their tiny feet thumped down against the wood of the shelves, creating a miniature rumble. Ronnie could see their blank-eyed smiling faces, and a severe terror filled up his stomach like ice water.

Then they were all speaking at the same time in chittering voices, one word overlapping a hundred times.

"Trofonag!" they squealed. "Trofonag, Trofonag, Trofonag!"

The word made him feel unutterably filthy, and sick to his stomach. Images flashed through his head, surfacing from his subconscious without permission, horrible things he'd seen, terrible things he'd done.

Yet it was so hypnotic.

Ronnie slapped hands over his ears. Andrew, not having the benefit, shouted, *"STOP!"*

At his command, the chanting quieted. All at once the dolls rushed forward off their shelves, tumbling down in an avalanche of silk dresses and cloth diapers. They crashed to the carpet, falling all over one another, then got up and trotted toward them with hands outstretched, like children begging to be held. Ronnie and Andrew backed away in unison.

Scrabbling behind them. Ronnie turned to find more dolls of all sizes marching out of the closet, an entire army. They spread out in a rough semicircle, moving to form a ring around them with their brothers and sisters.

"Get back!" he shouted, raising the gun. "Leave us alone!" It didn't faze them.

"Just run!" Andrew told him.

They charged the door, Ronnie in the lead. The dolls covered nearly the entire floor now, and he was forced to step on some and kick others. Their squirming bodies felt disgusting underfoot. The ones that weren't trodden snatched at his legs as he ran, a few of them gaining handholds on his jeans. He ripped them off and flung them away.

In the hallway, dolls poured out of every other doorway in impossible numbers, climbing over one another in their haste to get to them.

And now they were singing.

"*Calling all lost souls, calling all lost souls,*" they crooned, to the time-tested, multi-purpose theme of "Nanny-Nanny-Boo-Boo." "*Trofonag is here...to bathe in your fear...*"

"*Stop it!*" Ronnie screamed. He fired the pistol this time as they closed in. The bullets punched through several dolls at a whack, shattering porcelain limbs, lopping off plastic heads, but for every one he incapacitated, three more came forward to take its place.

"...*Where did He come from, where did He go?*" they continued. "*Took the Filament for a ride and now its open wiiiiiide...*"

Ronnie waded into them in a frenzy, kicking and stomping like Godzilla in the middle of Tokyo. They grabbed and clutched, their collective weight bogging down each step as though he were wading through a mud pit. He kept moving, pushing through their growing masses and knocking them from his legs until he reached the dim living room. The front door was open, letting in enough light to see more of the little bastards come running in from outside, into the already packed floor space. The stairs were the only open avenue. He scrambled up them.

"*Ronnie!*"

In his frantic terror, he'd forgotten about Andrew. The cop made it through the living room, to the base of the stairs, but then the armada of fake babies overwhelmed him, probably because he had no hands to use for defense. He went to his knees with his arms still behind him. The dolls swarmed over his waist and shoulders, trying to pull him back into their midst. His face was a study in wide-eyed horror.

Ronnie hesitated, looked up the remaining stairs at the relative safety of the landing...and then turned and leapt down toward Andrew.

He grabbed the man's shirt front—dolls instantly leaping for his arm and dangling from his wrist—and hauled. Andrew fell forward, landing full out on his stomach against the stairs. He got his feet under him and shoved. With Ronnie pulling too, they freed him from the clutches of the glassy-eyes monsters. They were both on their butts now, climbing upward a step at a time, kicking at the dolls that tried to follow.

The delay gave the ones in the living room time to mount the side of the stairwell. Their cute little limbs dragged them through the bars of the banister. Ronnie pushed Andrew ahead and started punching them with his free hand, knocking them into the teeming mass filling up the living room like the middle of an ant hill. He put the barrel of the gun right up against the face of one with painted Kabuki features and saw its microscopic black eyebrows draw up in surprise just before he pulled the trigger, turning it into melted plastic. When he saw Andrew was at the top and on his feet again, he crawled up after him.

"Here, c'mon!" Andrew shouted. He stood in a doorway just ahead. Ronnie ran through and slammed the door shut, then put his back against it. This was another dark bedroom, a kid's room judging from the cartoon posters, but at least there were no dolls.

Within seconds, tiny fists beat and clawed at the other side of the door, just like at the fence. It shuddered from their sheer volume. And these things were smarter than the zombie mutants; the knob rattled as they tried to turn it.

"What now? There's no lock on this door!"

"Get me out of these cuffs!"

Ronnie shook his head. "No way!"

Andrew nodded toward the room's window. "We have to go out on the roof. I can't do it with my hands tied behind me."

Ronnie gritted his teeth, then reached in his pocket for the handcuff keys he'd taken off the cop. "Fine, come here!"

Andrew backed up to him, and Ronnie undid both bracelets. When the cop turned to face him, he expected to get punched—and knew he probably deserved it—but Andrew only said, "Give me a chance to get the window up."

He crossed the room, pulled the latch, and raised the glass. The fake night outside rushed into the room. Andrew slid out feet first and disappeared momentarily, then his hand came back to wave Ronnie out.

As soon as his weight was off the door, it swung open. The dolls had formed a ladder with their bodies to reach the knob. They rushed after him as he climbed out onto the narrow, shingled ledge beyond the window.

Andrew was to his left, at the edge of a jutting eave over the backyard porch. "We can jump to the next house!"

Ronnie came up next to him and looked over. There was a gap of two yards from the edge of this roof to that of the next, with a wickedly-sharp fence below. "No way, we can't make that!"

"It's either jump, or stay here!" He pointed at the dolls already crawling onto the roof. Without another word, he backed up for a running start and jumped across the distance, not even stumbling on the far side. Andrew stood on the slanted surface and waved for him to follow.

Ronnie gave himself the same running room. He took off, pelting down the slope, but as first one foot and then the other left the safety of the roof, he could tell it wasn't enough, he wasn't going to make it.

He hit the other side on his stomach, legs dangling off the edge. Andrew grabbed his wrists and dragged him the rest of the way up. He flipped over on his back and watched as the dolls lined up along the edge of the roof they'd just come from, all of them still bouncing and holding their arms out. It reminded him of the mosh pit at a metal concert, with less Goth clothing and metal studs.

"Yeah motherfuckers, whatcha think about that?" he taunted.

"I believe that's mine." Andrew plucked the pistol out of his hand during his distraction.

"Aw, shit." Ronnie looked up at him. "So what, you gonna put me back in the cuffs?"

"I think we're beyond that by now."

There were howls from the direction of the street.

Ronnie got up. "Jesus, what now?"

The crowd of freakish suburbanites raced up the sidewalk toward them, at least fifty of them now, clawing at the air in their direction.

"Goddamn it, they heard the gunshots!" Andrew said. "We gotta get out of this house before they catch us!"

But it was too late. They raced across the roof to the nearest second floor window, which Andrew kicked out. Ronnie sliced his hands on a few shards as they rolled through onto a neatly made bed. By the time they could get out of the room and into the hallway beyond, the entire house was alive with the sounds of glass breaking on the lower floor and pounding at the doors.

"*What do we do?*" Ronnie demanded. He couldn't figure out if the shrieks and growls of the mob tearing its way into the house were worse than the singing of the dolls.

"*I don't know!*"

There was a rusted squeal behind them. They spun and clutched at each other in horror.

At the other end of the hallway, the wide air-conditioning vent in the base of the wall was raised. A gray-haired man in a tweed suit had his head poked out through the opening, staring up at them with calm clarity.

"Step this way, if you would gentlemen," he said, with the most snobbish non-British accent Ronnie ever heard.

They looked at one another, still holding each other like schoolgirls.

"I would recommend haste," the man added, withdrawing into the dark depths of the vent shaft. "As you may have realized, time is something of a factor."


After a few minutes of slithering on elbows and stomach, with Ronnie practically up his ass and the older man's Oxford shoe soles in his face (and the pistol ready to be whipped up at a moment's notice, in case either of them should try something he deemed threatening), Andrew began to suspect the air vent was no longer an air vent. He didn't know when they'd crossed the line in the dark tunnel, but the narrow metal walls had turned to rough stone and widened until they had room to crawl on hands and knees with room to spare. The sounds of the horde diminished behind them, and ahead was a clean, white light.

Finally, there was a squeal of hinges and the man in the brown tweed suit climbed out into another room. Andrew followed, ready for anything.

They were in what appeared to be a basement, an L-shaped room with cinderblock walls, concrete floor, low wooden ceiling, and a staircase in front of them that led up to a closed door. Coleman electric lanterns hung at regular intervals from the rafters, casting a soft but thorough glow around the room. The place was lined with mounted shelves of tools and other junk, a few pieces of dusty exercise equipment in the far corner, and a bicycle leaned against the stairwell.

Ronnie crawled out beside him and got to his feet while the man who led them here hurried across the basement to the far wall. He was a few inches shorter than Andrew, average build, with silver hair and a neatly cropped mustache and full-beard to match. He placed his palms flat against the cinderblock thumb-to-thumb with fingers splayed and paced to the right, crossing one hand over the other, like someone taking approximate measurements.

"Is this…is this the same house?" Ronnie gawked at their new surroundings.

"And if it is, how did that vent shaft get us down to… the…" The wall they'd just come from was solid cinderblock, not so much as a chip missing. The vent or hole or tunnel or whatever got them here was gone. Why this should surprise Andrew after everything else was a mystery, but he could feel his brain stretching like Silly Putty to encompass the contradiction of yet another physical law.

"It's actually a rather stately Victorian Gingerbread from three streets over," their savior said, while still continuing that odd hand-over-hand appraisal of the basement wall.

"One of the nicer houses in this suburb, but I daresay the owners paid far too much over market."

"H-how—?"

"I shifted us between the two locations." The man had a voice that screamed upper crust, the kind of cadence and diction Andrew would've expected from a New England prep school graduate. He stopped his inspection long enough to turn his head and tell them, "Time and space have little meaning here, gentlemen."

Ronnie glanced at Andrew, and hooked a thumb at the older man.

"*Time* and fuckin *space?*" the kid asked. "What the hell does that mean?"

"Ah yes, the profanity." The other man's lip curled peevishly as he reached the corner of the basement and turned to the wall that ran to their right. "Never a challenge to tell when one is from the twenty-first century."

"Hey old man, I've had my nose broken, my ear bit off, and just nearly got torn apart by a bunch of Cabbage Patch rejects! It's been a helluva day, so I'll cuss if I want! And what's with the wall anyway? You two wanna be alone?"

"I'm checking for weaknesses."

"Jesus, he's as nuts as everything else around here!"

"Ronnie, cool it for a second," Andrew told him. He waited till the older man had finished up his examination and faced them with hands clasped behind him. "I saw you earlier. You were in the house I went in after the accident, weren't you?"

"Yes. I was hoping you would both come in. I couldn't afford to risk making contact with only one of you."

"And you opened the gate," Ronnie said. "When we were running from those messed-up people, you waved us into that backyard."

"Correct. I was attempting to keep you safe until I could approach you unseen, in order to bring you to this haven I prepared."

Andrew nodded. "Well, thanks for helping us out. I'm—"

"I'm aware of your names, Mr. Horner."

"Okay then, how about telling us who *you* are? Do you know something about what's going on?"

The older man nodded crisply and rubbed at his thick, gray beard, cupping his entire chin as he did so. "My name is Edward Manners, if such titles really apply anymore. No one has called me that in…well, eons, I suppose. As to your second question, yes, I know a bit about what's going on. I am, after all, the one that set it in motion."

"You did this?" Ronnie was back across the room in a flash, in Manners' face. "Then *un*do it, put things back the way they were!"

"Perhaps I should clarify. My research and preparation made this staging dock possible, but I had nothing to do with its actual execution, and I have no means of curtailing events at this juncture."

"*What?*" Ronnie cocked a fist. "Speak English you old fuck, or I swear to Christ, I'll cave your face in!"

Manners cast a blithe eye on him, not flinching from the aggression. "Young man, if you think anything you could threaten me with will make a difference, or even frighten me in the least, be my guest. But we have only minutes, so I suggest you listen to what I have to tell you about your present predicament."

"Ronnie, step away from him." Andrew clicked the hammer back on his pistol without raising it. "Right now."

Ronnie's fist hovered another few seconds before he let it fall. He snorted through his clogged nose and plopped down on one of the bottom steps in defeat.

"I have a son out there," Andrew told Manners. "So, please, just tell us what happened to the world."

"I assure you, nothing has happened to 'the world,' as you put it. It's still ticking along with the same callous indifference it always has. You are just no longer in it."

The silence was so deep in the wake of this offhand statement Andrew felt like he might've gone deaf. "What does that mean? We're on another planet?"

"Not anything quite so easy to explain, I'm afraid. This is more of an alternate reality. An engineered, imperfect, and very limited parallel universe." When they continued to stare, Manners sighed exasperatedly. "Think of your dimension, of everything you know and accept as reality, as occupying a finite space. And everything that is finite, must have a boundary, yes? A skin, so to speak. We are currently within a bubble on that skin, a sort of...cancerous growth. And, just as with a cancer, everything appears sane and orderly on the surface—the same way this might *look* like a common neighborhood—because the cells that make up the cancer are, for the most part, nothing but clones of other healthy cells. But beneath that surface is disease and rot, an area that does not follow the established set of rules governing the rest of the body. Does that make sense?"

"Not really, dude," Ronnie chimed in. "What about all those freaks? They cancer, too?"

"Absolutely. They're not the real residents that inhabited this neighborhood, but defective—and quite dangerous—copies."

Andrew considered the senselessly constructed people, sprouting hands from elbows and growing feet out of their backs. And Mr. Childress, dead at his desk with a head that was almost inside-out. Now that Andrew thought about it in this new light, the man's bloodless wound had seemed more like a severe birth defect than an injury.

*They're all just Xerox copies*, he thought, *except the toner's out and the picture is all…fuzzy.*

Ronnie was still asking questions. "So then how'd we get into this 'parallel universe,' huh?"

"That question has, in my opinion, a quite philosophical answer, but for sake of time, I'll give you the mechanical one: you entered the affected zone just as the boundaries which define it were sealed off."

"We colored outside the lines," Andrew murmured. The words were out of his mouth before he even realized he'd said them. That image of Joey at the kitchen table burned like a lighthouse in the center of his forehead, the crayons sliding over those fat, black lines that marked the edges of Donald Duck's shirt or Barney Rubble's hair, out into those empty planes where formlessness ruled.

Ronnie arched an eyebrow, but Manners beamed, lighting up his dreary face. "Yes! That's an excellent analogy, I'll have to remember it!"

"You talk like a goddamn college professor," Ronnie said.

"That's because I *was* a college professor. Long ago."

"Yeah, 'eons,' right?" The kid rolled his eyes. "So you're telling us that's why all this crazy shit is happenin? Cause we're in some other universe?"

"This 'crazy shit,'" Manners said, wrinkling his nose, "is nothing but proof that reality as you know it has been suspended in this place. A side effect of its very creation. Madness and chaos reign here, brought about by potent and unpredictable forces."

"Okay, so we're in this reality, universe, whatever." Andrew held his hands in front of his chest, as though gripping an invisible box. "One where dolls can talk and Tyrannosaurus Rex is walking around in suburbia. I don't understand it, but I get the concept. But how did *it* get here?"

Manners held up a single finger. "Now we're getting to the important questions. Unfortunately, they will have to wait until my return." He moved toward the staircase.

Andrew rushed over to grab the man's arm. At the same time, Ronnie jumped to his feet, blocking the stairs.

"No way, dude, you're not goin anywhere!"

"You can't just leave us, what are we supposed to do?"

Manners looked from one of them to the other with clinical detachment. "I'm afraid I have other matters to attend to, gentlemen. Otherwise the Incarnates might find me here and then we'll *all* be in a mess. When I am able, I will return for you and attempt to secure a passage back to your own world. In the meantime, if I have calculated correctly—which I am positive I have—as long as you stay within the boundaries of this room, you should remain invisible."

Andrew frowned and ran a tongue over dry lips. "Can I… can I talk to you for a second? Privately?"

Manners sighed, removed a highly polished pocket watch from his suit coat to check the time, and nodded. Andrew led the man over to a corner of the basement. Ronnie watched them from the stairs with a scowl.

"This is kind of awkward," Andrew whispered, "but I'm a cop. This kid is my prisoner. He robbed a bank."

Manners blinked. "And why should this concern me?"

"Well…you know…he's a criminal."

"Again, Mr. Horner, I fail to see the connection."

"He needs to be contained someplace! Locked up! He tried to kill me just a few hours ago!"

Manners shrugged, already starting away from him.

"That is something you will have to sort out for yourselves. The forces at work here don't care who you are, or *what* you are, so I suggest settling your differences and staying put until I can return."

He climbed the staircase, waited patiently for Ronnie to raise an arm and allow him room to slide by. At the top of the stairs he paused in the basement doorway and called down, "I put some medical supplies in the cupboard beneath the staircase. I didn't know what you might need, but I believe there are, at the very least, a supply of painkillers."

The door closed, and they were alone.

The old guy had to be crazy. Nuttier than a Snickers. Talking about 'alternate realities' and 'parallel universes'. It had all the ingredients of a SyFy Channel original movie.

Ronnie wanted to say all these things to Andrew, but didn't.

Partly because he was afraid it would come out too much like he was trying to convince himself of those claims, but also because he didn't want to answer the inevitable question: if the story was crap, then how were they supposed to explain what the hell was going on?

So instead, in the few minutes after Edward Manners left them, and Andrew slid into the floor of the basement next to the stairs to bury his face in his hands, Ronnie went around to open the half door beneath the staircase. A leather satchel sat inside. He pulled it out to the middle of the floor, sorting through bandages and iodine until he found what he was looking for.

The bottle's label said "Percocet," right next to a little caricature of a sneering, cross-eyed devil. Below that was

"Strangewood Pharmacy," and the address was listed as "666 Filament Drive, Somewhere Over the Rainbow." Further down, he caught sight of the prescribing doctor's name.

Trofonag.

Just reading the word was like taking a skinny dip in raw sewage. He popped the top, shook one pill into his hand, then added another after a moment's thought, and dry-swallowed. His nose and ear would thank him once they took affect.

"Any aspirin in there?" Andrew asked.

Ronnie fished another bottle off the bottom of the case and tossed it across the room. The cop frowned at something on the label before opening it. After taking a handful, he rested his head back in his hands.

"What was with that 'outside the lines' crap?"

Andrew didn't look up; his response was filtered through his hands from the cave formed by his knees. "My kid. He likes to color. Gonna be an artist. It was the only thing I could relate all this to."

"Ohhhh. Outside the *lines*. I get it now. Cute."

Andrew didn't respond. The only sound in the room was the barely audible buzzing of the electric lanterns.

"So…how long are we gonna sit here waiting?"

"Until he comes back, I guess."

"And what if he never comes back?"

Andrew shrugged wearily. "We'll cross that bridge when we have no other choice."

"I'm just sayin, it's been a while since breakfast. Sure would be nice to get some food up in us, right? We could go check out the kitchen in this place…"

The cop finally raised his head. "Manners said to stay down here, so that's where we're staying. Just because you're not in handcuffs anymore, don't start thinking you're not under arrest."

"I know. I heard what you said to him."

"Good."

"I also heard what he said back, that we're supposed to work it out."

Andrew put a hand on the pistol between his feet. "Fine. This is me working it out. Cops and crooks, remember? Not a democracy."

Ronnie kicked at the case on the floor in front of him, tossing the contents across the room. It made him feel childish, but he was too angry to care. "This is bullshit! I get it, you're a cop, you take guys like me to jail, that's the natural order of things! But you *didn't* take me to jail, man, and this *ain't* the natural order! This stopped bein about cops and crooks when my life got put in danger!"

"Says the guy who beaned me in the brainpan the first chance he got."

"Okay, that was wrong, I'm sorry. All I'm sayin is, this shit is happenin to both of us, and it ain't fair that you're makin all the decisions!"

He sat there after his unprepared speech ran out, the rattling of that many words through his skull making his broken nose throb. Andrew sat across the room for a long second.

"You know what? You're right."

"...I am?"

"Yeah. This bust stopped being worth it a long time ago. As usual, I was just too stubborn to see it. You want to go, there's the door."

"What, seriously?"

"Yes, Ronnie, you're free. Get out of here, I don't care."

No way was he going to look this gift horse in the mouth or anywhere else. Ronnie jumped to his feet, started up the stairs, and stopped halfway, staring up at the door. Thinking about the world beyond. It was easy to discount talking dolls and mutated 'burbers down in this safe—*sane*—basement, but probably not so much once he went back out there.

He turned back. Andrew had his head down again. "Um…sure you don't wanna come?"

"No. I'm staying here."

Ronnie still hesitated. This was his chance to get away scot-free, an offer that could expire if Officer Andrew changed his mind. Hell, if he left now, maybe he could even find his way back to the cars and get the money.

*And do what with it, Ronnie-o? You think the stores around here are still takin cash?*

Defeated, he came back downstairs. He strolled around the perimeter of the basement, poked into the junk on the shelves, and asked, "I guess that means you believe him?"

"You're still here?"

"Where else am I gonna go?"

Andrew leaned his head back and stared at the ceiling. "I don't know what I believe. I knew all along that something was off about this place, but I kept denying my instincts. Hell, I think I knew something was off before we even got here. What Manners told us, it's absolutely insane, but…so is everything we've seen with our own two eyes. Until I have some better way to rationalize that, I'm going to listen to the one person who hasn't tried to rip our heads off."

"I got a way to rationalize it, dude. We're both in the hospital after that mondo car accident, on the hardest morphine trip in history."

Andrew cracked a half-smile, and nodded. "Believe it or

not, that's kind of comforting."

"And what happens if the good professor don't exactly have our best interests at heart? He already said he's responsible for all this."

"Then we're not much worse off than we were before. But he helped us out back there. If there's a chance he can get me out of this, I have to trust him. I've got to get back to my son."

Ronnie wheeled the bicycle leaning against the staircase out to the middle of the floor, turned it to face Andrew, and straddled the seat. "You know, you keep talkin about your-kid-this and your-kid-that, but no mention of a wife. She dead or what?"

"No. We're divorced. I get Joey every other week."

"Yeah, I remember the little dude. So, if you're half-Chinese, that's make him a quarter, right?"

"*Korean*. I'm half-Korean."

"Right, whatever. I'm just sayin, he didn't look, you know, chinky."

Andrew made a hissing sound between his teeth. "From you, I'll take that as a compliment. He looks like his mother."

"Gotcha. Do you miss her and shit?"

Andrew sighed. "Look, if I'm stuck with you, I'd rather not give out my life story, all right?"

Ronnie shrugged and looked away. The room blurred a bit when he moved his head. Those Percs must be taking effect. "Fine, whatever. Just makin conversation."

"I'm fine with conversation. But if we're getting personal, I think a much more interesting question would be, how'd you know you'd get away with it?"

"With what?"

"Robbing the bank."

"You call this gettin away with it?"

Andrew waved a negation. "No, I mean if we hadn't crossed over into Oz, and I didn't just happen to be there. You were practically safe even with me on your tail. Did you case the joint, test reaction times?"

"Naw, I'm no pro. It was just the first place I saw, man."

"Wow. Talk about getting by on stupid, blind luck."

"Again, I don't know if I'd call endin up here instead of jail 'luck.'"

"Point taken." Andrew grunted. "But *why?* Why'd you do it? You're a young guy, you've got a long life ahead of you, and something like this could get you put behind bars for the rest of it."

Ronnie frowned. Cleared his throat. "I needed some travelin money. And I didn't have time to apply for a loan."

"Traveling money? To go where?"

"South. I was…headin down to my brother's place in Tijuana."

"That's perfect." Andrew raised his hands and slapped both knees simultaneously. "You tried to kill me just so you could go to Mexico and party with your deadbeat brother. Why am I even surprised?"

"He's not deadbeat," Ronnie said flatly. "He's just dead."

"Oh."

The Percs were definitely hitting the bloodstream. He could feel goddamn tears welling up in his eyes again, but he didn't want to wipe at them and call attention. So he rubbed at his freezing cold, goose-pimpled arms instead. "He was pretty bad as a kid, sellin drugs and whatnot. We were always close, but my parents—or really just my dad—ran him out of the house when he turned seventeen. He straightened up, got some job with this American logging company and followed it south. I hadn't seen him in, like, six years. Meantime, I got into some shit of my own. A lot of theft. But nothing like this! Anyway, my dad disowned me too, only it wasn't quite the...the slap in the face it was for Mark. Then I get the word yesterday, he was killed in some accident. I just...I wanted to be there, ya know? To see him one last time before they put him in the ground..."

Andrew's breath plumed in front of his face in a white cloud as he spoke. "Look Ronnie, I'm sorry. I didn't know."

"No biggie, man." He wanted to stay with that pain, the grief he'd been keeping at arm's length, but he was too far gone on the meds.  Ronnie grinned sleepily. "Hey...is it just me, or did this place get a lot more sub-zero all of a sudden?"

# V. THE CREATURES

It happened so fast, Andrew didn't notice until Ronnie called his attention to it.

The temperature in the basement had dropped…fifty degrees? *Sixty?* The place felt like a meat locker. Each breath hung in the air in front of him, freezing so hard and fast that the moisture droplets in it grew heavy and dropped into his lap, like crystalline confetti.

It was the exact opposite of that other room he'd been in, the one with Mr. Childress' hollow head.

And the phone with that awful voice on the other end.

Andrew was too numb to even be scared.

One of the floorboards above them gave a long, sighing creak.

"*What the fuck is that?*" Ronnie asked hoarsely, his voice slurred from the painkillers he'd taken. He jumped off the bike he was still straddling, letting it crash to the floor.

"Shhhh!"

A series of sliding, slithery noises drifted down from the house above. They moved across the basement, toward the door at the top of the stairs.

"N-no way, man!" Ronnie said, teeth chattering from the cold. "The P-Professor said we'd be hidden if we stayed d-down here!"

Andrew jumped up, clutching the gun in both hands, and pressed back into the corner. From this angle, he could see most of the way up the stairs. If anything came down them, it was going to get blasted as soon as it came into his line of sight.

Ronnie took a few steps in his direction. At the same time, the knob at the top of the stairs rustled and the latch clicked. If the kid tried to come to him now, he'd have to cross the foot of the staircase, in full view.  Andrew waved him back. He nodded and moved around to the far side of the room, got down on his hands and knees, and crawled into the shadows beneath the shelves.

Andrew waited, shivering and tense.

The door squealed open, and those squelchy sounds got louder as they descended. A voice preceded them, one high-pitched and burbly, with elongated S's, the way snakes always talked in fiction.

"Yesss, yesss, *here* it issss. Thisss isss what Marglo ss-sensssed. Sssee the lightsss?"

Andrew aimed the pistol and held his breath, trying to steady himself enough to fire at whatever was coming.

But even with as broad a definition as he was giving the term 'whatever,' he still wasn't mentally prepared for the creature that entered the basement.

He saw its pitch black tentacles first, a plethora of short, eel-ish appendages as thick as his flexed bicep that boiled over one another, propelling the thing down each step. Its body was nothing but a protoplasmic blob of dark, squishy, glistening flesh, adorned with several crablike pinchers on stalks, and a bloated head the color of a rotted plum that came up no higher than Andrew's waist. Two beady eyes glared out from the depths of a fold in it. It might've been cute if it was a creature on a cartoon, but there was a repugnance inherent to it, a vileness in its very structure that he could only liken to the gut reaction people had been conditioned to feel when they saw a swastika. He was so horrified by the abomination he completely forgot to pull the trigger.

A second voice spoke up. Their visitor wasn't alone.

"Never mind the lights!" it demanded, rough and deep compared to the monster now on the concrete floor of the basement. "What do you sense, maggot?"

The owner of this voice was much less interesting than the first. He was a large, broad-shouldered man, the type of hulking workout drone for whom steroids were a way of life. Andrew might've been inclined to believe he was just another of the rabid Xerox copies if not for the fact that all his parts seemed to be in the right places, he was speaking coherently, and, whereas their clothing had still been new and clean for the most part, this person was filthy and dressed in discolored rags that looked like they'd been sweatpants and a t-shirt long, long ago. He also wore the thickest pair of sunglasses Andrew had ever seen, and, even with these on, he raised a hand to shield his eyes against the lamplight. A rash of black boils stippled his face and exposed biceps, the kind of skin condition that would've sent Andrew to the nearest chemotherapy facility. Still, he was far more identifiable than his companion, and the recognizable form and gender was a strange comfort.

He stepped onto the floor in his disintegrating shoes—the Nike swoosh was barely visible on their worn sides—and stood behind the squid-thing, scanning the basement with his hand still over his eyes in a salute. Andrew tensed as those black lenses moved to him...

And kept moving without a pause.

He frowned. There was no way to miss him, he was just a few yards away, right out in the open.

A dull ache in his chest made him realize he was still holding the breath he'd taken earlier. He let it out in a visible cloud and lowered the gun, afraid the movements would snag their attention, but they remained oblivious.

"It'sss…a protection field," the gelatinous creature finally answered, its pinchers clicking excitedly. There was no mouth; Andrew couldn't even tell where it's gurgling voice came from. "Ringsss the room, it doesss! Yesss, powerful artcraftsss here, Marglo knowsss, Marglo ssseess!"

"Protecting *what?*" Sunglasses growled. "If you have brought me away from the hunt for the mortals for a trifle, I will make sure the Fires of Magdemnon are stoked to their fullest before I toss your wormy hide in." Again he glanced right over Andrew, and suddenly he understood.

Manners hadn't said they would be hidden; he'd said they would be *invisible*, and apparently they were. The only problem was, it hadn't stopped these beings from detecting whatever Manners had done to the room itself.

The squid—Marglo—shied away from the man and made a series of tweeting, whistling noises. Sunglasses raised a foot and stomped it in the side, causing the thing to bleat in what was either terror or ecstasy. "I told you maggot, quit speaking that slave tongue!"

"Marglo doesssn't know itsss function, Massster!"

"Then figure it out!"

The cold was bitter, numbing and burning his skin all at the same time. Each breath hurt. Andrew raised a hand to the side cautiously, directly in front of them, and waved to get Ronnie's attention. He could see the kid across the room on the floor around the writhing bulge of Marglo's tentacles, watching them with his lip curled up in disgust. His gaze flicked up, and Andrew pantomimed as best he could that these things couldn't see them. He wasn't sure if 'invisible' also meant 'unable to be heard,' but he wasn't going to risk opening his mouth to find out. Ronnie seemed to get the gist anyway.

Marglo was on the move, heading into the middle of the room, away from Andrew. The case of medical supplies lay scattered across the floor next to the overturned bicycle, and the creature squatted on its tentacled-haunches over it. "Massster, look here!"

Sunglasses came to him and examined the case's contents for a long moment. Then he looked up at the nearest lantern, as though reconsidering their significance. "Can you bring this field down?"

"Yesss, of courssse, Marglo can do it!"

"Then be quick about it!" He cast a suspicious look over his shoulder. "We may not be alone."

Marglo began emitting a high-pitched humming sound as he (or she) turned in a circle in the middle of the room. His master stood aside, taking in the rest of the basement from behind his thick lenses.

Again, Andrew contemplated shooting them. Would they even hear the shots or see the muzzle flash, or did this cloak Manners put around them extend that far? Even if not, he could still probably be fast enough to gun them both down before they could get a bead on his location.

*And what if bullets don't even do the job? Or what if you kill them and something worse comes looking for them?*

He took his finger off the trigger as Marglo's buzzing reached higher ranges. On the other hand, if they just waited until this squid undid Manners' spell or field or whatever, they would be completely revealed.

Escape was the most viable option. To either find another

place to hide or stay on the run until Manners could find them again.

He beckoned to Ronnie. The kid crawled out from the shadows. He stood, but a dizzy look crossed his face, and Andrew cursed his stupidity for letting him take the medication. He wobbled on his feet, and threw out a hand to grab the mounted shelf next to him to keep from falling. The violent motion caused the assembly to shift over a few inches, rattling everything on it. Ronnie closed his eyes and grimaced.

Sunglasses spun to face that side of the room, his back now to Andrew. "You're here, aren't you, little humans?" he asked aloud, over Marglo's noises. Taunting undercut each word. He took measured steps forward, arms up at the elbows, cocked and waiting for further confirmation of his quarry. "I don't know how you managed this, but we have seen through your magics. Come to me. Trofonag wants His keys, and He's getting impatient."

That word. Trofonag. Andrew thought he could scrub his skin with a wire brush and acid soap and he would never get the feel of those three syllables off him.

Ronnie stood against the wall, watching as Sunglasses closed in and narrowed his avenue of escape. Andrew signaled him to edge around the still-humming Marglo before he was trapped.

"You only try my patience, sin cow." Sunglasses flashed an arm out, sweeping junk off the nearest shelf. Ronnie jumped away, narrowly avoiding getting hit by a glass jar full of nuts and bolts that shattered against the wall where he'd been standing. Sunglasses pressed on, arms held out wide now in a bear hug, grasping at the air like a blind man, driving the kid back into the corner.

There was no way to help him. He would be caught in a matter of seconds.

*So let him. He's nothing to you. You have Joey to think about.*

It was true, but it did nothing to assuage his guilt. Andrew started up the stairs, taking each step slow and silent. He could see through the narrowing crack between stairs and ceiling as he worked his way up that Ronnie was watching him over Sunglasses' shoulder, his face caught between a silent plead and a scowl.

God, he couldn't do it.

Andrew fired his pistol down into the basement.


That Jappy pig was leaving him. To serve and protect. What a crock. Ronnie gave him the blackest look he could muster over the broad shoulder of the man closing in on him.

Andrew paused on the last stair before moving out of view entirely. Their eyes locked. He hesitated before pointing his pistol down at them and shooting a round.

If he intended to hit this linebacker, he was way off target; the concrete floor chipped a good two feet behind the behemoth in the sunglasses. The man spun, forgetting all about whoever he might have trapped in front of him, and bolted for the stairs. Andrew ran—Ronnie heard the sound of his footsteps overhead—and then the man with the ultra-dark sunglasses was in hot pursuit, leaving him alone in the basement with the thing called Marglo.

The gunshot and subsequent departure of his master hadn't phased the slimy creature. Its eyes remained closed, those irritatingly high-pitched tones still drifting from what passed for its face. Ronnie was freezing cold and only getting woozier from the pain meds, but he had to move. He circled to the far side of the room, wanting to sneak by and go after Andrew. He got as far as the door leading to the closet beneath the stairs when the humming cut out. There was a *whoosh* in the room, an invisible rush of wind, and Ronnie got the idea of something suddenly deflating, like a popped balloon. The sensation was gossamer, only detectable on the outermost layer of his skin, but the room began to heat up immediately afterward.

Marglo's eyes opened.

And focused on Ronnie.

"*There* you are," Marglo purred, with a newfound slyness its previous subservient tone had lacked. It squelched around on its tentacle legs to cut him off, dangling claws clacking in anticipation.

"Yeah, here I am." Ronnie puffed out his chest and stood on his toes to look as intimidating as possible. His height advantage gave him a good two or three feet over the creature, but it carried its mass wide and low enough that their weights were probably the same. Even so, he didn't anticipate a problem if he showed some dominance; this thing had turned bootlicking into an art form. "And if you thought your pansy-ass 'master' was bad Squidward, just wait and see what I'm gonna do to ya."

Marglo's eyes narrowed. "Do not threaten Marglo, human."

"Oh yeah, you gonna squirt ink on me?" He moved forward, whapping the knuckles of one hand into the palm of the other.

That bulbous lump that formed its head rippled. Its gelatinous flesh peeled back, taking those beady eyes with it. Its whole body was changing and unfolding, expanding and rearing up, like Play-Dough flattened out into a sheet for wider surface area, revealing a dark black, impossibly big gullet lined with razor-sharp incisors in a spiral pattern. That pit was big enough to swallow him without even chewing.

"God*damn* it," Ronnie moaned.

The giant mouth came at him, the hole in the middle contracting in great, hungry swallows. Ronnie dodged away, backing into the corner of the basement again. Marglo followed. When he reached the shelves, Ronnie scooped up everything he could lay his hands on—in this case, a metal child's fire truck, something that looked like a Thighmaster, and a heavy wrench—and chucked them all at the creature, one after the other. The wide fan of its bruised lips caught each one in midair and sucked them down with a slurp.

Before he could find a better weapon, Marglo darted forward and wrapped tentacles around his left leg in a vice grip. It yanked, pulling his foot out from under him. Ronnie grabbed the shelf to stay upright and ended up bringing the whole thing down with him. The world spun and blurred. He landed on his back amid an avalanche of tools and junk, knocking the air from his lungs. Marglo stuffed the appendage into his mouth, shoe and all, and Ronnie's leg disappeared up to the shin. Those little needle teeth sliced through his jeans and into his flesh in a 360 degree bear trap.

Ronnie found his breath and screamed as Marglo sucked him in. He thrashed, digging at the floor, and his hand found the rubberized handle of another tool. He lifted it.

A hatchet.

Marglo was up to his knee now, the entire lower half of his leg somewhere down inside that disgusting tentacle body, and Ronnie sat up to swing the weapon, aiming for the fleshy circle of teeth above his leg. The hatchet blade sank through mottled flesh, and a black ichor spewed from the wound.

The creature shrieked and spit him back out. His leg was bleeding, he was missing the lower third of his jeans, and his shoe was covered in yellowish bile, but other than that, he was intact. Ronnie scrambled to his knees and hacked at the tangled knot of tentacles like he was Paul Bunyan. Rubbery flesh split. More of its putrid blood flowed. Sometime during the assault Marglo transformed back into his previous form, and Ronnie buried the hatchet right between its beady eyes.

It made a pitiful mewling noise and sank to the concrete in a bleeding heap.

He got up, ignoring the way his brain sloshed inside his skull. He was streaked with gore, but he wiped at only the worst chunks of it and ran for the stairs.

Andrew fled the basement and heard the 'roid freak pounding up the steps behind him.

The cold ended at the threshold, just as the heat had in the other house. He didn't stop to marvel this time. Beyond the basement doorway was a lightless corridor leading to his right. He charged down it, and passed a branching hallway on the left before he even knew it was there. Not only was he navigating unfamiliar terrain again, but he was doing it in the dark. No time to turn around and explore though; when he looked back, he saw Sunglasses hurtle through the basement door. The big guy honed in on him like a guided missile. Before taking flight, Andrew saw him remove the huge sunglasses and caught a glint of something stark red beneath, glittering deep in his eye sockets.

The hallway ended, and Andrew careened into a larger room filled with the low shadows of furniture. Here he did stop to goggle. This had to be a living room, but there were no windows in here, no doors, no other way out. The construction felt forced, unnatural, designed specifically to halt his progress, but that wasn't the source of his amazement.

Along the walls of this room were glowing handprints. They were small, the slender digits those of a child, placed at random angles in a haphazard line about waist high. A soft, white radiance poured out of each one, bright enough to cast a gloomy pall across the entire room, like the Batman nightlight in Joey's room.

But there was nothing comforting about this illumination. It made him feel disgusted and diseased.

From all around came the laughter of children.

He thought of the voice on the phone, the one that sang those awful lyrics. These high-pitched giggles turned his muscles to stone. They came from everywhere at once, from *inside* his skull like a metal plate picking up radio stations, a blend of a hundred, a thousand, an infinite number of merry childish peals invading his thoughts, throwing him out of his own head, and worst of all, even in that miasma of laughter, he thought he could hear one that sounded like Joey...

He was hit hard from behind. The laughter cut off, and Andrew realized he'd been distracted just long enough for his pursuer to catch up. A shoulder slammed into his lower back with the force of a linebacker moving to not only sack the quarterback, but break bones. He flew forward. His ankle hit the edge of a recliner and zipped out from under him. He fell, arms pinwheeling with the pistol, and landed face down on a glass coffee table in the middle of the room. The surface shattered under the weight of his stomach, dropping him to the floor through the metal frame with his feet still in the air.

Andrew twisted around onto his back, shards of glass cutting his arms and chest. Sunglasses no longer wore his namesake; those pitch-black lenses had been covering two ovals of fiery red that burned in his face like hot coals. The man came for him, hands outstretched and kneading the air.

"Stop! Get back!" Andrew raised the gun. When the guy didn't slow, he squeezed off a round. In the combined light of the muzzle flash and the wan glow from the handprints, he saw the bullet strike home high on the chest. Blood flowed, but it did little to faze his target.

The man reached him and grabbed his wrist. He held the gun away while he pummeled at Andrew with his free hand.

"It's...OUR...time!" he screamed, each word in rhythm with his blows. His eyes burned so hard they generated actual heat. "We will take your world and you...will...LET US!"

Andrew was caught in the table and couldn't get into a position to fight back. The pistol fell out of his grip. One of the guy's punches struck the lump in his temple, knocking him woozy.

His free hand landed on a piece of glass still stuck to the frame. He snatched it up and jabbed it into his opponent's throat. It sank deep.

The flesh around the wound sizzled momentarily, and then crimson spurted over Andrew. The creature with the red-eyes let go and stumbled back, clutching the glittering triangle jutting from his neck.

Andrew climbed out of the table frame. The room was back to its original construction, with a big picture window, a front door, and no radioactive finger paint. He watched his adversary collapse against a nearby ottoman and grow still, the fire in his skull dimming as smoke dribbled out.

He knew he should see if Ronnie needed help, but claustrophobia swept over him. Andrew wanted out of this house, this neighborhood, this universe—at least into some fresh air—or he was going to hyperventilate. He left the pistol behind and ran to the door, found a lock and threw it open, then went onto the porch outside.

It was still unnatural night—a night without moon or stars or any kind of interruption in the bluish-black void above—but at least it was open space and breathing room. As he pelted onto the lawn, an arm came out from behind one of the wide columns that flanked the porch's entrance and clotheslined him.

Andrew went down hard enough this time to knock the wind out of him. As he gasped for air, he saw another burning-eyed man step out from his hiding spot. Except this one's skin condition was more advanced than the last one; huge, cancerous stretches across his skin appeared to be eating him from the inside out, making him look halfway dead.

And there were more closing in, crossing the lawn to surround him.

"Go and find the other," he heard the newcomer lean over him and growl. "I'll get this one to the Facilitator."


Ronnie had time to make it to the back door on the opposite side of the house just as he heard the front crash open. Heavy feet stomped inside and spread out, like the Gestapo sweeping for Jews. He limped along the outside of the house to where the fence line met a decorative row of tall, thorny bushes and pushed into the small space behind them. From there, he was able to shimmy through the dirt down to the front yard without being seen.

By now, the medication was in full swing, turning his muscles to jelly and urging him to fall into the sweet arms of sleep. He shook it off and watched from the shadows as a group of men with glowing eyes milled about the lawn, standing guard over Andrew, one of them with a foot planted on his chest to keep him down. Whatever these things were, there were more arriving all the time; ranks of filthy men dressed in ancient rags made their way up the dark streets. Various parts of their bodies looked rotted, and some of them had creatures like Marglo on leashes, like hunting dogs. Ronnie was afraid they might sniff him out as the squid had done with Manners' magic spell or whatever the hell it was, but they remained oblivious.

More of the red-eyed men came from the front of the house a few minutes later, carrying the bodies of Marglo and his master and dumping them both unceremoniously on the porch. When Ronnie saw the big guy from the basement covered in blood, he gave a silent cheer for Andrew.

The ones that had run through the house reported him missing. A search party was quickly organized, and a large chunk of this Nuclear Brethren were sent to look for him.

After that, he did fall asleep. The sound of a revving engine startled him awake, and he opened his eyes to find a huge tire rolling toward his head on the other side of the bushes. Ronnie's lips clamped shut just before a scream could escape.

It was a school bus looming over him. He recognized the shape and color even in the perpetual twilight of this insane place. They backed it up over the curb and onto the lawn, the tires digging furrows through the lush grass. The back bumper was inches above his head.

The remaining thugs lifted Andrew under the arms and carried him, feet dragging, through the side door. The engine revved as they prepared to pull away.

Ronnie knew this was where he and Officer Andrew part-ed ways. Probably forever. The man was caught, and Ronnie could do nothing to change that. Besides, he would likely want Ronnie to go and tell his one-fourth Jap kid that he died bravely, saved his life, all that heroic, line-of-duty shit.

There was absolutely no need to go through with the insanity his brain was pushing him toward.

But he slithered under the bus anyway, working his way to the middle section where the wide metal struts gave support to the vehicle's heavy interior. He'd done this before, on a field trip in the fourth grade that the school had banned him from. Of course, he was a hell of a lot smaller and a hundred pounds lighter back then, but *que sera, se*-mother-fucking-*ra*.

Ronnie squeezed into the guts of the vehicle and stretched himself across several supports just before it rolled away. He was almost unconscious now, his eyes drifting shut every few seconds. He managed to get in a snug position almost like a hammock that kept him from being pitched out when the bus bounced back over the curb.

"Fuck, fuck, what is *wrong* with me?" he muttered. Ronnie let sleep take him as the bus roared up empty Strangewood streets.

# VI. THE SCHOOL

Andrew's forehead leaned against a pane of glass.

On the other side, nighttime scenery rushed by: houses and lawns and cars, all fake somehow in the eternal twilight, more like cardboard cutouts than actual items. Manners' 'imperfect' universe. He could understand now why he'd had that feeling of vague wrongness when he first awoke here. If you accepted it at face value, it might fool you, but when you stepped back and tried to take it all in at once, it all looked rickety, like you could poke holes right through it with your finger.

He looked away from it all before the dizzy panic in his chest could spread.

He'd passed out sometime after being carried onto this bus, but now he could examine it at his leisure. It was a long, metal tube. Brown, imitation leather-covered seats marched away from him in rows, some of them with pen-scrawled graffiti. Several were occupied, the backs of scruffy heads the only thing visible to Andrew as they faced the driver. The person at the wheel was obscured by a padded wall and the overhanging mirror was too cracked and shattered for a reflection. A sign right next to the driver's seat had a picture of a menacing, shadowed figure holding out a fistful of candy to some cartoon children that looked eager to take it.

Below this, the caption read, "Always talk to *Strangers*."

In the seat directly across the narrow aisle from him was the gaunt, shirtless, almost skeletal figure that had knocked him on his ass outside the house where Manners hid them. He was a complete contrast to the hulk Andrew just fought, but he had those same burning eyes. They were bright enough to light up a muted halo around his face.

He turned them on Andrew. No pupils in there, nothing but a shifting sheen of blood red and burnt orange, like staring into a volcano. The man displayed chipped teeth in a grin. Part of his lip on the bottom was blackened and rotted away down to the gum line. "Wakey, wakey, little sin cow."

Andrew said nothing.

"Too bad." He gave a forlorn shake of his head. "I would have enjoyed removing parts of your body until you regained consciousness."

"Where's Ronnie?"

"You mean the other mortal? He has eluded us, for now. But it matters not."

"Who are you people? *What* are you?"

"You really wish to know?"

Andrew nodded.

"Very well. We are the—" A tangle of syllables spilled out of his mouth that caused something right in the center of Andrew's forehead to seize up, like the painful spike of a cold headache. At first he thought it was his multiple head injuries finally catching up to him, an aneurysm or blood clot popping to kill him, but then he realized his new friend was grinning even wider as he waited for the echo of his words to fade away.

"Did you get that? Should I repeat it?"

"Please." Andrew coughed miserably. Coppery blood filled his mouth. "Please, don't."

The other man—if this thing *was* a man—laughed. It was a gruff sound. "We wouldn't want to damage you. Not yet. Since before time began, your kind has called us Incarnates. I see no reason why that will not suit our purposes now."

The name rang the dullest of bells for Andrew. Manners. Manners had mentioned these things. He'd been afraid they were going to find him.

"What do you want from me?"

"We are the emissaries. The hands, eyes, and mouth of Trofonag the Depraved, the Outer Terror, He who, in turn, serves the whim and will of the Stranger."

Trofonag. That word dove into his mind—he imagined it in there thumbing through the ridges of his brain like a prospector panning for gold—and what it unearthed was a painful memory: the time he'd blackmailed another student in the second grade, threatening to tell that the boy had been the one to break the drinking fountain if he didn't give up half his lunch money for the week. Christ, he hadn't thought about that in nearly thirty years. "I...I don't understand."

"Of course you don't. But your understanding is inconsequential. The Dark Filament brought us, its armies are massed, and after we breach the thin wall that separates us, your world will be but a footnote in our conquest."

"Outside the lines," Andrew stated, almost robotically. "You want to break through. To get from this universe...to mine."

The Incarnate's eyes narrowed, those blast furnaces slitting. "How do you know that? Who have you spoken with? Who crafted the magics that hid you and the other human during our search?"

"I don't know what you mean," he said, too quickly. "What do you want with my world? What's going to happen if you get through?"

"Chaos, death, and darkness. A return to the old ways, when your kind was sludge on our boot heels. And do you know how we will start, sin cow? Do you know the first thing we will do when we enter your reality?" He leaned across the aisle as though telling a secret, that rotted smile combining with his glowing eyes to make a skin-covered jack-o-lantern. He held up a picture of Joey, taken from Andrew's own wallet. "We will spill the guts of every *single* child your world has to offer."

The anger swept out of nowhere, burning through every cell in Andrew's body, coating his thoughts in red haze. He screamed wordlessly, pure rage expressed in sound, and surged out of his seat to pound at this hideous creature.

His attack was fruitless. The Incarnate grabbed him by the throat and forced him back into his seat with more strength than a normal person his size could possibly have. His air supply vanished, and Andrew had no choice but to go slack until he was released.

As he fought for breath, the Incarnate stood over him without a shred of sympathy. His ribs poked at his pale skin, forming a ladder up to his scrawny neck. "And the best part is," he continued, "*You're* going to make it happen."

There was a squeal as the bus brakes engaged, and a lurch when it stopped. Andrew was still recovering from his throttling when two of the Incarnates yanked him up by the arms and carried him from the vehicle so roughly he couldn't get his feet under him. One of their hands was nothing but a skeleton with a few scraps of muscle clinging to it.

The bus sat in front of a school. Arthur J. Filament Elementary, according to the sign out front. The name was circumspect, but, if he had the right understanding of this place now, then the school itself actually existed back in the real world. Just another perk for the residents of Strangewood. The building was two stories, lots of windows, a flagpole with the American flag in front. It only had one star on it, but still. The place should've been cheerful and inviting for the kids—most of them around Joey's age—that attended class here everyday, but the pollution of this world made it more terrifying than any haunted house or dreary forest. The brick exterior was infected with the same darkness that had taken over the sky.

Andrew didn't want to go in there. His stomach clenched at the thought, his testicles drawing up.

But his captors weren't asking. The one that had choked him led the way as they carried him up the paved walkway and in through the front doors as he squirmed. Inside, the hallways were dark and silent on the surface, but buzzed with an undercurrent of energy that he imagined he could only feel in his bones. There was potential here, expectation, and when they passed over the threshold he drew in a sharp breath as though he'd just put his hand in fire.

That was okay, he decided. As long as there were no glowing handprints or impish voices that spoke madness, he could bare it.

They took him deep into the building's interior, into a maze of lockers and closed classroom doors. His head throbbed, pulsing in sync with that latent power bleeding from the walls. He slipped in and out of consciousness, and only one moment in the journey stood out enough for him to recall.

They approached a door on the left that said, "FURNACE."

It was black. Blacker than night, blacker than outer space, blacker than any color ever conceived by man. It gulped at the little bit of light in the hall, sucking it in, forming an aura of darkness that bulged in front of it.

And here those licks of energy peaked into a jangled disharmony that set his hair on end.

"Nooo," he moaned, and then screamed, "Please, no, *dontakemeinthere!*"

The two Incarnates holding him were as distressed as he was. They quivered and halted, unwilling to go past. The one leading waltzed by, then turned and spat, "Keep moving you wastes of flesh, or what's behind that door will be a paradise compared with what I do to you!"

They crossed to the far side of the hallway and moved on.

Finally, when Andrew's arms ached and he was sure this would never end, they turned into an open door and dropped him on the threshold.

It was a classroom with multiple desks. There were more electric lanterns around the entrance, on the teacher's desk and several of the students', casting steep shadows from their sphere of weak radiance. The Incarnates shielded their eyes from the light.

In the middle of the room a figure stood with its back to him, speaking to a group of six or seven more Incarnates. The figure was giving orders. It pointed angrily and the mass disbanded, filing out of another door on the far end of the room.

"Facilitator!" Andrew's tormentor barked. "Here is one of the mortals! Let us begin!"

The figure turned and crossed the linoleum, entering the circle of light cast by the lanterns. Andrew looked up at the face above him.

"Well," Edward Manners said. "You certainly gave us quite a chase, sir."

~ ~ ~

Ronnie wasn't sure how long he napped beneath the bus, but he came aware when it stopped. The Percocet had worn off enough for him to not feel woozy, but his nose and ear once more throbbed in tune with his heartbeat, and now his ankle joined the chorus where Marglo bit him. He waited until he was sure the passengers had all filed off before lowering himself to the pavement, and then crawled cautiously out.

He was alone. The bus was parked at the curb of an elementary school from hell. That wasn't exaggeration; he'd seen less ominous buildings in Freddy Krueger movies. So of course, with his current streak of luck, he had no doubt this was where the Nuclear Brethren had taken Officer Andrew.

Any direction he went from here would expose him. The closest cover was a low brick wall that started at the edge of the school lawn about ten yards away and then led up past the left side of the school. He hesitated, still not sure if he wanted to risk his neck any further for the cop, but the point was moot. He'd come too far to turn back now.

He crawled across the lawn on his belly, thinking about when he and Mark used to play 'army men' in the backyard as kids, and then shying away from that memory just as fast. His ankle radiated waves of heat up his entire leg, but he didn't stop to check it until he'd covered the sixty or so yards to the building.

The anklet of wounds just above the shredded top of his sock was angry red and swollen. Perfect. Who knew what diseases were in that thing's saliva?

"Now what, Ronnie-o?" he muttered. "What's the brilliant plan?"

He was flying by the seat of his pants, and that was what had gotten him in this mess in the first place. He needed to think. Well, step one was get into the building. No, scratch that. Step one, above all else, was to not get himself caught. Step *two* was get into the building.

Ronnie crept along the exterior. All of the doors he found were locked. Near the rear, he found a maintenance ladder bolted to the brick, high up so it would be out reach of young hands. He had no trouble leaping to grab the last rung, hauling himself up, and then climbing to the black-tarred roof of the school.

An access door next to an HVAC unit was unlocked. He slipped inside and sealed it back. Utter darkness greeted him in the stairwell down to the second floor. He waited for his eyes to adjust, but they never did. He finally limped down a stair at a time, until he came out into a main hallway almost as pitch.

A full body shiver worked its way through him. This place was not right, in a cosmic, back-of-the-eyeballs sort of way. He was never a big fan of the educational institution, but the walls here felt alive and watching. They buzzed beneath his fingertips, like the vibration of distant machinery. He moved on, listening for voices, but the school's silence was so thick it was claustrophobic.

By the dim evening light coming through windows at either end, he found a door labeled 'CUSTODIAL.' After tripping over a mop bucket and almost severing his pinky on a disassembled paper shredder, he found a working flashlight whose bulb wattage was high enough to be used as a prison guard tower search beam.

There was also a fire axe in a wall-mounted glass box. He thought of the hatchet he'd used to kill Marglo and mentally gagged. As little as he wanted to perform any more wet works, he needed a weapon. He unsealed the case and hefted the axe in one hand.

Then it was back out into the hallway, the flashlight kept off and shoved in his waistband. Now he only had to check every room in the school until he found Andrew. He turned the corner into the next dark cross hall...

And almost ran into the broad, rotting back of one of the Nuclear Brethren.

The guy spun at the sound of either Ronnie's approach or his mad scramble to back away. Those deep red orbs drilled into him, scattering shards of light in all direction like a prism. The man wore an NHL hockey jersey for the New York Americans, which, if Ronnie remembered his favorite sport worth a damn, had disbanded sometime in the early forties.

"Little mortal came to us," Jersey growled. He gaped in surprise for only a moment before recovering his wits. "How convenient."

Ronnie brandished the axe. "Let's see how convenient it is when I chop you into firewood, asshole! Now where's Andrew?"

Jersey came at him with spooky silence. Ronnie swung the axe blind. The blade thunked into the other man's upper chest, releasing a dribble of brackish, partially-coagulated blood. He grinned and wrenched the handle out of Ronnie's grasp, then pulled the weapon from the wound with a wet, sucking *shhhhluck!*

"We have the other human. I don't think Almighty Tro-fonag will be too angered if I turn your body into a flesh sculpture in honor of His greatness."

The only other thing Ronnie had that was even close to a weapon was the heavy-duty flashlight. He pulled it out just in time for the creature to knock it away. It planted a hand on Ronnie's chest and shoved, throwing him back against the corridor wall. Ronnie hit hard enough to knock the wind out of him, then rebounded into the floor. Jersey moved in, axe raised.

When the flashlight hit the tile floor, it switched on, throwing a shaft of pure white radiance back at them. Jersey screamed, dropped the axe and threw up a hand to cover his eyes. The reaction was so violent it could've been acid thrown in his face.

Ronnie scrambled for the flashlight as it rolled away down the hall. Jersey shook off the blow and came after him. Ronnie got in one good kick at the creature's chest—a few ribs snapped like kindling—and then it landed on him.

Luckily, he had the flashlight by then.

He shone the beam right in the thing's face. Jersey cursed and flailed away. He followed with the beam, chasing the creature into the corner of the nearest locker, where he buried his head in his hands. Ronnie kept him pinned there, blind and writhing, while he retrieved the axe.

"All right, let's try this again, dickhead."

A few minutes later and Jersey was a bloody mess on the floor. The fire in his eyes extinguished, and Ronnie thought he saw black smoke wafting from the empty sockets in its skull just before he turned away.

He suddenly had a much better idea how to go about this.


Andrew stared up into Manners face for a full twenty seconds. The professor gave no indication he even recognized him as he looked down his nose.

"Where was he?" Manners asked the Incarnate from the bus. The other two still stood on either side of Andrew, ready to grab him if he made a move.

The creature lowered his hand, but still squinted in the pale lamplight. "Cowering in a basement like the vermin he is."

"And the other one?"

"He...escaped. My men are searching the area for him even now."

Manners glanced once more at Andrew. He couldn't figure out what was going on, and his exhausted brain was throwing suggestions at him half-heartedly, that this man had been duping them all along, or that this wasn't even the same person. Anything was possible in this insanity; hadn't that been proven time and time again? He opened his mouth to just ask for an explanation—it probably couldn't make things worse than they already were—but Manners rushed to cut him off.

"Good. Take this one somewhere and guard him until you've found the other."

"No. We'll continue the search, but we don't need the other. Begin the ritual with this one immediately."

"We should wait."

"*We've waited long enough!*" the Incarnate snarled. "Open the doorway so we can feast on their world!"

Manners turned a stern gaze on the creature, a look that could probably freeze any poor undergrad student in their tracks. "Who is the Facilitator, demon, you or I?"

"You are, but don't forget your place. You hold no dominion over us. Your part in this is all but finished. Open the doorway or I'll do it for you."

Manners glared for another few seconds before relenting. "Fine. Let me collect my things and we will go downstairs." He turned away from Andrew and started across the room to a satchel on the windowsill.

"There is...one more thing," the Incarnate said, a sly touch to his words, and Manners froze with his back turned. "These cows had help."

"Help? What do you mean?"

"Powerful artcrafts protected them; magics far stronger than they would ever be capable of. That's why they eluded us for so long."

Manners froze with his hand on the strap of the leather bag. "What are you suggesting?" he asked over his shoulder.

The Incarnate crossed the room, coming up close enough behind him to speak directly into the professor's ear. Andrew leaned forward to listen to what was whispered, but there was no need; the creature spoke at the same barking level.

"I'm *suggesting* that there's a rogue force at play in this reality you constructed," he said, "because if I thought for even a second your leash had grown long enough to allow such duplicity, I would tear your puling guts out."

The moment stretched, and just as Andrew thought he was beginning to grasp the situation, a new sound filled the room: a brief, high-pitched whine, followed by a rustling.

Everyone in the room raised their heads and stared around in confusion, but Andrew recognized the noise.

The open hum of a PA system.

"Attention faculty and students," a familiar voice boomed over them. Andrew grinned. "This is Principal Pearson."

"*The other human is here!*" the Incarnate screeched. He pointed at the two guarding Andrew. "*He's in the headmaster quarters! Go now! Gather the others! FIND HIM!*" They tromped out of the classroom.

"Officer Andrew, if you can hear this," Ronnie continued over the loudspeaker, "would you please meet me in the place where your son would do that thing he likes to do? And just in case you need some assistance..."

The room blazed as the overhead fluorescents came on, both here and the hallway outside, unnaturally bright after so long in the dark. The kid must've used the master override; since Columbine, all schools had them in case the police needed to search the premises fast. The bony Incarnate screamed and clutched at his face, stumbling backward into the first row of desks like a man trying to get away from a swarm of bees.

Andrew didn't waste the opportunity. He swayed on his jelly legs as he got up. The creature thrashed, throwing wild punches while hiding his eyes in the crook of his other elbow. That anger from the bus came back. Andrew dove into him, throwing them both over a desktop and into the floor. They fell in a pile with Andrew on top, and he straddled the hideous thing, pulling its arm away so he could pound that rotten face with both fists. He could feel bones snapping beneath its mushy skin.

"Stop!" Manners pleaded. "You'll kill him!"

Andrew got in a hit that made his knuckles ache. "I hope I do!"

"Yes, but you don't want to be that close to him when he dies, believe me! Run, while you have the chance!"

Andrew reached into the pocket of the creature's faded jeans and pulled Joey's picture out. The Incarnate coughed and twitched, reaching weakly for him as he got up. Andrew kicked him in the head. The left side of its putrid face collapsed beneath the toe of his sneaker. "Let's go, you're coming with me!"

"What? I-I can't, I have to stay!"

Andrew grabbed the professor around the back of the neck and shoved him toward the door of the classroom. "I don't remember giving you a choice!"

"You have no idea what you're doing!"

"No kidding. That's been par for the course since the beginning of this whole mess."

In the hall, Andrew saw that all the lights in the entire school were on. It made the place much less terrifying. Several yards away, the other two Incarnates writhed on the ground.

"Do you know this school?" Andrew asked.

"I built this entire universe from the ground up. I assure you, I know every inch of it."

"Good. Then take me to the art classrooms."


The room Ronnie waited in was rectangular, with long windows and cabinets of art supplies along one side, and children's pictures covering the other in a collage of the damned. They were full of the glopped-on paint and primitive characters indicative of any kindergartener, but the kids that created these needed serious help. Beasts of all shapes and sizes were depicted as they tore human beings apart by the handful. Red and black seemed to be the predominant colors. He resolved to wait only another minute before he declared that he'd done the best he could and make a run for it, but Andrew entered before he'd counted to thirty, shoving the good Professor ahead of him.

"Holy shit, it worked?"

"Yeah, thanks. That was some damn good thinking, but I'm sure those things will find a way to come after us any minute." Andrew forced Manners into the closest desk with a hand on his shoulder.

"How'd *he* get here?"

"He was already here, giving out orders to these things." Andrew's eye was caught by the collection of nightmare-inducing art. He scanned across them as he continued talking. "He's their 'Facilitator,' whatever that means."

"Oh, you old douchebag fuck," Ronnie spat. "I knew you were in on this, I just *knew* it."

"I told you to stay put!" Manners snapped. "All you had to do was sit there and wait for me, and you incompetents couldn't do that correctly!"

"Yeah, well I got news for you, genius! Your spell or whatever didn't work! It led them right to us!"

"It…it did? Oh, I didn't compensate for…" His reserved face twitched with emotion warring beneath the surface. "I apologize, I don't normally perform that kind of work. In any case, you have to let me go back! They can't know I tried to help you!"

"Not this time." Andrew crossed his arms. "We want answers. Right now."

"Uh, right *now?*" Ronnie went to the doorway of the classroom and glanced up and down the bright hallway. "Andrew, don't you think we oughta be, uh, hittin the ol dusty trail?"

"I'm not moving another inch until I understand what's going on." He leaned over Manners. "Tell us everything. What this place is, how it got here, what those Incarnates want with us…everything."

"And about this Trofo—!"

"SHHHHH!" Manners pushed past Andrew and leapt up from his desk chair, wagging a finger at Ronnie. Absolute panic filled his face. "Do NOT say that name! He will know, he will hear it, and then whatever time you might have bought yourselves will be wasted!"

Ronnie blinked. Even just the two syllables he'd gotten out were enough to make him dizzy, and sent the time when he'd stolen fifty dollars of his mom's grocery money shooting to the surface of his consciousness. Saying the word was even worse than seeing it or hearing it.

"Explain," Andrew bade the old man softly. "And if you convince me fast enough, we might let you go."

Manners threw up a hand and paced away from them. "Believe me when I say, there are forces at work here so grand you couldn't imagine them. It would be like trying to explain quantum physics to a golden retriever."

"These things want our universe. That son of a bitch said he wanted to kill my son. That's not too hard for me to understand."

"*Start talkin!*" Ronnie shouted.

"*All right!*" Manners thundered, and launched into his scholarly teaching voice. "I would hope the theory of multiple parallel dimensions is familiar to you. There is an infinite chain of universes just like yours, each with its own alternate earth and alternate timeline, many of them containing their own versions of Mr. Horner and Mr. Pearson, although they are, most likely, radically different from either of you. So it has been, since the beginning of whatever concept of time you subscribe to."

Ronnie found himself nodding along. Other versions. Maybe a version where he'd made something of himself. Or one where his father hadn't been such a dick.

Or one where Mark was still alive.

The idea actually gave him some comfort.

Manners was still talking. "But now...they're being plundered. Extinguished like candle flames. As I said earlier, your world is safe for now, but it may not be for much longer. This place is what's known as a 'staging dock,' a preparation for... well, an invasion, to put things bluntly, which is all we really have time for. Going back to my cancer example, just as the cells within that growth want nothing more than to spread and infect the rest of the body, the forces contained within this small growth clinging to your plane of existence intend to breach the boundary separating them and claim your world as their own. As they have done countless times before."

"*Who?*" Andrew pressed. "*Who* has done it countless times before?"

Manners' next answer was longer in coming, and he swallowed several times before saying it. "Evil. The purest, most distilled form of the concept you could ever want. He goes by many names. The Dowser Beast. The Great Obligath. The Dark Stranger."

"I've seen that written all over the place here. That Incarnate mentioned it."

"I imagine so. This dock is built to His specifications, in His image. You are not dealing with Him directly, but your dimension will be claimed in His unholy name. If they succeed, it will be written across the sky in fire."

"Then who are we dealin with?"

"The taking of your world was delegated to one of His generals, the name which you so carelessly almost blurted out, Mr. Pearson. And trust me, that creature is almost as bad."

"You're the one that makes all this possible," Andrew said suddenly. His face reminded Ronnie of a borderline retarded kid that had been in his high school chemistry class, the day he finally understood what a milliliter was. "You're the Facilitator. You said you built this place."

Now Manners looked downright miserable for the first time, and as ancient and exhausted as a desiccated Egyptian mummy. "I was a man once, long ago, on another world much like yours. I learned something terrible, dug too deep behind the fabric of things, and I was taken forcibly into His service, along with several of my colleagues. We were given more knowledge and life than any being should ever have.

He needs men like me, you see. Men who…who understand the codes, can see the…ways. We open these staging docks, to prepare the way for His conquest."

Before Ronnie was even aware of what was happening, Andrew grabbed the professor by his jacket lapels and drove him across the room, smashing him against that wall full of hideous drawings.

"*And you just do it?*" he shouted. "*You help them take over entire* worlds?"

"Please understand, I have no choice—!"

"Yes, you do, you *always* have a choice! How many people—how many children?—have died because of you? In my book, that makes you no better than this Stranger!"

Manners looked haunted by the accusation. He remained pinned in Andrew's grip as he said, "I've sat by so many times and watched as world after world after universe after universe fell to the armies of the Dark Filament, and this time, this *one* time, I saw an opportunity to stop it."

"Look, I don't care about your life story," Andrew growled. "Just tell us how we fit into this whole mess, and how we can stop it."

Before Manners could speak, the lights went out. Or rather *exploded* out, hard enough to pierce the plastic coverings over them and spray florescent bulb glass in all directions. As they plunged back into darkness, Ronnie felt a thousand tiny daggers slash at him, and covered his face.

"Andrew," he said. "I think we better save that one for another time."

Andrew released Manners, grabbed him by the back of the neck instead, and slung him toward the door. "C'mon, let's go."

"No, you said you would let me go back!"

"I said if you convinced me, and the only thing you've convinced me of is that you have to be kept out of their hands."

They entered the hallway, now in total darkness. For the first time, Andrew realized Ronnie had an axe. He held the shaft in both hands out in front of him.

"I w-won't go!" Manners sputtered.

"Fine. But if they catch us again, I'll be sure to tell them who helped us."

"You wouldn't!"

"*C'mon*!" Ronnie hissed.

He led the way down several corridors by the light of a cannon-sized flashlight, limping badly. Andrew didn't even try and navigate mentally or count how many turns they made, he just concentrated on keeping his hand clamped on Manners' wrist, dragging him along.

At last the younger man stopped and glanced around one more corner. "There's a fire exit way at the end of the next hallway," he whispered. "Don't know what we'll do after that, but at least it'll get us outta the building."

"That's all I can ask for right now," Andrew said, thinking about that power in the walls, emanating from that door labeled FURNACE.

The three of them eased into the next hallway. Andrew could see the doors at the end, visible only as a slightly less dark rectangle. They looked a football field's length away.

From behind them came the clang of a door, and the scurrying of feet.

All of them stopped and looked back.

"Oh god," Manners moaned. "They released the *Elohaman*."

Coming down the corridor after them was an unending pack of children. Ages anywhere between four and seven, all hairless, all naked and sexless, all so pale and white they glowed in the dim light. They spilled out of a doorway just up the hall and came at them with uncanny speed, filling the passage from side to side, some of them on all fours, some almost floating, some defying gravity outright and scurrying up the walls. Claws stretched from their delicate fingers and fangs lined their smiling mouths. None of them made a single sound, but he heard their laughter in his head all the same.

These were the creatures that sang to him on the phone. The ones that tried to distract him with their handprints in the living room where he'd fought that first Incarnate. The ones that had painted those terrible images in the art room.

A terror as he had never known bashed its way into Andrew's brain, leaving him a quivering shell.

"RUN!" Manners bellowed. Now it was him tugging at Andrew as he sprinted away from the ghastly monsters. Andrew felt his feet start to move, but it was like someone else behind the controls.

They passed Ronnie, who was sweeping his flashlight beam along the faces of their tiny pursuers.

"That won't work! They're not Incarnates!" Manners called over his shoulder. "The *Elohaman* are nothing more than vampires! We have to get outside!"

Andrew pulled his hand out of Manners' and pumped his legs. He couldn't be caught by those things, he couldn't bare to be touched by them, because he *knew*, he knew there would be one in that pack of innocent-looking demons that looked just like Joey and if that happened, his mind would break.

The length of hallway to the doors had tripled. He and Manners were just about dead even with Ronnie a few steps behind, and the sound of their pursuers was like muted thunder.

He put his arms out and hit the metal of the fire door with his palms, shoving it open, and ran into the unnatural night. Manners did the same with the other door.

Ronnie screamed.

Andrew turned in time to see him go down, one of the white creatures clinging to his hurt leg.

The axe flew out of his grip and hit one of the doors as it started to swing back closed. Andrew leapt forward and grabbed it. The creature that tripped Ronnie was towing him back down the corridor, and Andrew swung the blade of the axe into its skull. The entire top half of its bald head tore away. It fell back, caterwauling.

"SHIT, GET 'EM OFF ME!"

The others had reached them. Tiny hands latched around Ronnie's feet and ankles. Andrew dropped the axe and snatched up his arms, trying to yank the kid out of their grasp and through the double doors. The tug-of-war lifted Ronnie completely off the ground.

Something scrabbled at Andrew's waist. He looked down to find one of the monsters had slunk underneath Ronnie to grab at him. He pulled his stomach away, over the threshold of the door, and when the thing tried to follow him, smoke poured from its pale skin. It screeched and jerked the appendage away.

"They can't enter nature, not even one as false as this!" Manners yelled.

"Professor, get over here and help me!"

Manners grabbed one of Ronnie's arms and helped Andrew pull, but they were swarmed. There must be twenty of the impish creatures hauling at the kid, and more crowding around the doorframe to swipe at them.

And then one of them jumped atop Ronnie's back and thrust its face almost into Andrew's.

It was Joey. Just as he predicted. Joey with no hair, a little albino chemo patient, Joey with more malicious glee in his face than Andrew had ever seen, but unmistakably Joey. It hissed at him through incisors as long and narrow as toothpicks.

Andrew screamed and pushed away, letting go of Ronnie, falling back on his ass outside the doors of the school. Without his strength, the kid was yanked from Manners' hands.

"ANDREEEEEEW!"

He watched as Ronnie was dragged down the hallway, carried on a pale tide of small bodies, receding into darkness. His face was the last thing to disappear, mouth stretched open and still screaming Andrew's name.

The doors of Arthur J. Filament Elementary School swung closed.

## VII. THE RITUAL

Andrew stayed where he landed, staring at the smooth metal of the school's fire door. His brain felt sluggish, confused and disbelieving. Seconds became soupy. He could still feel Ronnie's hands in his, just before he'd let go and the kid had been pulled into the mass of those...*things*.

Manners backed away quickly and then spouted a string of gibberish. The world rotated around Andrew with the precision of a clock gear, and then he was no longer sitting on the walkway outside the school. He was on the concrete in the middle of the street, staring at his and Ronnie's ruined vehicles. The change of scenery only added to his mental disarray.

"I still have a few tricks up my sleeve," the professor muttered.

"What were those things?" Andrew gasped.

"I told you, they are called *Elohaman*." His pronunciation of the word sounded like something from the Torah. "I've rarely seen them in the flesh. They're mostly used to play mental tricks on enemies of the Filament, distractions, that sort of thing. The Incarnates had them looking for you the whole time, trying to keep you off balance long enough to be captured."

"Then...they're not really children?"

"Oh no, they certainly are. Or *were*, once. Children tend to be the only ones that survive the...process." He turned and hurried toward the cars. "Come, Mr. Horner. It won't take the Incarnates long to get organized and come after us again."

Andrew got up. He was so exhausted, in every sense of the word. And he couldn't tear his thoughts away from that awful look on Ronnie's face as he'd been dragged back into the darkness of that terrible school. He ran after Manners. "But they have Ronnie!"

"I know. That's unfortunate."

Andrew reached out and grabbed the man's shoulder, forcing him to turn. "We have to go back!" Even as he said it, a more primitive part of him recoiled. The thought of seeing those pale creatures again curdled his blood.

Especially the one wearing Joey's face.

Manners spun and pushed his hand roughly away. "Unhand me, sir! I regret ever laying eyes on either of you! I hoarded what little power He gave me for close to a *millennia* just to hide you two cretins from His all-seeing eye, and look what it brought me!" He clutched great handfuls of his silvery hair and pulled at them. "Good Lord, even though I failed here, I could have tried again another time! I could have worked from the inside to save even an infinitesimal number of universes! But now that He knows what I've done, I'm no better off than you! You're a selfish ingrate!"

Andrew slapped the man across one bearded cheek. His head rocked to the side and then swiveled back with a look of shock. "To be honest, I don't really care anymore about your problems, Professor Manners. Just tell me what they want with him. What they wanted with me."

Manners gently touched the place where Andrew's hand struck flesh, but when he spoke, his voice was still full of disdain. "I thought you might figure that out yourself by now. You're the keys."

"Meaning?"

"Meaning that armies of the Dark Filament need permission to enter your world, acquiescence from a representative. The cosmos is in great upheaval, but it still holds to some rules. An effort to keep balance, I suppose."

"So they need us…to tell them…it's okay to wipe out our planet?"

"Correct. They only need it from one of you, and now that they have Mr. Pearson…I imagine they'll start trying to get it."

"Oh my God." Finally it all made sense, an order in this chaos. "What will they do to him? That Incarnate mentioned something about a ritual."

"Ritual. Ha!" Manners shook his head. "No need to pretty it up. It's nothing but a glorified torture session. They'll take him apart piece by piece to get what they want and then put him back together to start all over again if necessary."

Manners sighed heavily and let his gaze fall to the ground. "Make no mistake. That young man is going to be in unimaginable torment in the very near future."


All was darkness.

Ronnie could feel their small hands on him, carrying him above their heads like a champion quarterback after a winning game, but he could see nothing. The corridors of the school (if that's even where he was anymore, and he wasn't entirely sure) had become choked with blackness.

He struggled and squirmed, but their grip was absolute. He couldn't hear their impish giggles anymore, could hear nothing at all but the sound of his own panicked breaths. They moved along for an undetermined length of time before he felt a different surface under his back, cool and flat.

Those hands pulled his arms above his head and held his legs down while they bound him to whatever he now lay on.

And then, all at once, the darkness was gone. Whisked away from his eyes, like a veil thrown aside. He raised his head and looked around.

He was in a room that brought to mind medieval dungeons. The walls were dark, stained brick with shackles bolted into them. Ronnie was bound tight by wrists and ankles to a table made of white stone or marble. No windows; the only light came from a roaring fire in a round pit beyond the foot of the table. The flames produced no smoke; so there wasn't even a chimney to break the solid façade of the walls. The place was long and rectangular; to his left was a flat wall with a door, but on the right it stretched beyond the limits of the flickering fire-light into a cauldron of darkness.

Except it really didn't feel like his right, not in the spatial sense of the word. What he actually thought, looking into it, was that it led *down* somehow, deep into the bowels of the earth, either on a steep slant or by some quirk of physics that twisted direction.

The creatures that brought him here—Manners' Aloha Men, or whatever they were called—were gone. Disappeared along with the darkness. Instead, one of the guys that Andrew had been calling 'Incarnates' leaned casually against the far wall on the other side of the fire pit with one leg up. Part of his face was crushed in, bone poking through the black, flaky skin. His eyes glittered even brighter than the flames illuminating him.

"Welcome," he said, and started around the fire.

"What's up?" Ronnie replied. He coughed. The noise echoed away from him for what sounded like miles. "Did Andrew and the Professor get away?"

"For now. We'll find them. Manners will pay for his deceit. His rebellion amounted to nothing, considering one of you is still strapped to that table."

"What about your little friends?" Ronnie asked. "What happened to them?"

The Incarnate reached his side and raised a gangrenous eyebrow. The dent in his face was sickening. He wore no shirt, and the skin along his narrow chest was riddled with black boils. "Little friends?"

"Yeah, the bald kids with the bad teeth."

He shone a smirking grin down on Ronnie. "The *Elohaman* are back in their confinements. Their minds reach far, but their physical forms are exhausted so quickly."

"Well, whatever, dude. Where I come from, running around with a pack of naked kids'll get you lynched."

Now the Incarnate was really beaming, both through his smile and his eyes. "I'm so glad it's you. I think you'll turn out to be so much more fun than the other mortal, in the end."

Before Ronnie could inquire or quip, the man's spidery hand flashed out. It latched onto his calf, where the bite mark from Marglo still pulsed below the torn hem of his jeans leg. Fingers found the puffy, infected holes and squeezed.

The pain was indescribable. An acid that shot through his nervous system. It wracked his body, arched his spine so hard his butt lifted off the table. And just when he didn't think it could get any worse, the fucker's fingers slid *into* the holes, digging at warm underflesh. White tracers shot through the blackness behind his eyelids.

He thought he blacked out, but if so, it was only for seconds. When he came around, the Incarnate still leered down at him, and the heat in his leg was dying down.

"That hurt, yes?"

"No, it was better than a hand job." Ronnie heard tears in the hoarse retort and hated himself for it. "What the fuck do you think it felt like, asshole?"

"There will be more of that," the Incarnate told him matter-of-factly. "So much more. Unless…"

Ronnie refused to give him the satisfaction of asking for the rest of the sentence.

"Unless you say one word. Just one."

"And then you'll let me go?"

"Of course."

"That was said waaaay too fast to be anything but a lie."

The Incarnate shrugged. "Why wouldn't we? Once you say this word, you're of no further concern to us. Do you want to know what it is?"

"I hope it's not your boss's name, cause that shit gives me diarrhea."

The Incarnate reached for his leg.

*"Okay, yes, yes, I wanna know!"*

"There!" He clapped his hands together. A flake of blackened skin landed on Ronnie's cheek. "You just said it! The word is 'yes!' See how simple that was?"

"All right then, I said it, now lemme the fuck outta here!"

"You have to wait for the question."

"Then ask me if you're an uncircumcised cock, and I'll be glad to give you your yes!"

The Incarnate's eyes flashed. Literally; the red centers pulsed angrily. He leaned in until his crumbling nose was almost touching Ronnie's. The stench that hung around him was a torture all its own. "Little sin cow…" he whispered. "May we enter your realm of existence?"

Ronnie swallowed. He had no doubt his days of cruising in the Mustang and living off his wiles were over no matter what this talking corpse said, so he'd been prepared to give an affirmative to just about anything as long as it meant going out painlessly.

But this question stopped him cold.

He wasn't even sure he heard it correctly, but he understood it was important. More important than anything he'd ever been asked in his whole miserable life. The image of his mother came to him for some reason, and Mark, and even his father.

The Incarnate waited.

"No." The word was more a quivering sigh than anything. He suddenly didn't have the strength for anything else.

"I knew you wouldn't disappoint me." The Incarnate turned and looked into the dark hole to Ronnie's left. Ronnie did the same. He could discern nothing in that nest of shadows, but he could *feel*. It pulsed with energy that made him want to tear at his flesh, like an alcoholic with DT-induced bugs on their skin. The Incarnate seemed to get the answer he sought. He walked to the fire, bent, and picked up a sharp metal rod that had been roasting in the embers. The tip glowed the same hideous red as his eyes.

"Feel free to stop me at any time," he said.

Ronnie laid his head back against the table and tried not to cry.


Andrew heard glass break behind him. He jumped and wheeled around, ready for whatever nightmare this place wanted to throw at him next.

No one was there. It looked like the front window of the house right behind them—the first one Andrew tried knocking at when they woke up here, where he'd imagined another life—had fallen right out of its frame, hit the lawn and shattered.

"It's unraveling," Manners told him. "This universe is unstable. They weren't meant to last forever. The Incarnates wasted a lot of time looking for the two of you after my little trick."

Andrew peered closer in the gloom. He could actually see the house frame sagging under its own weight, like a giant, invisible hand pressing down on it. The walls looked even more worn and thin, almost fading out of reality. "What will happen to it?"

"It will keep falling apart until it collapses in on itself. The pressures outside are massive."

Andrew faced him again and jumped back into their previous conversation. "Why didn't the Incarnates just grab one of those deformed people and get them to agree?"

Manners waved a hand impatiently. "Because they don't represent your dimension. As I said before, those are just twisted duplicates of the people that actually lived here. The only beings currently within the boundaries of this staging dock that are from your world are you and Mr. Pearson."

"And once Ronnie gives them permission, that's it, they can just waltz right in like they own the place?"

"There's a bit more to it than that, but yes. Once the path is open, your dimension *will* fall."

"And if he doesn't give them the okay?"

One of Manners' bushy eyebrows took a hike up his forehead. "Do you really think someone of his social standing would give the slightest hesitation?"

Andrew grimaced. For some reason, the aspersion on Ronnie aggravated him, especially coming from Manners, whom he now equated on a level with Nazi officers in charge of concentration camps. "But if he doesn't?"

"He will. I've seen it happen more times than you can count. They'll torture him until there's hardly enough brain function left to resist."

"Yeah, I guess you would know," Andrew snapped. "You're their Facilitator after all, right? You were in charge of the torturing."

Manners said nothing. A dark ghost of truth and memory flitted through his eyes.

"What if this place collapses before then?"

"First of all, don't hang your hopes on that. They have more than enough time to coerce him. But…*if* he could hold out…then that would be that. Your universe remains safe. They move on to the next one."

"Couldn't they just build another one of these things, these 'staging docks?'"

"Absolutely not. That's another balancing measure the cosmos enforces. The same way they need permission from a representative, they can also only try each link on the dimensio-axial chain one time."

Andrew brought his arms up and let them drop back to his sides. "Jesus Christ. One time. Why us, huh? Why did this responsibility fall to us?"

Manners clenched his jaw. "Because God determined it should. Or Buddha. Or Fate. Bad luck. Take your choice, Mr. Horner."

The curb was a few feet away. Andrew barely made it over before his legs gave way. He sat and stared at Ronnie's overturned Mustang in front of him and then at the rest of this godforsaken world. Without stars, the night was more of a smothering blanket than a natural occurrence. The streetlamp illumination looked more sickly yellow than the last time he'd been here, the houses more broken and dilapidated by the second. But there were more noises now. From all over. The sound of the buildings crunching and cracking was almost a constant mutter. It reminded him of a documentary about Antarctica in summer he'd watched: the brittle sound of melting ice rubbing together.

It all made him feel numb, and unimaginably far from home.

Manners softened. "Listen, the building of these docks is by no means an exact science. Or science at all, really. They are just a net that is cast, and we see what we reel in. Sometimes it's a movie star. Sometimes it's an entire religious congregation. Sometimes it's no one, and in that case, the builders are punished severely. This time, it just happened to be the two of you. I tried to help you escape before the Incarnates got a hold on you, and I failed." He took a few paces across the street and squatted in front of Andrew, plucking at the hems of his tweed pants to keep them from touching the concrete. "But we can *still* escape, my friend. Back into your world. I know how to do that much."

"What good will that do? If what you say is true, won't they be coming in right behind us, after Ronnie gives them the okay?"

"Yes," Manners agreed. "But we can run. We'll have plenty of time for me to gather the necessary elements for another jump. For you to find your son, if you want. Then we can all flee to the next dimension. And keep fleeing, if need be. But we must...go...*now*."

Andrew considered that. At first, the urge to get back to Joey—to see the boy with his own two eyes and make sure he was all right—was so strong he wanted to demand Manners do it immediately. But what then? A life full of running across worlds that weren't even his sounded more like hell than this place. He just couldn't reconcile himself to the fact that this morning he had a future—maybe not a great one without Michelle, but there was still Joey, and his job, and hope—but now, no matter what he decided, that future—*everyone's* future—was gone.

"So just leave Ronnie to the Incarnates? Not to mention the rest of my world?"

Manners nodded slowly.

"No. I can't do that."

"Be reasonable and save yourself. There's nothing you can do."

"We can get Ronnie back."

Manners sprang up, guffawing all the way. Andrew did the same. The professor jabbed a finger into his chest. "You listen to me, Mr. Horner, and you listen good! Here's another natural law: two beings entered this staging dock, and only two can leave it. At the moment, that's you and myself. Even if you were to somehow reach Mr. Pearson and safely extricate him from their clutches, I would be unable to transport all three of us across the barrier."

"Then send both of us, like you were going to anyway!"

"That was *before* you revealed my rebellion and made me a hunted man! If I send the two of you back, your world is safe, but what about the rest of the cosmos? I'm one of the few beings in all existence that knows of the invasion being perpetrated, and that makes my life far more important in the long scope than either of yours! I can still do a lot of good by spreading a warning to the right people! Look beyond your own petty concerns and realize that!"

"Okay, fine! But there must be some other way!"

Manners didn't speak. He squinted at Andrew, and then cupped his chin in that scholarly way of his. Andrew wondered if being a professor was half about imparting knowledge and half about theatrics.

"What?"

"Suppose…" he began, holding it out with the pomp and poise of a gifted lecturer, "You *were* to reach Mr. Pearson. I could get you as close as possible, and then the rest would be up to you."

"That's pretty much my plan so far."

"Yes, but let me finish. Suppose you were to reach Mr. Pearson and then…well…the Incarnates couldn't very well coerce him if he were dead, could they?"

The words made the pit of Andrew's stomach feel even heavier than it already was. "You mean…kill him? Me?"

"One life to save many; it's a concept as old as time. We leave him here, and your world dies. Mr. Pearson can't have given them anything yet or I would know it, so there's still time. If you can get within striking distance…"

Andrew didn't answer. He stepped around Manners and walked across the street to the driver's side door. As he opened it, a familiar moaning came from somewhere up the street, but he ignored it. On the driver's seat was his makeshift Spiderman evidence bag, filled with cash, Ronnie's gigantic revolver and a box full of ammunition. He snapped open the cylinder, loaded it, and held the gun sideways in his hands.

Manners came up behind him. "I could shift you back there. I can't guarantee what kind of resistance you'll meet, but I can get you as close as possible. They'll have him—"

"In the Furnace room," Andrew finished for him. "I know."

"You understand, of course, that you can't allow yourself to be captured either."

Andrew turned around with the gun still clutched tightly in his fist. "One of those vampire things…it looked just like

Joey. That was another version of him from some other universe…wasn't it?"

"Undoubtedly."

"If they take my world, will that happen to the children?"

"Only to the most unfortunate."

Andrew nodded. "Then take me to Ronnie."

A whole chorus of pathetic moans drifted up the street this time. The Xerox people were back.

"We'd better move fast," Manners told him, drawing away.

"Wait a minute." Andrew looked over the truck bed at the crowd of mutated fiends in bathrobes and housedresses headed their way once more. "How many things can you *shift* at one time?"


"*NO! OW, FUCK OWWW! OH GOD, PLEASE, STOOOOOOP!*"

Ronnie's screams felt loud enough to pierce his own eardrums. He was stripped down to nothing more than his underwear, his clothes shredded in a game with razors that left his torso a bloody mess.

The Incarnate removed the superheated clamps away from the pinky toe he'd been so lovingly reducing to a burnt stump. His eyes blazed. "May we enter your dimension?"

Ronnie screamed with laughter. Or wept. He was having a hard time discerning what was coming out of his mouth anymore. "*Mother may I take three baby steps forward?*" he screeched. "*No, you may not! May I take eight giant leaps forward and tear this maggoty, shit-eater's head off? Yes, you can fuckin well d-do thaaaaaaat!*"

The Incarnate took down a new device from the wall, something with a narrow scoop on one end and a spike on the other.

*"Bring it on, bitch! I've done a lot of shitty things in my life, but I don't want 'Ended the World' on my resumé!"*

But he would. He knew it. His mind felt like squashed Play-Doh. He couldn't take this forever, and he thought the Incarnate probably knew it too. Fact is, he didn't know why he hadn't already given in before now. It's not like he owed the world anything. It certainly hadn't done any favors for him.

So why not just give them what they wanted?

*Because you believe Officer Andrew is coming for you... don't you?*

*He is. I came for him, and he's gonna remember that.*

*Then that makes you the stupidest high school dropout that ever lived. Why would Andrew risk his ass coming back for you? He and Manners are probably halfway to Hawaii by now, sipping coconut drinks and laughing at you for taking the fall.*

Ronnie knew he probably should believe that—past experience had given him no reason to trust in others, that was for damn sure—but he didn't. Not even a little bit.

He just hoped the Jappy son of a bitch got here fast.

His torturer cranked some kind of wench below the table. The chains on Ronnie's ankles pulled, opening his legs an inch at a time.

The Incarnate pointed the scoop end of the device at the exposed crevice. "I'm told this one is especially uncomfortable."

Ronnie giggled, and he thought something in the darkness to his right laughed along with him.

# VIII. THE END

Three Incarnates had been designated to guard the front doors of the mortal educational facility which the Almighty Trofonag had chosen as his mainstay. One of them paced back and forth across the entrance in front of the others, so fuming mad his eyes had turned to a pulsing blood-red.

"We are missing the hunt," this one said.

"There will be no bloodshed," another answered. The words were a bit mangled due to his loose jawbone; he expected this body to give out any time now. "You heard the orders. Manners and the other human are to be found and brought here unharmed."

"We should kill them *both*," the first growled. "There is no reason to leave them alive."

"The human is insurance, in case the mortal now in our custody does not break fast enough. Manners however... Manners will be sent back to stand before the Stranger for his actions. He will pay for his betrayal."

"And what if he escapes across the barrier?" the third asked.

"Then finding him in the mortal world will be our first priority once we secure a connection between universes."

The pacing Incarnate turned and started back across the paved walkway. He pulled the ragged blade from the sheath at his side and waved it over his head. "I tire of this place! This endless boredom! I want to be back in a sinning world again, I want to rend children with my bare hands and watch the Light drain out of their accursed eyes—!"

"Freeze, all three of you!"

The Incarnate was so surprised by the sudden intrusion, for a second he actually did halt. When he looked up, he was shocked to see the human all the way at the end of the school's pathway, wielding one of the projectile weapons they loved so much. Manners cowered behind him.

The other two drew their own weapons. None of them paused to wonder at this turn of events or the mortal's stupidity for coming here; their ways were brute force and immediate gratification over thoughtful consideration. They started forward. "Fire that, if you think you can hit all three of us before we reach you. You will only bring a hundred more of us down on your head."

The human lowered its weapon. "Then I guess we better try something else."

Manners spoke the Old Language. Artcrafts beyond the Incarnates' understanding. There was a shift in the air between the two groups, a rush of displaced air, and suddenly a crowd of thirty deformed mortals appeared on the lawn.


The first thing the Xerox mutants saw were the Incarnates. Manners had been careful to make sure they appeared turned the right direction, so the murderous rampage didn't backfire. The assemblage shrieked and ran to meet the three decaying demons, crooked limbs reaching.

The two forces clashed. The Incarnates waded into the fray, swinging their long daggers and hacking apart the mindless men and women, but there were just too many. Once they got their hands on the red-eyed fiends, they tore at them, pulled in different direction until rotted limbs separated, and then threw themselves on the ground to feast on the decayed flesh. The grisly sight was enough to make Andrew gag.

"C'mon!" He grabbed at the professor while the Xerox suburbanites remained distracted.

"Oh no, I never said I would accompany you!"

"Tough! Now move!"

Manners planted his loafered feet. "Shoot me if you must, but I'll not walk willingly back into their arms on this addle-brained mission of yours! If they get their hands on me, I'll suffer far more than Mr. Pearson, I assure you!"

Andrew paused. Manners had called him selfish before, and maybe that wasn't far from the truth. The intent of returning here had been to save his world—to secure a future for Joey and Michelle even if he didn't make it back—but if these creatures took possession of the professor again and put him back to work making these staging docks, then *all* worlds would be in danger.

A trillion other Joeys and Michelles on a trillion other worlds, if he understood the situation.

He released the man and looked into his eyes. "Don't you leave me, Professor Manners. Don't you go back without me."

"I can only promise to give you as long as possible. Mr. Pearson's resolve won't hold forever; frankly, I'm surprised he lasted this long. And, as I said, this staging dock is collapsing."

He pointed. Andrew looked past the still feasting clones at the school. Stress fractures stretched across the brick and concrete front of the school. The whole midnight sky felt heavy above them, like it was squeezing in, to such a degree that Andrew imagined he could even feel the pressure change in his eardrums.

"Those *Elohaman*…you're sure they won't be around?"

"No, they couldn't. Their influence on the physical world will be exhausted for a while."

"And there's not any other nasty surprises waiting for me in there?"

Manners flinched. It was barely perceptible, but as someone trained to watch for lies on the faces of drunks and criminals, it could've been a neon sign. "No. Just whatever Incarnates were left behind. But once they're aware of your presence, the others will come running."

*What aren't you telling me, Professor?* Andrew thought. He gave no sign of his suspicion. There wasn't enough time to coerce information the man wasn't willing to give.

Manners straightened his suit coat. "I must set about preparing for our exit. I'll shift back and collect you once the deed is done."

"How…" He swallowed to wet a suddenly bone-dry throat, brought about by the thought of 'the deed' in question. "How will you know?"

"Trust me," Manners said, and rattled off a string of those guttural words. He disappeared, not all at once, or with a puff of smoke, but more like a door had been closed in front of him; the term 'shifting' made complete sense. He took the deformed cannibals with him, leaving only Andrew and a collection of gnawed Incarnate body parts strewn across the school lawn.

He hurried to the front doors, taking no great pains to be quiet. He could hear the place creaking and groaning as he entered, slowly being crushed. One of the interiors walls buckled beside him.

An Incarnate raced down the hallway at him, drawn by the noise of the battle on the lawn. Andrew took careful aim with Ronnie's huge revolver and squeezed off a round when the creature was just a few yards away. The bullet hit it square in the forehead. A few dribbles of sluggish blood came out, and he went down. These things were tough, able to take a lot of punishment, but their bodies (and Andrew got the idea the flesh and blood was the equivalent of a cheap suit) could be killed. A wisp of black smoke wafted out from its eyes as the fire in them died. Andrew was careful to stay away.

He ran. Down the cracking hallways, killing two other Incarnates along the way with well-placed shots and then reloading. His memories of being carried through the school before were vague, but in order to find his destination, he only had to keep his palm against the wall and trace the titanic flow of power beneath its surface. Before he knew it, he was standing in front of a door marked FURNACE.

The black aura still surrounded it. A dark halo that ebbed and grew in waves, pulsing outward from the door's surface. The murk reached out for him when it was at the height of each cycle, with wispy hands made of a substance like the smoke that came from the dead Incarnates' eyes. A fountain of ill thoughts sprang up in his head as he regarded it, awful memories and hidden desires he'd never told a soul and base, vile fantasies dredged from the deepest depths of his id. He had trouble believing such things could even originate in a human mind, let alone his own.

Andrew's heart squeezed up into his throat, where its frantic pulse threatened to choke him.

He couldn't open that door. To reach into that oily mass and turn that knob was lunacy. Doors were made for a reason, and whatever was on the other side of this one needed to stay here. His instincts—not just those honed by his cop background, but the ones that came with being human—urged him to run from here, find Manners, and beg the man to lead him out of this hell. And something told him that once his resolve broke, there would be no second try.

He wished he could say that it was the thought of Ronnie that stopped his flight—the punk had come back for him, after all, and Andrew believed in returning favors—but if he was being honest, he would have to admit it was Joey. God, he loved that boy *so much*. From the second he held him in the delivery room, Andrew knew there was nothing he wouldn't give up for him. All he wanted in that second was to hold his son again, to kiss those slender, artist fingers of his, and tell him it was all right to color outside the lines once in a while.

But in order to do that, Andrew had to get himself back *in*side the lines.

And ensure there was still an inside-the-lines to go back to.

Andrew reached into the layer of smog covering the door, wincing at the slimy feel against his skin, found the knob, and pulled it open, waiting for whatever lay behind it to pounce.

No monsters. Nothing lay in wait. Only a staircase leading down into darkness. He started down them, knowing that it couldn't be this easy.


The pain.

The pain was.

The pain was all consuming. Everywhere. Around him and in him. The past, the future, and the present coming together in one mind-blowing mental cataclysm.

Inescapable.

His mind was a blank. An empty landscape colored a screaming shade of red. He couldn't even remember his own name anymore, let alone why this was happening.

And then it stopped. Something swam through the haze of his vision. He (*wait, Ronnie, that was his name*) blinked away tears and stared up into the leering, cancer-ridden face hovering over him.

"*Plea...se...*" he rasped. His lips had forgotten how to form words. Each breath made him shudder. "*N. No m-more.*"

"Only you can make that happen, human."

He couldn't remember what, exactly, the Incarnate had done to him during this last session, but it had involved a pair of gardening shears, thumbscrews, and a toilet brush. Ninety percent of his body was either contused or burned, with several small wounds along his extremities cut down to the muscle and one on his right side exposing ribs. A puddle of his own blood squelched beneath him on the table.

What he wouldn't give for the days when the only thing hurting him was that piddly broken nose.

"Your species is so sensitive," the Incarnate rasped. "So delicate. You haven't learned to ignore the sensations of the flesh. I have seen pain do fascinating—and amusing—things to your kind. Unlocking long dormant abilities. Devolving into all manner of lower life. Agreeing to absolutely any-thing. All just to escape that which your pathetic minds should be capable of blocking out."

Ronnie didn't respond. No strength left in him to crack jokes. He used his tongue to raise the blood in the back of his mouth up and let it dribble down the side of his cheek.

The Incarnate went to the wall of torture implements and selected a new tool. He held it up where Ronnie could see. It was a steel rod with a crank on one end, and a metal bulb on the other, several inches in diameter.

"Do you know this, mortal? It is called a Pear of Anguish. Another instrument from the medieval period of your history. Exquisite era; torture, religious persecution, plagues by the dozen. It exists across almost all dimensions, no matter how different the timeline. Which I believe just proves you humans are as eager to be rid of each other as the rest of the cosmos is." He held the bulb over Ronnie's face. "If you do not tell me what I want to hear, I am going to insert this down your throat. Then..."

The Incarnate turned the crank at the other end. The bulb separated into four pieces, opening wider with each turn of the handle until it became a shiny blossom of sharp metal.

Ronnie wept. Blubbered as never before in his life.

His torturer leaned closer and crooned, "The internal damage will be massive, but it is not likely to kill you. You should even be able to speak enough to proceed."

"*Don't. Oh God, please don't.*"

"Then TELL ME!"

"*I don't remember what I'm supposed to say!*"

"TELL ME I MAY RIP YOUR WORLD ASUNDER!"

Ronnie opened his mouth to give this creature what it wanted. He couldn't remember why he'd held out so long in the first place. It seemed like he'd been waiting for something, hoping for something, but whatever it was obviously wasn't going to happen.

He got as far as the letter Y when the door set into the brick wall to his left flew open. A man burst into the room. Ronnie didn't recognize him.

But he surely looked Jappy.

~ ~ ~

It took Andrew several moments to realize the bloody, beaten, burnt sack of meat in front of him was Ronnie. The kid was chained to an ornate little pedestal in his underwear, shaking like a palsy victim.

He couldn't see the opposite wall; this room stretched away (or was it down? Looking over there gave the impression of depth, like staring over the lip of a tall building) into impenetrable shadow. But on the far side of the table was Andrew's old friend, his seatmate for the bus ride. The last time Andrew had seen this particular Incarnate was when he'd caved in the demon's skull with his foot, back in the classroom where they brought him to Manners. Even with those smoldering eyes and the dent along the side of his head, the surprise on the creature's face was obvious when Andrew burst into the room.

"*YOU!*" he screeched, coming around the table with a metal pole in his hand held back to swing.

"This is what you get for threatening my son," Andrew told him coolly. He raised the gun and fired, emptying an entire cylinder into the Incarnate. The flesh was so necrotic, so eaten up by whatever cancerous disease ravaged them, the large-caliber bullets tore gaping holes right through his torso. He didn't so much crumple as he disintegrated, splattering wet, blackish chunks across the cobblestone floor. The remains of his face released that puff of smoke which, Andrew suspected, were these things' true form.

From the darkness across the room came a roar of purest fury. He couldn't tell if he actually heard it or if it was only in his head, but he felt it all the way to his bones. It seemed to come from an impossible distance away, echoing across miles, oceans, light-years; distances so far they didn't have measurements. After it faded, he could feel a slight breeze against his skin, a wave of displaced air with a fetid under stench.

Something was coming. Something large and fast, hurtling up the brick-lined tunnel toward them. He could feel the power crackling from it, the source of all that latent energy running through the school.

And he did not want to be here when it arrived.

Ronnie had looked the same direction when the blast of sound came, but now he twisted his head back around. The Incarnate had done a real number on him. He bled from more wounds than Andrew could count, but even more startling, the punk attitude was gone, wrung out of him like blood from a rag, leaving only a terrified, hurting young man. "Andrew," he gasped, as though recognizing him for the first time. "Help. Please."

Help. There was only one way to help him now, one way to help both of them, and no time to waste talking, not even with himself. Especially with himself.

Andrew opened the cylinder of the revolver, fed in more bullets with a shaking hand, then snapped it closed. He crossed to the table quickly and pressed the barrel against Ronnie's forehead. The least he could do was make this quick and painless.

Ronnie gaped, crossing his eyes to stare up at the revolver. The confusion on his face smoothed out into understanding and, even worse, acceptance.

"I'm sorry," Andrew said, feeling moisture on his cheeks. "This is the only way."

Ronnie nodded beneath the gun. "D-do it. Put me outta my fuckin misery."

Andrew looked away. Squeezed the trigger. Felt the tension in the metal as the hammer pulled back. Wondered if he could ever face Joey again.

A few seconds later, the gun went off.

And the chain holding Ronnie's arms over his head was blasted apart.

"You don't get out of this that easy, you little shit," Andrew murmured. He turned and shot the chains holding the kid's feet, leaving steel bands around both his ankles. "C'mon, can you walk?"

"Walk? Man, I don't even know if I can *move*." Ronnie leaned up on the table and cried out, clutching a gaping wound in his side. Blood seeped between his fingers.

A crash swept out of the horizontal hole, the sound of smashed brick and collapsing mortar, definitely auditory rather than mental this time.

It was hollow and dull with distance, but much closer than the roar.

"We gotta go," Andrew said. "Right now."

Ronnie struggled up and swung his legs off the table. Andrew tossed him his jeans and the shredded remains of his t-shirt from the floor by the fire-pit and he slipped it over his head, hissing through his teeth when the material touched his tender skin. Every movement fired pain up somewhere on his body as working muscles reopened fresh wounds. Two of his toes on his right foot were gone; one by heat, the other by blade. His Marglo bite pulsed heat.

But he didn't slow down. Not for a second. A chewing, grinding noise came from that darkness behind him, like a freight train barreling at them and crashing through anything in its path. Ronnie remembered the Incarnate looking into those shadows as though seeking guidance just before starting his torment. There was increasing vibration in the floor and the walls as whatever had been at the other end of the—tunnel? hole?—approached at tremendous speed, a worm tunneling up from hell.

*Oh, c'mon Ronnie-o, you know what's comin just like I do, his name starts with T, ends with G, and makes you feel like you just masturbated in the middle of an orphanage when you hear it. And he ain't gonna fit inside this tiny room when he gets here; this motherfucker is BIG.*

He hopped off the torture table and his feet almost went out from under him. Andrew caught him before he went down. Ronnie put an arm over the man's shoulder and hawked a monstro loogie on the remains of the Incarnate.

"There's your permission, bitch," he wheezed.

Andrew half-led, half-carried him through the door and up the dark staircase beyond. Ronnie ignored the screaming aches and sharp pains from all over his body as best he could. By the time they emerged into the hallway of the school again, the entire building quaked hard enough to drop plaster ceiling tiles from above. And Ronnie didn't think it was all because of whatever was burrowing up beneath them either. The place was flattening out like a pancake, the walls scrunching up. The roof seemed at least a foot lower than the last time he'd been through here.

"It's collapsing!" Andrew yelled over the constant, unnatural grind. "The whole place, the entire universe!"

"It's the fuckin trash compactor from *Star Wars*!"

"We have to find Manners!"

They moved as fast as they could toward the front doors, Ronnie in his t-shirt and underwear and Andrew supporting him while keeping the gun ready. The vibration beneath them continued to grow all the time.

Outside, the night sky was threaded with cracks. *Cracks*. Ronnie felt like he could go mad staring at that sight. Something bled through those chinks in the very air, an inky black that made the false night feel as bright as high noon in the desert. He imagined this world as a giant bubble suddenly, a delicate boundary of soap separating them from whatever lay beyond.

What would happen when the stress became too much, and the bubble finally burst?

He shivered, wincing when something in his side flared.

"Manners!" Andrew screamed, wandering out toward where the school property met the street. Ronnie hobbled after him. "*Where are you?*"

"What do we do, man, what's the plan?" Time seemed to be slipping away like water through a breaking dam. Ronnie only knew one thing: he would rather die than go back into their custody.

"*I don't know, he said he'd be here!*" From the panic in Andrew's voice, Ronnie figured he probably felt the same.

The front doors of the school banged open again. A throng of Incarnates came sprinting out through them.

"Then we better think of something fast."

Too many to fight. All they could do is run. Andrew urged Ronnie across the lawn of the school, but the kid's injuries were slowing him down too much. Andrew took a few potshots into the closest members of the mob on their heels, giving him time to get a little further. Everywhere the ground shook, like the few earthquakes he'd been in, making them wobble as they moved.

When he turned back to sprint, he saw his truck shift into existence at the curb, the front end complete and undamaged once more. Even the bullet holes and shattered windows were repaired, all as new as the day he drove it off the lot. Manners appeared beside it, hurrying over to meet them, but stopped when his eyes landed on Ronnie.

"What is *he* doing here?" he cried.

"He's escaping, just like us!" Andrew shouted as they reached the professor and continued past to the truck. "We'll just have to find another way!"

"I told you, there is no other way! You weak fool, *you've doomed us all!*"

The Incarnates were still coming, a forest of red eyes and snarling mouths. Andrew yanked open the driver's door of his truck and let Ronnie slide in first. "Worry about that later, and let's get out of here!"

Manners ran, skirting around the hood and hurtling through the passenger door. Andrew dove behind the wheel and twisted the keys that were already dangling from the ignition.

"*Go, go, go!*" Ronnie screeched.

Andrew put the car in gear, floored the gas, and rolled all of two yards before the street in front of them cracked violently open.

The pavement rippled and thrust upward in a rough circle approximately thirty feet in diameter. Chunks of dirt and concrete—some of them the size of small automobiles—rocketed into the air, leaving a dark, round pit. At the same time, the trembling underneath them stopped.

And from the hole climbed…something.

Andrew coasted to a stop and stared in awe. Two gigantic, spider-like appendages rose up and found purchase to either side of the hole. They heaved, and, like a slow-motion jack-in-the-box, up came a head as big as his truck, a conglomeration of disgusting creatures, parts from rats, snakes, bugs, and more all jammed together in a Frankensteinian stew. It had pincers on either side of a mouth filled with grimy fangs, any of which was longer than a human body. Two iridescent green eyes—orbs that looked like they should be staring out of a forgotten swamp—regarded them as it roared, emitting the same sound Andrew had heard in the furnace room of the school. That mashed, misshapen face kept rising as it climbed from the hole, towering over them, revealing the eel body it was attached to, from which a thousand wiggly legs dangled in twin rows.

Andrew suspected this was the source of the shadow they'd seen, just before the doll attack. The king surveying his dock before nestling back into his putrid nest beneath the school to watch the torture show.

"Uh, maybe we don't go this way," Ronnie whispered.

"That's Trofonag, isn't it?" Andrew asked. The word twisted his stomach into knots.

"Yes," Manners answered.

"And you knew he was down there all along. You were going to let him take me, too."

"You insisted on going back. I never expected you to make it all the way in, much less out. And certainly not with Mr. Pearson in tow. I assumed, one way or another, that your world was finished."

Andrew didn't have time to get angry. He stomped the gas and twisted the wheel, swinging the truck away from the three-story tall Lovecraftian monstrosity in the road. From the edge of his vision, he saw one giant limb take a lumbering swipe at them and miss. Trofonag bellowed.

Before he could get the truck up to speed, the group of Incarnates reached them and swarmed over the vehicle. A body climbed the hood, obstructing his vision momentarily before sliding off. Glass shattered as the truck windows broke for the second time this day. They pulled away fast, but not before several of the demons climbed into the truck bed.

In the side mirror, Andrew saw the beast destroy the school with one swing of its jointed leg, before wriggling the last of its bulk out of the ground.

There was hardly time to breathe, let alone think. No sooner had they left Trofonag behind than the back window of the truck rained down glass on Ronnie's head. Rotting hands reached through and hauled at him. They yanked him out of his seat and had his head and shoulder through the window and hanging over the truck bed before he could grab onto anything. The remaining chunks of glass in the frame tore at his back.

Three Incarnates stared down at him. One moved to put a rusted blade against his vulnerable throat.

The truck swerved. All three of them stumbled sideways, one so much that it flew over the side. Ronnie thrashed in the grip of the other two, his tortured body screaming at the effort, and tried to worm his way back into the cab.

Gunshots blasted next to him. Andrew had one arm twisted backward out the window while he drove, firing the revolver over Ronnie's chest. One of the Incarnates let go of him after a bullet hit it in the shoulder. It crashed against the tailgate, which popped open and spilled the demon into the road.

That just left one. Andrew would have a hard time hitting it from his angle. Ronnie reached out, grabbed it around the head, and sank his thumbs into those glowing red ovals in its face.

The Incarnate howled. Ronnie expected blood or liquid of some sort, but got smoke instead. Like a miniature tornado, it funneled out of the creatures eyes…

And headed straight for his.

The movement was unnatural, denying the direction of the wind whipping around them. He shoved the dying Incarnate away, which sent it tumbling off the back of the truck with its brethren. The first wisp of smoke brushed against him, and, for just a moment, he felt a *presence* in his head, something clawing at the insides of his brain for purchase like a man about to fall off a cliff.

Then it was gone, and he slid dazedly back down into his seat just in time for the front windshield to be filled with the monstrous form of Trofonag.

Andrew drove as fast as he could while trying to help Ronnie with the Incarnates in the back. Since leaving the school, the streets had been empty, so he didn't have to worry about weaving. But no sooner was the kid safe than a giant shadow swept over them from the right, and suddenly Trofonag scuttled into the street, trampling an entire row of houses along the way.

All three occupants of the vehicle screamed.

Andrew had no idea how the monster had gotten in front of them. Probably the same way he and Ronnie had ended up back at their vehicles after taking a stroll this morning. One of its huge legs smashed into the pavement right in the truck's path and he yanked the wheel to swerve around it at the last second.

Then they were sweeping under its reptilian belly, staring up at mottled flesh. Trofonag moved fast, turning in a circle to stomp them. Andrew flew around a corner fast enough to lean them up on two wheels. They sideswiped a car that deflated like a popped balloon before the truck shot back into the open. This time, Trofonag gave chase, the ground and car jumping every time one of its limbs thudded down.

Andrew leaned around Ronnie and shouted, "Where do we go?"

"*THERE ISN'T ANYWHERE TO GO!*" Manners screamed back at him. "Not for all three of us! This vehicle is bonded to take us back to your world, but I told you, only two can cross the barrier!"

"He's gaining!" Ronnie yelled, twisting around to look behind them.

"That's only one of our worries! This dock is dying!"

Andrew glanced at the suburban houses running alongside the street. The ones that hadn't faded away were badly crushed out of shape, that invisible hand steadily mashing down on them. Even these looked more like cartoon drawings than reality now. The sky seemed right on top of them, claustrophobically close. For the first time, he realized even Trofonag was keeping his head low as he scrambled after them.

"It isn't too late! One of us has to die or stay behind!"

"Definitely die," Ronnie said softly. "You don't wanna be alive if they get their hands on you, believe me."

Andrew coaxed a little more speed from the truck, bringing the odometer up to 90 miles per hour, an insane speed for streets designed for no more than 30. "What do you suggest then, Professor? Draw straws?"

"There's no need for that! I already told you, I'm too important, and you have a child!" Manners jabbed a finger at

Ronnie. "Eliminate this thug! He's nothing to us, nothing to your world! Shoot him and be done with it!"

Ronnie turned to Andrew. The kid's eyes looked clearer than the entire time Andrew had known him. He wasn't sure where or how the metamorphosis had occurred, but this wasn't the same bankrobbing punk he'd chased down a scant few hours before. "He's right, man. If that's the only way, you gotta do it. Prob'ly be quicker than what ol' Red Eyes started."

Andrew made the hardest decision of his life in less than a second. "No. I didn't shoot you before, and I'm not going to now."

"*Think about your world!*" Manners screeched, absolute desperation on his face now. "*Think about your SON!*"

"I am," Andrew said, and stuck the barrel of the revolver in his own mouth.

He intended to pull the trigger immediately, no hesitation, but Ronnie moved fast, pulling his wrist away and knocking the gun out of his hand with an elbow. It hit the seat and rolled into the floorboard. "It ain't happenin like that, Andrew!"

Behind them, Trofonag roared and snapped at the back of the truck. Andrew could hear the beast in his head, speaking an alien gibberish that tore at the anchors of his sanity.

"*I'll not die like this!*" Manners declared. "*If either of you are too weak to do what needs to be done, then by God, I WILL!*"

He leaned down and retrieved the weapon.

"Look out!" Andrew yelled.

Manners fumbled the revolver, trying to get it turned correctly in his hand. He might be comfortable with quantum mechanics and the laws of the cosmos, but he was a ditz when it came to firearms.

Ronnie leapt on him. Manners snarled and fought with the kid. One of them must've hit the handle in the struggle, because the passenger door popped open, forcing the professor to grab at the seatback with one hand to keep from falling out. Andrew reached over, trying to get a grip on him while keeping his eyes on the road and the titan in their wake. The passenger seat became one big tangle of bodies.

The revolver went off.

Ronnie fell back in his seat, covered in fresh blood.

But Andrew saw immediately that it wasn't his. Manners sat up in the open truck door, looking down at a hole in his tweed suit vest the size of a quarter, from which a maroon flood gushed. The gun was backward in one limp hand, and Andrew plucked it away.

The professor's bewildered eyes came up to them. He muttered, "But I was going to save worlds…"

"Sometimes you can only save your own," Andrew said, "And let the rest worry about itself."

He fired the revolver again.

The bullet pushed most of Edward Manners' face through the back of his head. He flopped over backward and fell out of the vehicle. Andrew saw his corpse roll in the street before Trofonag crushed it flat with a careless step.

He and Ronnie said nothing to each other as the kid leaned over and pulled the door closed. The monster was almost on top of them, but so was everything else. The sky was falling, those cracks widening and black slime running through in steady streams. The houses on either side disappeared, the street beneath them losing definition, becoming one big, black, featureless plain and even that was *squeezing* in around them…

And suddenly the road ahead was awash with light. Pure light, clean light, *sun*light. It came from nowhere and everywhere, brightening so hard and fast that it blinded him, made the truck glow at every angle where it kicked up sparks of light. He felt the tires leave the ground, and then they were travelling toward the light at incredible speed.

The last thing Andrew saw before his vision blotted out entirely was the neighborhood behind them shrinking to a pinprick in the rearview mirror, an island in the middle of rich, deep darkness, and Trofonag screaming as it closed in around him.

The sunlight was too bright. Ronnie covered his face and peered out through his fingers.

The truck sat diagonally across the access road, the freeway just ahead and below them. Cars whizzed by without taking any notice.

"Are...are we back?" Ronnie asked.

A horn blatted from his left, and an angry driver edged through the narrow space between truck hood and guard rail, shaking his fist at them as he passed.

"Yeah, we're back," Andrew answered.

He opened his door and stepped out. Ronnie did the same, leaning against the side of the vehicle for support.

Behind them sat the red brick wall that flanked the entrance to Strangewood Homes. Except it wasn't called Strangewood Homes anymore; now the sign read '*Stern*wood Homes.' People drifted out of the houses closest to the entrance—real people this time, limbs all numbered correctly and in the right location, folks in bathrobes who peered curiously at their stopped vehicle.

Ronnie imagined what they were seeing—two bloody men, one of whom looked like he'd been through a paper shredder—and began to laugh.

~ ~ ~

Andrew pulled the truck over against the curb, out of the way of the minimal traffic. Far down on the opposite side of the freeway, right about where the bank would be, he could see an ocean of flashing red and blue lights.

Joey would be down there. Andrew wanted to see him so much.

But first things first.

He left the door of the cab open and stood outside, loving the feel of sun on his face. He knew what the Beatles meant now: it did feel like years, in his heart. And though his head told him it had at least been hours, as near as he could tell they'd only been physically gone for a few minutes, if even that.

Ronnie was a few yards away, sitting on one of the wooden guard rail posts with arms wrapped around his own torso. His arms were caked in dried blood and filth, but his face—aside from his lumpy nose—looked surprising clean. Andrew went over and sat down beside him.

"I would ask if that really happened, but I'm still in too much pain for it not to've," the kid said.

"We have to get you to a hospital."

"It's all good, dude. None of what that fucker did was designed to kill me, so there ain't no rush." Even so, he winced when he moved his arms and put his hands in his lap. "So you think…it's okay? They're not gonna get through or whatever?"

Andrew turned to look across the street. The Sternwood residents were gathering at the mouth of the housing development, staring down the street at the cavalcade of cops around the bank, more arriving all the time, glancing warily at the two of them every few minutes. He didn't know what it would be like if Trofonag and the Incarnates breached the boundary between worlds—if it would be immediate chaos or a far more subtle infiltration—but the feeling in his gut told him they were safe.

"I think it's all right," he said.

A wistful smile crossed Ronnie's face as he whispered, "We saved the world. Awesome."

"No, not we. *You.*" Andrew held out a hand, the way he had when this whole mess was first getting started. "I don't know a lot of men who could've held out during what you went through. So…thank you. Thank you for giving my son a chance."

"Yeah, yeah, just be sure to tell the judge that. I'm sure they'll let me out in a couple of decades." Ronnie accepted the hand with a roll of his eyes. Then a cloud seemed to move over his disposition. "Back at the school…or even in the truck… Why didn't you do it, Andrew?"

He didn't have to ask what the kid meant. He also didn't have an answer ready.

"I would say you didn't have the balls, but you blew away Manners when it came down to the wire."

Andrew frowned at the mention of the professor. He could already feel guilt gnawing at him, and he only expected it to get worse in the days, months, and years ahead. The man was a monster—a different kind of monster—but his death was a further tragedy.

How many worlds had Andrew doomed by killing him? How many *universes?*

He answered, "You didn't shoot me when you had the chance. And you came back for me when they had me in the school."

"Yeah, but that's different. We didn't understand the stakes yet. But you knew you had to kill me to stop them from gettin through. You *knew* you had to do it if you ever wanted to go home again."

"But I didn't kill you, and yet here we sit."

"Goddamn it, you know what I mean." Ronnie spun on the post to face him. Andrew saw the stark need to understand in his eyes. "Manners was right. I ain't nuthin to you. I ain't nuthin to anybody. Nobody here would shed a fuckin tear if *I* was the sacrifice needed to make sure the world kept on tickin. To make sure the Sternwoods of the world got to keep watchin bad Michael Bay movies and eatin themselves to a heart attack. So why were you ready to throw your life away for me?"

Andrew grabbed Ronnie's wrist and pressed the truck keys into his open palm.

"Because everyone deserves a second chance to color inside the lines, Ronnie."

The kid stared at the key ring for several seconds. "Does this mean you're not arrestin me, Officer Andrew?"

"Can't have the savior of the world rotting in prison. Just go. Fast. They're going to come looking for us any minute. I'll buy you as much time as I can."

"Sure you won't get in trouble?"

"Not looking like this, I won't. Just don't get caught, because I'm going to have to tell them you did all this to me. In the glove box, there's $200 I keep for emergencies. Find someplace to clean yourself up, then ditch the truck and grab some new wheels. I hope I don't have to tell you—"

"—not to try this again. Yeah, I'm way ahead of you."

Ronnie got up and hobbled for the truck.

~ ~ ~

He backed up, intending to go the wrong way on the access road for the short distance it would take to get to the overpass. His body still hurt, but besides the toes, the ear, and the nose, he didn't think it was anything permanent. Even his Marglo infection felt better; apparently germs couldn't cross the barrier either.

Mark's funeral. He probably still had time. But after that, he had no idea where he was going. Usually that realization thrilled him, but at the moment it just made him very, very sad.

Andrew stood at the open passenger window. "Take care of yourself."

"You too." He grinned. "Thanks, Jap."

"Thank *you*, shithead."

Ronnie pulled away. A glance in the rearview showed Andrew waving his arms and running after him. He braked.

Andrew yanked open the passenger door, leaned into the floorboard, and came up with a plastic bag with Spiderman's face on it.

"Everyone deserves a second chance," he said, "but not *this* much of a second chance."

Ronnie laughed, and drove toward the dazzling California sun.

# My Boy

Thomas waited with hands clasped and head bowed while the drawer was pulled out in front of him. The slab seemed to take an hour to trundle all the way out of the wall, revealing the long, shrouded shape on top, but he refused to lift his head to look at it. He sensed the man in the lab coat come around behind him in preparation to raise the sheet, but Thomas stayed stubbornly hunched inside his tweed blazer.

"Mr. Oberman." Detective Kenneth prompted him with a gentle touch to the elbow.

*It won't be him*, Thomas thought. *It won't, they made some awful mistake, a terrible clerical error, and the sooner you look at what's under there, the sooner this nightmare will be over.*

He lifted his head. The morgue worker pulled the sheet back unceremoniously.

Beneath was Thomas' son, eyes closed, dark skin tinged with the waxy blue of death.

A reedy, pain-streaked sigh escaped his lips.

At his side, Kenneth asked softly, "Mr. Oberman, can you verify that this is your son, James?"

For a moment, the use of the young man's first name actu-ally threw him. Eugenia had always been the one to call him *James*, all of his school friends used *Jimmy* or, later on, when the trouble started, *Jam*, but to Thomas, he had always been *my boy*. As in 'My boy, why don't you mow the lawn,' or 'My boy just turned twelve and is already hittin the hoop from midcourt.'

Or 'My boy robbed a liquor store with his idiot friends and got sent to juvie for six months.'

Thomas forced himself closer to the morgue drawer slab. Part of him was still thinking this might be a mistake, reinforced by a cruel trick of his mind. He wasn't even confident he knew what his son would look like after so much time.

James did look older, his face covered with fading acne scars and old fight wounds, but he was still recognizable as the boy who had once tried to get Thomas to help him build a spaceship out of cardboard. That night behind their old house on Wilton Avenue seemed like a thousand years ago. The memory was obscured by so many other, far less pleasant ones, but now, laid out on this slab, he looked peaceful, more like that child Thomas had watched sleeping so many times.

"That's him," Thomas croaked. His voice sounded as scratchy as old sandpaper on a rough wooden plank. "That's my boy."

The morgue worker pulled the sheet back into place without a word. He started pushing the drawer on its long trek back into the wall. Thomas had the briefest urge to beg him to stop. After a few seconds bordering on eternity, James Oberman was nothing more than a jutting handle amidst a sea of other handles that covered every wall in this cruel, cruel room. Thomas wondered if the other drawers were all occupied, and if their families had been called in the middle of the night to drive here and identify their bodies.

He followed the detective back out of the room. The morgue was in the basement of the hospital, at the end of a depressingly bare concrete hallway. Only a cargo elevator came down this far in the building, but it was strictly for corpse transportation, so they had to walk up an endless staircase to reach the first floor, where the admission desk sat across from the ER entrance. The people in the waiting room chairs watched them as they passed.

When they reached the glass doors, Thomas asked, "What happens now?"

"I'll finish up the paperwork in the morning. Once I close the investigation, James will be turned over to you. If you want to start making arrangements, the body should be available for pickup tomorrow night."

"Arrangements," Thomas repeated numbly. That meant another funeral, another grave to visit. Tears. Not as many as had been shed for Eugenia surely—James had worn out his welcome with family, and Lord knew his hoodlum friends wouldn't care enough to show—but more tears all the same.

Thomas turned toward the doors, where the first skirling drifts of winter snow were drifting from the November sky. He didn't want to go out in it.

"Why don't you have a drink with me?" Kenneth asked, as if reading his mind.

"I don't drink."

"Some coffee then. I'm buying."

"No. Thank you. I have to go." But he didn't move.

"C'mon, stay for a bit," the detective pressed. "The coffee in the cafeteria tastes like shit, but it'll warm you up."

"All right. Reckon I'm not gonna sleep tonight anyway."

The hospital cafeteria was on the other side of a row of glass windows looking out on the ER. Detective Kenneth ordered them coffees and brought the Styrofoam cups over to the table Thomas had chosen. He sat in the opposite chair and began pouring creamer into his, so much that Thomas wondered why he hadn't just ordered a milk.

"When was the last time you saw him?"

Thomas didn't even have to pause to figure the answer. "Be four years ago in March."

"He would've been, what? Fifteen?"

Thomas nodded. "Woke up one mornin to find a brand new convertible Mustang in the driveway. Him and them other idiots had all stole it, but James was the only one stupid enough to bring it home. We fought, both of us said some things, and he left. Started living with his gang in some rundown hovel over on Foster."

"I know the place." Kenneth took a sip of coffee and smacked his lips. "Lotta kids from the neighborhood end up there. You ever try to get him out?"

"Not me. For a while, I was just glad to be shut of him. Boy'd been nothing but trouble from the time he turned thirteen. But Eugenia—my wife—she went. Begged him to come home. He all but spit in her face. She said it was like he was a different person." Thomas had expected to see the boy at Eugenia's funeral last year, but the ungrateful little bastard hadn't even been there to send his own mother into the ground.

"That's how these street gangs operate," Kenneth agreed, sounding like Thomas' preacher when he started to get ramped up in the pulpit. "More like cults. They take in these bad seeds and—"

"My boy wasn't a *bad seed*," Thomas said brusquely.

Kenneth must've seen something in his face, because the enthusiasm was gone from the detective's voice when he spoke again, replaced with quiet respect. "Of course not. I didn't mean to imply that he was."

"Eugenia and I did the best we could. Raised him up in the church, taught him right from wrong, but in the end…it just didn't matter."

Kenneth opted for silence this time, staring down into the steam drifting from his drink.

Thomas sighed. It was a weary sound. He realized he hadn't even tasted the coffee, had just been warming his dark, shriveled hands around the cup. He lifted it to his lips now and winced as the bitter liquid washed over his tongue. "You have any children, Detective?"

"Two. My son is eight; my daughter's five."

"Then you know fatherhood is like one of those chemistry sets they used to give kids back in the fifties, the ones with all sorts of dangerous chemicals in them."

Kenneth grinned. Thomas decided, despite everything, that he liked this white boy. "I think that's a little before my time, Mr. Oberman."

"Well, take it from me, they was real. My own mother scrubbed motel toilets for six months so I could have one for Christmas. They came with this list of instructions on how to mix the ingredients to create all manner of reactions, but every red-blooded boy on earth did the same thing I did: threw chemicals in a pot to see what happened. Most times, you got nothing. Sometimes, you got a beautiful smear of color. But every once in a while…you got an explosion. You see what I'm gettin at?"

"I think so."

Thomas studied the detective's face and saw that he did. "Fatherhood is constantly second-guessin yourself. It's throwin those chemicals in a pot, to see what you get. And when you get an explosion—like I did with my boy—you lose a lotta sleep tryin to figure out where you went wrong."

Kenneth sat forward. "But sometimes, even the most trained chemist can't predict those explosions. Sometimes they just happen."

"That's true. But you still can't blame the explosion, like I did for so long."

That seemed to stump the detective. They sat in silence for a moment, until the ER doors slid open on their automatic tracks, letting in a burst of howling wind and two paramedics wheeling a gurney between them. Before the doors could close, another woman burst through behind them, a white woman with curly, auburn hair and a white sweater splashed with a shock of blood, like an exclamation point. She was sobbing as she caught up with the gurney and held the occupant's hand. The paramedics wheeled it up in front of the admissions desk, where one of the nurses paged a doctor over the intercom.

"Do you think it hurt him?" Thomas asked suddenly, over the cries of the woman beyond the glass. "My boy, I mean."

Kenneth hesitated. "He was…DOA. You'd have to ask a doctor to be sure, but with the severity of those wounds, he probably went fast."

Thomas nodded, and then heat stung his eyes, and the next thing he knew he was crying himself, shuddery sobs that made his spine ache. "*I wanted to bring him back!*" he wailed suddenly, his voice startling the few other people in the cafeteria. "*Don't you think I did? I practiced what I would say to him every day! But you always think you have tomorrow, and the day after that, and the day after that, until you don't! Ah god, what I wouldn't give for one more chance to see him, to make him understand that I loved him, to make it all different!*"

The detective didn't seem to know what to say. Was, perhaps, rethinking this entire invitation to coffee. Thomas' cries competed with the woman in the ER lobby, but, as he listened, hers seemed to spiral up, drowning his out, and then he realized it was because she was no longer sobbing, but screaming.

He and Kenneth looked over. On the other side of the glass, the person in the gurney had sat up. It was a man, but the entire left side of his face was crushed in so severely that Thomas didn't understand how he could be alive, much less sitting up. And apparently the paramedics agreed, because both of them were backing away in horror.

The woman couldn't, however. The man in the gurney had clamped down on her hand, and now she thrashed and yanked hysterically, trying to free herself. As Thomas watched, she was pulled down until the man got a grip on her mop of curly hair, and then he buried his mouth in her throat. A crimson flood rushed over the ruins of his face and rained down into his lap.

"Jesus Christ!" Kenneth exclaimed. "Stay here!" He slid out of his chair and ran toward the cafeteria exit.

Thomas stayed where he was, transfixed by events on the other side of the glass.

The paramedics had overcome their fear and moved forward to help the woman, but as soon as they were within range, the man on the gurney leapt at one of them, bearing him to the ground and out of sight. The other paramedic reached the woman, now slumped across the foot of the gurney, and put three fingers across the ragged hole in her throat to stop the flow of blood.

In response, she bit one of them off.

He pulled away, staring at the stump in the middle of his hand as the nurses shouted for security over the intercom.

Someone in the waiting room on the far side of the lobby screamed. People were out of their seats now, running and limping toward the exit, but they were forced to slip by the gruesome scene at the admission desk to get out. The man from the gurney and the paramedic he'd fallen on both rose and proceeded to grab people from the crowd and bite at them. Thomas saw their teeth rip flesh wherever they touched. Those people that made it by unharmed were stopped at the ER doors by a crowd shambling the opposite direction, a mob of people covered in blood with fatal wounds and missing limbs. Some of them even looked withered and ancient, skin like sandpaper hanging from visible bones.

*They're dead*, Thomas thought in wonder. *Every last one of them.*

Kenneth had finally reached the admission desk. He pulled his revolver, yelled out a warning to one of the walking corpses as it came at him, and then opened fire. The bullet slammed through the front of the creature's forehead. It dropped to the tile floor.

Thomas stood up with a jolt, banging the table so hard his coffee tipped over. He started moving then, following the same path Kenneth had taken, out of the cafeteria exit and down the corridor back toward the admission desk. A doctor and two people in hospital gowns flew past him, fleeing deeper into the building. One of them told him not to go that way, but he kept walking.

A few seconds later, he arrived beside the detective and surveyed the scene.

The crowd of the dead was forcing its way in through the ER doors, arms outstretched and reaching for the living. Those that had been killed rose to join their ranks. With the exit blocked, the folks from the waiting room herded back into the lobby, defending themselves as best they could. More people were arriving from elsewhere in the hospital, doctors and patients trying to see what the commotion was. All told, better than a hundred people were packed into these narrow corridors, and the living were being driven further back with each passing second. Kenneth picked targets one at a time, dropping as many of the creatures as he could, and telling people to keep back. Two security guards joined him, using their own weapons on the crowd, but they didn't seem to be as good a shot.

Thomas concerned himself with none of it. He moved past the detective, pushing into the sea of people, heading back across the lobby toward the opposite hall.

Behind him, Kenneth shouted, *"Come back, there's no way out down there!"* And then, as he understood, *"Don't do it, Oberman! It's not him! IT'S NOT HIM!"*

Thomas ignored him. The press of bodies was like a battlefield around him, people fighting, screaming, bleeding, dying. But he seemed to float through it all, unscathed. Only once did one of the creatures come at him—a young blonde woman with one eye socket chewed out like a rathole in a baseboard—but he grabbed her by the shoulder and shoved her away. On the opposite side of the hall, the crowds thinned, and he was able to walk quickly down the passage he and Kenneth had come from before. Ahead, a sign pointed the way back to his destination.

Just before he reached the door at the top of the stairs, it was pushed open from the other side. Heeding instinct, Thomas ducked into the nearest open hospital room. He pressed himself back into the shadows and watched as another horde of corpses stumbled by the door, these all naked and smelling of formaldehyde. Their moans were piteous. He tried to imagine what it must've been like for them, to wake up in those awful drawers. After they had passed by, and he was sure the one he sought was not among them, Thomas eased back out into the hall and through the morgue entrance. When the door shut behind him, it sealed off the noise of the riot and gunshots down the hall.

The lights were off in the stairwell, and he couldn't find the switch to turn them on. He had to feel his way down the steps in the dark. At the bottom, the concrete passageway made a right turn, where the fluorescents buzzed and flickered. The morgue worker waited for him here, a hole in his white lab coat from which half-eaten intestines dangled. He snarled and lunged.

Thomas grabbed a fire extinguisher from the wall and swung it against his face, stripping flesh down to the bone. When the man came at him again, Thomas smashed the metal against his skull, driving him to the ground. He brought the extinguisher down again, over and over, until the man stopped moving. When Thomas straightened, something in his 61-year-old side shrieked with pain, but he stepped over the twice-dead body and kept going.

In the morgue, Thomas gazed around at the destruction. Most of the low-hanging bulbs had been broken, leaving the room in steep shadows. From what he could make out, the dead people must've busted their way out of the drawers, leaving behind splintered remains. He could hear a few still in their tombs, battering at the enclosures. His eyes skimmed over the handles until he found the one James had been in.

It, too, was open, a jagged hole bashed through the wood from the inside.

As Thomas stood staring into that black drawer, a long, hoarse moan sounded from the darkest corner of the room. He turned.

A figured lurched out of the shadows. It was a young man that had once asked his father to help him build a spaceship to the stars, the grown-up face of a boy that Thomas would know anywhere, that he would never be able to forget. He could even see the holes that riddled the figure's bare torso now, from the bullets a rival gang member had fired at it earlier this very night.

Elation surged through Thomas, a joy that threatened to burst his heart wide open.

"*My boy!*" he cried, holding his arms open as the corpse of his son shambled forward.

"*Faaaa. Theeeer,*" James Oberman groaned, and fell into the man's embrace.

# That Old Rugged Cross

The box of Bibles bounced on the seat next to Beecher as the car hit another uneven patch on the winding dirt road. One of the tomes on top, already precariously balanced, slid forward and made a valiant effort at escape.

Beecher took his hands off the wheel and snatched it out of the air before it reached the filthy floorboard of the vehicle; not much to worry about hitting if he ran off the road. The last house was miles back, nothing more than a dilapidated little log cabin with no air conditioning. He'd given his sales pitch there yesterday to a farmer with a craggy face and his rapidly balding wife. Both were sweating profusely and reeked of B.O. and they made it abundantly clear they had little use for the word of God, even when offered in a handsome and convenient leather-bound travel size.

There were only extremes when these simple folk realized what he pedaled; out here they either foamed at the mouth in their religious fervor to buy a bible or ran him off their property with shotguns and pitchforks.

But the wife offered him a glass of water for which he was thankful—he'd been on foot taking orders all day, and the Mississippi sun had wrung every ounce of moisture out of him—until he followed her through the kitchen doorway. He at first thought heat waves caused the interior of the kitchen to shimmer, until he looked closer and realized it was a layer of flies, a thick carpet of tiny jostling bodies covering every surface of the room.

He politely declined the water.

And that was about par for the course out here in the backwaters of the country. For a kid from suburban Chicago, rural America might as well be another planet.

Beecher stacked the Bible back on top of the others and glanced at his watch. Thirty-five minutes after nine in the morning, and that meant he had a bigger problem than the local population.

He had to find a church, and he had to find it fast.

"Never happen," he muttered to himself. "You'll never find a church with a service this late out here. Screwed yourself real good on this one, Beech."

These country folk liked their worship services at eight o'clock on the nose, nine at the latest. His own fault for going out this morning to deliver product to as many customers as possible before service, but the shipments were in, he had orders to fill, and he really needed the money or his current diet of tomato sandwiches was going to get even skimpier. He had intended to take a short trip and then double back to a tiny Church of Christ on the edge of his selling territory, but somewhere along the maze of unnamed back streets he made a wrong turn and got lost.

And just why did he have to get to a church so urgently? They weren't allowed to sell at the houses of God after all, so why should he be so worked up about attending, other than, you know, the salvation of his soul?

"Because the people who run this business are damned Nazis," Beecher answered his own question. "Nazis disguised at Bible-thumping business moguls."

He never expected a summer of Bible-selling to be like this. Sleeping in a communal bunkhouse outside Biloxi every night with his fellow salesmen, up by six for a rigorous morning of calisthenics and 'optimistic reinforcement,' wherein they got one another fired up for a day of *grrrrrreat* sales (always *grrrrrreat*, like they were hawking cornflakes), and then out on the job from eight till dark. There was a whole manual of do's and don'ts for the selling aspect of the job, but as far as personal lives went, the only restrictions were no smoking or drinking.

And one other.

They must attend a church service every Sunday morning, or forfeit all bonuses for the week.

Most of the time it wasn't a big deal. They had Sundays off, and he just rolled out of bed and went with the other guys and the regional sales manager to a Baptist outfit in the city. But, if they went off on their own, they were required to bring back a signed pamphlet or some other form of authorization proving they attended elsewhere.

Nine forty-five now. He was out of options.

Beecher topped a short hill and came around a corner guarded by a thick copse of sycamore trees. He would settle for civilization now, somewhere he could stop and ask directions, get back to the main road and finish his deliveries.

And there, lo and behold, rising against the sky like a lighthouse beacon, a wooden arrow pointing the way toward salvation, he saw that old, rugged cross floating above the stand of trees. The road split off ahead, one branch curling back behind the copse, and Beecher followed, knowing services must be over already but hoping for a miracle.

He began to catch his first glimpses of the temple through gaps in the thinning trees. The structure was made entirely out of badly rusted corrugated sheet metal, welded together at crude angles in a rather slapdash display. The wooden cross was mounted at the top of a steeply sloping metal roof that couldn't be more than a single story high, canted crookedly and badly pitted and weather beaten. No foundation whatsoever; the whole horrid thing just sat right out on the dirt, ready to be picked up and moved or blown over by a strong wind.

A handmade church, no way it could have central heat or air or even electricity, and small enough for a congregation of no more than two dozen people.

And right now it looked like heaven.

A dusty dooryard with a rickety screen door set into the metal indicated the entrance to the building. In front of this, close to the road running in front of it, was a faded, hand-lettered sign nailed to a stake in the ground that read, 'SERVICES HELD PROMPTLY AT TEN.' That was all, no church name or catchy Biblical quote, just short and to the point.

Beecher smiled. He had to be the luckiest SOB in the universe.

*Well, Mr. Lucky, if worship is about to start, where are all the cars?*

The thought popped into his head, and Beecher's smile faded. Maybe they weren't meeting this Sunday. Maybe they were on an annual pilgrimage to see some tortilla with Jesus' face on it. Maybe they just figured it was too damn hot. He felt panic start to rise up and quelled it with a possible answer.

This was a church slapped up only for the benefit of the locals, all of whom were probably within walking distance.

*You haven't seen a house in the last ten miles. You telling me they walk all the way here in this heat?*

Sure. Why not? He'd been to a place just last week where he pitched to a nice-looking couple on their front porch while the three of them sipped tea—all very nice and elegant, how he imagined the deep south really would be—while their approximately one-hundred and fifteen children played, screamed, and chased one another all around them. As he flowed into his bit about how a new Bible could enrich their lives, a naked boy of no more than eight came strolling out of the house. Beecher, to his credit, hadn't missed a beat as the child crossed the porch to stand next to him and began urinating with reckless abandon on the tacky green Astroturf. The parents seemed not to notice, so Beecher took his cue and did likewise. Continued to do likewise, somehow, as the child strolled over to the sparse flowerbed that ran the length of the house, ripped an elephantine palm frond out of a plant that looked half dead, and came back to the bright yellow puddle to begin slapping the frond down on it, splattering droplets of hot, foul-smelling urine all over the front of Beecher's best shirt and his demo Bible. The couple ended up buying a unit from him, but he had to wonder if his two dollar bonus was worth going home smelling of some hayseed brat's piss.

Just went to show, these people had a ton of eccentricities he would never understand. It was a different culture, a different lifestyle, and nothing should surprise him anymore.

*Okay then, at least tell me this: what denomination are they?*

He didn't care, and he was more than a little annoyed with this interior pessimist for bringing him down. He didn't care if they called themselves the Fifth Church of the Macarena Zionists. It was a *Christian* church—that beautiful cross up there couldn't proclaim it any more if it were written out in pink neon—and he just wanted to go in, sit through whatever kind of service they called worship, get the preacher to sign something for him, and get back on the road.

Beecher parked in the dirt beside the church under the shade of a stumpy sycamore and got out. The heat washed over him, beads of sweat popping out along his brow and arms at once. He walked through the dirt to the door, set under the shade of a metal eave that seemed to have been added as an afterthought to make the place look a bit homier.

He peered through the screen, but could see only a dim glow from within.

Beecher pulled open the door, which screeched on rusty hinges.

Dark inside, especially after the brightness of the day. No electricity just as he predicted; the only light came from rusted Coleman lanterns hung on the wall at irregular intervals. The heat rushed out in its eagerness to claim him, and Beecher grimaced at the thought of going inside.

*Snake handlers*, his mind objected desperately, *snake handlers can be Christians too, you know*, but he shook this off. To get that bonus, he might consider taking a few venomous bites.

He saw footprints in the dirt and followed them inside. The door swung shut, closing out a vast majority of the light so his eyes could adjust.

Directly in front of him was a small chamber, with a corrugated metal wall blocking off the rest of the church except for a hole with a curtain hung over it. On either side, two men stood solemnly waiting with hands clasped in front of them.

The one on the right came alive at the sight of him. "Welcome!" he shouted, rushing forward with hand outstretched. He was dressed in black, wearing what appeared to be a priest's cassock and robes, without the white collar. He was in his fifties and had a merry face—small glasses perched on a round bump-of-a-nose, twinkling blue eyes, and a quick smile. Beecher found himself accepting the dry, rough hand offered to him and smiling in return while he checked for snakebites.

"Welcome," the man repeated, pumping his arm like a water well. "I'm Brother Sweeney, I'm the preacher here at

Found Faith. How are you today, son? What's your name?"

"Uh, I'm fine," Beecher said, trying to free his hand from the preacher's enthusiastic grip and keep up with the speech. "The name's William Beecher."

"Brother Beecher, is it? Well, we're so glad to have you this fine morning! We so rarely have visitors here at Found Faith. Isn't that right, Brother Junior?"

Beecher glanced at the man on the other side of the door. He was rotund, a huge belly stretching out the waist of his filthy overalls. No shirt beneath, a carpet of thick hair covering his meaty arms and creeping on from under the front of the overalls on his chest. He grunted and nodded his piggy head, dull eyes taking in Beecher in one gulp.

"I'm...glad to be here," he answered, and then added, "I'm a Bible salesman, and I never miss a service."

"Did you hear that, Brother Junior?" Sweeney beamed at Beecher. "A Bible salesman! A spreader of the gospel! How nice!"

Beecher was getting the idea the man would stand here and talk to him all day if he didn't find a way to get the show on the road. Runners of sweat were already trickling down his back, and he didn't want to prolong his time in this hotbox. These two hardly seemed to notice the heat. "Well, I don't want to interrupt your service. I saw that you start at ten..."

"Nonsense!" Sweeney waved the thought away, and then his hand froze in midair as a new thought occurred to him. "You know son, you could be our *guest of honor!*"

"Oh no, I couldn't possibly." Beecher raised his hands in polite protest.

"Sure you could! We haven't had a guest of honor in such a long time! What do you think, Brother Junior?"

For the first time, Brother Junior showed some expression, his eyes livening and his lips curling up into the slightest of grins. He grunted like an ape. *Probably the product of champion inbreeding*, Beecher thought.

"See there, it would be our pleasure! Oh, please say yes! The congregation would be so happy!"

At the very least, it might result in a few sales appointments. Beecher nodded. "Sure. Okay."

Sweeney clapped his hands together once in delight, as exaggerated as a Disney character. "Wonderful! Let's get you dressed, then!"

"Dressed?"

Sweeney put an arm on his shoulder and guided him away from the curtain in the wall behind him, toward another hole in the metal to the right that opened onto a tiny closet-like room. The heat was so constant, worse than any sauna, and he felt like he was swimming through the air.

"Step right in here Brother," Sweeney said. "There's a robe right inside. You can just slip it on over your clothes."

Beecher frowned, sighed internally, and stepped into the little booth. On a nail to the right was a plain white robe covered in dust.

"Should have read the fine print," he muttered.

He comforted himself by thinking of the cross outside. Whatever their practices, they were still a Christian church, but, much like when a species becomes geographically separated and evolves differently, these worshippers had been away from any like-minded brethren for too long and developed their own ideas about running a temple. But it would still all be the same rigmarole he'd been through a thousand times: blah blah blah, Jesus did this, Jesus did that, forgive your sins, Amen.

He would worry if he saw snakes.

With a smile, Beecher picked up the robe, shook it out,

and slipped it on over his shirt, tie, and dark slacks. It hung to his knees and had a cloth belt that he cinched at the waist.

When he stepped back out, Brother Junior had changed into a robe of the same cut, but jet black and large enough to cover his gut. Sweeney held a large flat pan full of greenish water, and, before Beecher could protest, the preacher dipped his hand in and flung some of it in his face. At the same time, the other man rattled out a harsh series of syllables in a language Beecher had never heard, something that sounded like, "*Fer dim shaggoth Maymar mi opij.*"

Beecher recoiled, unable to stop a look of disgust slipping over him, and wiped at the substance on his face. Slightly greasy, with flecks of something in it that looked like spinach. It was too dark in the church atrium to examine the source as Sweeney placed it on the ground beside them.

"Come Brother," Sweeney said cheerfully, taking his arm and leading him toward the curtain. "Service must start on time!"

They stepped through the curtain with Brother Junior right on their heels.

The room beyond the curtain was much bigger than it looked from the outside. Like entering the narrow end of a barn, with the room stretching out in front of him for a good twenty yards and the vaulted ceiling falling away into darkness above. Here the heat was nearly unbearable, the stench of packed bodies and old sweat electrifying, and the few Coleman lanterns around the room were just sufficient to show him the backs of two rows of pews made from old wood. It was a packed house, at least thirty people, and the entire congregation stood in the pew aisles.

Men, women, and children, all wearing robes like the one Brother Junior had put on. They turned to watch Beecher with strange, solemn eyes.

"Brothers and Sisters!" Sweeney shouted, holding up the arm not around Beecher. "Brother Beecher has agreed to be our guest of honor! Let us begin our praise, so we may show him Found Faith has the gospel in our hearts!"

As one, the congregation of Found Faith opened their mouths and begin to chant one of the words in that harsh language Sweeney muttered when he anointed him with the spinach water, a rapid but steady repetition of the word, "*Maymar*." They turned away, toward whatever pulpit lay at the other end of the dim church.

The heat made him feel drugged, and Beecher suddenly wanted to be out of here, to run from this church and screw this week's bonus. They were growing louder and fiercer with each utterance of that hypnotic word. Sweeney's arm suddenly became ironclad, and then the man was leading him up the aisle between the two rows of pews.

They approached the front of the auditorium, and only with decreased distance was Beecher able to make out the pulpit. In front of him another, larger cross hung suspended from the ceiling, over a beautiful—and very out of place— white marble table with an ornately carved pedestal holding it aloft.

Both the tabletop and the dirt floor beneath were stained a dull maroon.

Beecher's breath caught in his throat, and he cringed against Sweeney.

From a side door by the pulpit, another man in a black robe led in a goat by a leash.

"No, Brother Adams," Sweeney shouted to him over the swelling noise of the congregation. "We won't be needing that today. Brother Beecher has agreed to be our guest of honor!" The man with the goat nodded and silently retreated.

Sweeney released him at last and turned to the suspended cross and held up his hands in supplication. He began to speak in that sharp, guttural language.

Beecher spun in a drunken circle. It seemed the congregation had closed in, cutting off the exit, but he was sure part of it was sunstroke from the crushing heat in this place. Their faces floated around him, each of them dead and expressionless, their mouths opening repeatedly around the same two syllables.

"*Maymar, MAY-mar, MAY-mar, MAYMAR!*"

He completed his turn, coming back to Sweeney, and froze with eyes bulging from their sockets.

In the air in front of the cross, a shimmering black hole appeared, a swirling vortex at least five feet across whose interior darkness made the church look as brightly lit as a hospital. From its swirling center came clacking, chitinous noises that set his teeth grinding and his hair on end.

Sweeney turned to him, his chest swelled with pride. "Behold the true god Maymar!"

From the hole, multi-segmented legs began to emerge, each half a car's length and as big around as sapling trees. They gripped the edges and strained, as though attempting to pull something too big for the circumference through the hole.

"But...but...b-but," Beecher stammered. "T-the cross! I thought this was a Ch-Christian church!"

"Well, son," Sweeney said, grinning at him and displaying an extra row of needle-sharp teeth from somewhere far back in his mouth, "you didn't think Christ was the only one to die on a cross, now did you?"

# In the Passing Lane

The car was nothing but a speck on the sunny horizon when Jerry first spotted it. The gently rolling hills caused the road to look like a roller coaster track, so it was hidden from view a second later, but at this speed he would be upon it in minutes. The speedometer needle of the Lexus hovered just above ninety as he flew down the lonely road through the empty Texas landscape.

But his mind was far from such trivial matters as 'the road' at the moment.

"Damn bitch," he mumbled. His voice sounded flat in the silence of the car. "When I find her, I swear to God…" His voice trailed off, but his hands finished the sentence by tightening around the leather-covered steering wheel almost convulsively.

The road began another quick descent following the curve of the land, and Jerry's speed caused the car to go airborne for a few seconds before reconnecting with the pavement. As the resulting jolt bucked his seat, he again saw the vehicle in front of him on the two-lane highway, now no more than a mile away and closing fast. It was white, but that was about all the detail he could make out from his current distance.

Jerry turned the air conditioner up another notch to the highest setting. Cold air blasted his face until his hair whipped around just as much as if he'd opened the window to the heat-baked air outside. He was still sweating beads of simmering water though, cooked by internal rage and frustration at the fact that there were no more flights out today.

"But that's all right!" he shouted, his voice rising on each word. "I'll get there one way or the other, and then she's gonna pay!"

The other car—he was close enough now so that he should be able to identify it, but the model remained indeterminate—was less than a quarter mile ahead, and he was zipping toward it like it was standing still. He depressed the brake pedal and watched as the tiny needle on the dash readout dropped past seventy, past the legal limit of sixty, and started its descent toward fifty.

"Oh, c'mon Grandma Moses! Take it on the shoulder!" The entire back window of the smaller car was piled to the ceiling with boxes, suitcases, clothing and the knick-knack paraphernalia of an obvious tourist. The edges of the glass were covered with stickers from famous Texas landmarks and cities, not a one of which Jerry had ever had the slightest inclination to see.

He blew his horn, a mighty bass rumble from under the hood announcing his presence. "Move it or lose it!" he yelled. The road started up another hill and the lane divider remained two solid yellow lines, as it had been for at least the past fifty miles of this wrinkled territory.

He tightened his grip on the wheel, his foot practically dancing on the gas pedal as he contemplated going around the other car anyway, but he couldn't quite summon the guts to pull it off.

It was laughable. Ridiculous, really. He was out in the middle of nowhere, hadn't seen another car for the past half hour, with that sorry excuse for a wife somewhere ahead spending his money, and he was scared to pull around a person who got their driver's license from a box of Cracker Jacks.

So he remained behind the car as it trundled along the highway, cresting the top of the hill and starting down the other side. He held his breath and looked for oncoming traffic, but before he had time to make a move, the land sloped upward yet again, blocking his view. He howled and pounded the steering wheel until he was sure he'd bruised his hand.

"For the love of God, don't you have anywhere to be besides in my way?" Jerry screamed. "Did you come out here to *die?*"

He noticed for the first time two odd bumper stickers on either side of the chrome-plated fender. The one on the left read 'I Brake for Wartletheps,' and on the right it said, 'Vote for Gorendathar.' Again he tried to identify the make and model of the sleek but economical car in front of him, which shouldn't have been a hard task considering he was once a mechanic. But the body shape was not comparable to any car he knew, and there were no identifying marks as to what type of foreign POS it might be.

He considered passing again, despite the limited visibility. Even on the downhill side, the valleys were just too short for him to zip around with any reliability. Jerry thought about his wife somewhere ahead, with all the money she'd withdrawn from his account, laughing it up with her new boyfriend, and the world was suddenly painted in red overtones.

The land dipped sharply and then started up again. For no apparent reason that Jerry could see, the brake lights on the car in front him came on.

It might as well have lit the fuse on a stick of dynamite.

"Forget this shit!" Jerry shouted. He yanked the wheel to the left, moving the Lexus smoothly into the other lane. His foot hit the gas pedal and jammed it to the floor. The engine growled beneath the hood as he surged ahead.

As he pulled even with the small white car, which was now doing about twenty-five miles per hour, he slowed just a little, his hand fisted on the seat next to him ready to shake at the driver, perhaps even to extend the revered middle finger, the greatest of motorist insults. He opened his mouth to shout, "Next time, buy American!" but the words dried up like sawdust on his tongue.

Through his passenger window, he had a perfect view of the driver alongside him.

It sat hunched over the wheel, its hands—gray-skinned with knots of bone at each joint—clasping the steering circle together at the very top, like kids when they first learn to drive or the way Jerry's own grandmother used to drive to church and bingo, barely able to see over the wheel of her Lincoln. The tip of its hairless scalp reached to the top of the window and its elongated face stretched down and forward, tapering to a pointed jaw. Ropes of saliva hung from several yellow-stained teeth. Two burning red, no-pupil eyes squatted to the sides of its face, buried in mounds of mottled gray flesh. There was no nose; just two dark jagged holes in the middle of its face.

Jerry's foot slid off the gas pedal and his speed continued to match the other car. As he stared, the creature pivoted its head to look at him—that exaggerated bottom jaw swinging in his direction—and fixed him in those large, ovoid circles of blood red. It raised one deformed hand to the glass and then a gelatinous coating slid down across its left eye, not entirely blocking it from view but dampening its glowing color, and then slid back up.

It was winking at him.

Jerry's hand started up with the intent to sketch a quick salute when a loud, high-pitched note rumbled through his head and shattered the encounter. He tore his widened eyes away from the slavering monster next to him and faced forward.

A large eighteen-wheel semi was coming over the top of the hill, bearing down upon him like a titan from the sky, sounding its foghorn siren as a warning that was far too late. Jerry stared at it stupidly, not quite comprehending what this development meant to him and his future existence on the earth.

The semi tore through the Lexus like a marathon runner through the finish line, the driver still blaring his horn in a futile attempt to move the car from his path. He pulled the rig to the side of the road and scrambled out.

The idiot that had been driving was plastered in a red fan across the grill along with chunks of car and gore. The driver, a short, squat fellow on his way to San Antonio, turned away in disgust, watching instead the little white car the guy had been trying to pass as it crawled away over the hills.

# DARK WORLD

It was Kylie's new habit of calling for water in the middle of the night that first led Harold to discover the other world in his living room.

The girl was five, all set to start school next year with 'the big kids,' but suddenly she couldn't make it through eight hours of sleep without a few gulps of lukewarm bathroom tap water, like she'd developed a set of gills. They'd tried leaving a glass beside the bed, but she insisted she needed it fresh. At first, he and Liz had alternated nights for this chore, but she made such a production of it when her turn came—throwing back the covers angrily, muttering that the girl must be part camel (a comment that really didn't make much sense anyway, when you stopped to think about it)—that Harold had taken over the duty on a full-time basis.

Secretly, he thought it was adorable.

But on the night Harold first crossed over into Dark World—as he would come to call it—Kylie's voice summoned him from the depths of a deep, dead sleep, and a dream where Liz had the body of a young Julia Roberts. In it, they made love at the foot of the bed with a fervor his wife had never possessed in waking life.

He sat up, peeling the lids away from swollen eyes enough to see the dim bedroom. Liz lay on her stomach beside him in a shaft of moonlight, arm over her face, breath like a whisper. The glowing digital clock on the nightstand read 1:30 over the curve of her bare shoulder.

"Daddeee!" The voice drifted from the other side of the house, muffled by several walls. "I need a glass of *waaaa*ter!" Always like that, emphasis on the *waaaa*.

"Harold, go get her some damn water!" Liz groused, without stirring. "I have a long day tomorrow and I don't need this!"

*Long day.* It seemed Liz' life was nothing but *long days* lately. And 'I don't need this'? That had been her catchphrase for longer than he could remember. A spark of annoyance shot through him, like a blazing ball from a Roman candle firework.

Harold stumbled out of bed and into the master bathroom. He grabbed the plastic glass he now set on their counter each night before going to bed, and filled it only half way. No need to give the girl too much; if Liz had to start washing urine-stained sheets, he would never hear the end of it. Then he opened the bedroom door and started across the living room.

It was utterly pitch out here at night. The small bit of moonlight that managed to trickle under the porch overhang and through the windows at the front of the house was cut off by a partition wall that divided the den from the dining room. Even the slight illumination from the bedroom windows behind him didn't reach very far, resulting in a darkness that grew deeper toward the left half of the room, particularly the far corner, too much for the eyes to ever adjust to. The effect was like a stygian cave.

He didn't need light, however. They'd lived in this house for eight years—the first place he and Liz bought, the year after their wedding—and he could navigate so well by the map in his head that he kept his eyes closed for most of this trip.

Harold inched his way forward with the glass of water, half his brain still asleep, only the barest thread of consciousness directing him. If he kept this careful balance, stayed in that queer land between waking and slumbering, he could slip into bed and fall right back to sleep. He should be passing between the television on the far wall to his left and a leather recliner on his right. Any second now, if he wasn't careful, he would bang his shin on that low coffee table Liz picked out at IKEA. He could usually find it with his toe and then turn right, lined up perfectly to pass through the dining room and into the hallway leading to Kylie's bedroom.

Except the coffee table wasn't there.

He'd taken a handful of half-steps from the door of the bedroom already. Harold surrendered and opened his eyes all the way, straining for any scrap of light with which to get his bearings, but the darkness around him was absolute.

Had Liz moved the damn thing? He could swear it was there when he went to bed. Of course it had been; hadn't he picked up his empty beer bottle from it after turning off the TV? His bleary head had just gotten him off course, and he'd passed to the side of it in the dark.

Harold continued forward with his free hand outstretched, seeking the couch or, missing that also, the back wall of the den as a new reference point. He could walk faster and easier now, knowing there was nothing to trip on. Any second he would feel it...any second now...

Nothing.

The entire stretch of the den couldn't be more than twenty-five feet. He'd taken more *steps* than that; maybe covered more area than the entire width of their little house on Meisner Street could possibly encompass. Harold turned in a disoriented circle, unable to see even the bedroom door he'd just come from, and wishing he'd just flicked the light switch on his way through. Lost in his own living room. That was one for the record books. He wasn't scared yet—oh no, that would be utterly silly, this was just a little sleepy confusion, nothing that wouldn't be forgotten in the morning—but the dial on his inner emotional thermostat was definitely heading toward panic.

He took another few steps, no longer sure what direction he was headed.

His foot came down on something that was not carpet.

He paused. The new surface under his toes was cool and smooth, like moist earth, but it seemed to move, to...to *squiggle*, was the word his mind jumped to, as if not entirely stable. It reminded him of the Halloween games they used to play as kids, games Kylie would be old enough for soon, where you made your friends mash their hands down into a big bowl of Jell-o and told them it was cow brains. He swept the sole of his foot back and forth and encountered crunchy, dead foliage.

At that point, Harold stopped relying totally on his eyes for input and opened *all* his senses up, like a blind person, and realized he was no longer indoors.

His ears detected none of the barely perceptible echoes that told the brain there was a roof over its head. The space around him was large and open, but still lacking any light source. It was full of other sounds though, both close and distant, ticks and pings and chirrups, the phonic indicators of life. As he stood there, an honest-to-God *wind* blew across his skin, warm and heavy...and brought a stink of something long dead and rotting.

His breath caught. He was dreaming. Had to be.

To his left, something moved.

It was a burst of scuttling, the same noise one hears when disturbing small creatures in woodland underbrush, as the rabbit or frog tries to decide if full-out flight is required. But something about it was so intricate—so starkly *real*—that he knew without a doubt he wasn't dreaming. That little needle in his brain shot right past panic and into dread.

*I sleepwalked*, he thought. *Walked right out of the house and into—*

*Into what? The jungle around the corner?*

He shook his head. If he was truly outside, what kind of place was this pitch black, even at night? There was no moonlight, no stars, *nothing*.

That scuttling sound circled around him from his left, as though evaluating. Harold spun to follow it, trying to swallow the acid ball in his throat. He had no idea where to go or what to do, but his skin crawled.

"Dadd*eeee!* Where ARE you?"

Kylie's voice floated to him from somewhere on his right. It sounded far away and muffled, but the security it offered was like a fishhook in his brain, reeling him in.

He moved toward it quickly. His ears (or maybe his imagination) told him that whatever was here lunged after him and missed by inches. That foliage crunched underfoot. He tried to cry out, desperate to hear the anchor of his daughter's voice once more, but no sound made it past his clamped throat.

Harold felt carpet between his toes, and a split second later he *did* fetch his shin up against the coffee table. He flew over it, only staying on his feet through sheer luck, and tried to get his bearings. Ahead, the darkness lessened in degrees, going from pitch black to a gray blur; somehow, he'd reentered the living room from the farthest corner, where no light could reach. He hit the wall beside the hallway and felt for the bank of switches on this side of the room.

The bulbs under the ceiling fan came on, blazing light in all directions, driving that darkness away like a bulldozer shoveling a mound of dirt. He turned on the ones for the hall and the end table reading lamps also, then checked over his shoulder.

His familiar living room stood there as it always had, comfortable walls enclosing a very finite space. He blinked around at it, panting for breath.

From the open doorway of the bedroom came, "Christ Harold, shut the damn lights off!"

"S-sorry," he called, but didn't do as she asked. Not yet. He was drenched in sweat, and below the waist his pajama bottoms clung to him in a huge wet patch down one leg. He thought his bladder might've let go, until he realized the water glass he still clutched had spilled in his run.

"*Harold!*" Liz shouted.

He stepped around the corner as far as he could, reached back, then flicked the switch and moved quickly down the hall.

The Eeyore nightlight in Kylie's room was a welcome sight. His daughter sat up in bed, watching him with huge eyes. He sat down on the bedside and handed her the glass.

"Daddy, that's not enough!"

"Drink that and I'll get you more if you need it," Harold said, twisting so he could see out the door of Kylie's room. Darkness reclaimed territory on the far side of the threshold, where Eeyore's feeble rays couldn't reach.

Was it real? Had it actually happened? Even now, it seemed far away and blurry, like the details of a half-forgotten dream, but the fear of whatever that place had been was still very much with him. If the girl needed more water, he might be able to make it to the guest bathroom down the hall, but he doubted he could force himself to go back through the living room until the safe light of day helped sort this out.

*Oh, this is a fine state of affairs. Forty-two years old and scared of the dark. You better not let Liz find out, buddy boy.*

He took the glass from his daughter—the child he had wanted for so long and had just about given up on ever having—and stretched out beside her small frame.

"Daddy's gonna sleep here, pumpkin."

"How come?"

*Because there's a forest in our living room.* "I'm too tired to go back."

"Oh. Okay." Her voice suggested even she didn't see the logic in this. The girl slumped against him. "Ew, you're all wet!"

"I know. Go to sleep, Kylie."

She passed out in seconds, but Harold's eyes were still open when sunlight filtered through the room's only window.

If Harold had ever been asked if he and Liz had a happy marriage, he would've answered 'yes' without a moment's hesitation.

If he'd ever really stopped to consider the question, even just for his own piece of mind, he might be forced to admit that he had no idea what a 'happy marriage' was. Deep down, he didn't think anybody did.

They'd never been a couple openly in love, not in the Hallmark-card, pet-names, kissing-in-public sense of the phrase. And if there had ever been passion between them, it was but a brief spark when they met, Harold at 34, Liz a year younger, both well past the age where such fantasies can be indulged. They'd met at a mutual friend's New Year's Eve party, been paired together out of necessity for an awkward kiss at midnight, and ended up having brusque sex at her cramped apartment two weeks later. Their union was one of functionality and an unspoken fear of being alone, the only commonality they shared was a desperate desire to have children.

An early miscarriage had crushed them both. They'd already named the child by the time it died: Samuel, after his grandfather. With Sam out of the picture, something had seemed to wither between them, but they kept trying, the sex almost mechanical, like two robots programmed for procreation.

Then Kylie had come into the world, and everything changed. At least, for Harold it had. He had expected the arrival of a child to wake them up out of their funk, and that's exactly how it felt for him, Rip van Winkle returning to life after a decade-long nap, but their daughter just hadn't seemed to thrill Liz in the same way. He'd always secretly wondered if the loss of Sam hadn't soured her on motherhood completely.

"Thanks for the wake-up call last night." She tossed a plate of toaster waffles down in front of him the next morning. "Maybe you can route a parade through the bedroom tonight."

"I couldn't see," Harold mumbled. "I banged my shin on the table. Got a bruise as big as an apple. Can I have the syrup?"

"You don't need any syrup. Too much sugar." This was the first he'd heard of the too-much-sugar law, leading him to believe this was a punishment. Her lip curled as she slammed the refrigerator door. "You never needed the light on before. I mean, Jesus Harold, I really don't need this."

He wanted to defend himself, but knew it would do no good. Judging from her tone, it would only start a fight. And he was too afraid that an argument would lead to the true source of last night's disturbance, and that wasn't something he could deal with just yet.

Kylie bounced into the kitchen dressed in the clothes he'd laid out for her, hair pulled back in a ponytail. She climbed into the chair next to Harold and announced, "Morning!"

"Morning, pumpkin."

"Don't 'morning-pumpkin' her," Liz snapped. She put their daughter's breakfast on the table, along with the syrup he'd been denied. "I'm sure you kept her up half the night with all that noise. And sleeping in her room, what was that about?"

He shrugged. The feel of that foreign soil beneath his toes was still with him. The first thing he'd done this morning— after making sure Liz was in the shower, of course—was walk the perimeter of the entire living room. He had no idea what he expected to find (*a gaping hole in the side of the house? A glowing portal?*) but he knew what he *had* found: nothing besides a few smudges of what looked like mud on the periphery of the room beside their entertainment center, far outside the normal lanes of foot traffic. He pinched it between both fingers, smelled it, but couldn't determine if it was proof of his nocturnal adventure or just some missed vacuuming.

Liz was still watching him with hands on hips, waiting for an answer.

Kylie saved him. "It's okay, Mommy, I like Daddy being there!"

She fixed the girl with a flash-freezing stare. "Finish eating."

Lack of sleep made Harold's workday a nightmare. His mind kept straying to those sensations from the middle of the night, the smells and sounds from that other place. Mostly he just wanted to forget, pretend the whole thing never happened. That had been his answer to a lot of problems in life though—especially the ones concerning his marriage.

He tried calling Liz' cell around midday, and got her voicemail. He could almost never get her during the day. At three, he left the office to pick up Kylie at day care. They went home, and while Kylie changed clothes, Harold stood in the middle of the living room and studied the empty far corner. He turned off all the lights, but there was still too much sun from the rest of the house to recreate the soupy murk that reigned in here after the sun went down. The texture of the walls stood out in rough patches to his tired eyes.

Kylie came out and plopped down in front of the television to watch cartoons.

"Honey, Daddy's gonna lay down for just a little bit before he starts dinner."

"Can we have mac and cheese?"

"Maybe." He kissed the top of her head. "Stay right here and watch TV and...and leave all the lights on, okay?"

"Okay!"

In the bedroom, he changed into a t-shirt and shorts. Liz worked late just about every day lately, so he had time for a nap before she got home.

Harold sat on the edge of the bed and reached to set the bedside clock, holding down the button that displayed the currently set alarm time.

The clock had always been on Liz' side of the bed, for as long as they'd been married. He couldn't even remember how it started. Certainly not with a conscious decision, but rather one of those random quirks that quickly evolves into marital law through routine. She set it, got out of bed before him in the morning, and then gave a shout—or in recent months, a grunt—when she was finished in the bathroom, so he could start getting ready. Once upon a time, they'd showered together, but those days were long gone.

Now, Harold looked down at the red digital numbers on the clock and tried to understand what they implied.

The alarm was set for 1:30. *PM.*

A time when—as far as he knew—their house should've been empty.

Liz arrived home at close to seven. She gave Kylie a perfunctory hug, then got out her laptop to work while she ate. Harold found himself watching her, scrutinizing every little move. His stomach twisted into knots so hard he ended up scraping his meal into the garbage.

When it was Kylie's bedtime, he escorted the girl to her room. Harold read her a story from *Maurice's Magical Adventures*, her favorite book. For the first time all day, he wasn't thinking about his strange adventure last night, or…

*1:30 PM…*

…or anything else. His daughter listened as raptly as though it was the first time, asking questions that had them both giggling. She was a guiding light, a beacon of sanity in a world that got crueler every day.

Harold finished the story and closed the book. "Time for bed."

"One more?"

"No more. You need some sleep, young lady."

She wiggled beneath the covers and he pulled them up to her chin. He was just about to stand when she asked, "Daddy…do you love Mommy?"

The question floored him, turned his skin to ice. He stammered, "W-why would you ask something like that?"

"I don't know. She's just mean sometimes."

"That's…no reason not to love someone, Kylie." He realized he had expertly avoided her question. "Don't *you* still love her? Even when she's mean?"

"Uh huh."

"Okay, then. There you go. Now go to sleep."

She nodded. "Okay Daddy."

"Goodnight, honey. I love you."

"I love you too."

Liz was already in bed when he entered the room, sitting up and reading a copy of *Forbes* with a highlighter in hand. She glanced up at him, but said nothing.

Harold stood in the doorway. For some reason, he didn't want to lie in that bed beside her. He had no real reason to believe the strange alarm clock setting meant anything, but his imagination—already revved up from last night—was working overtime.

"Good…" He stopped and cleared his throat. "Good day at work?"

"Busy," she answered, without looking up.

"I tried calling you. Around lunchtime."

"I was in a meeting."

"Oh? How long did it last?"

Liz slapped the magazine down on her covered thigh. "Jesus, Harold, is this the Spanish Inquisition? It was a meeting, I didn't check the time! Around 2, I guess!"

She flinched as she said it. Right around the eyes. He was almost sure.

Harold went into the bathroom and began brushing his teeth without another word. Kylie's question kept swirling around and around in his head.

~ ~ ~

Harold stared at the ceiling until he was sure Liz was asleep and then rolled over to study her in the moonlight. She still looked like the woman he'd married—still had a pretty decent ass and tits to match, in all honesty—but, in almost every other way, she'd become a stranger.

He didn't know when exactly that had happened, and it scared him. The change had no specific event that he could pinpoint; it was more like a houseplant that had been forgotten and allowed to die. The kind of difference you can see only when you look back at the entire length of the road stretched out behind you.

Something was growing between them. Had been, for years. Not a distance, but rather, the exact opposite: a weight, some super dense object whose gravity was slowly crushing them. You could say that Sam's death started it, but that wasn't true, it had been there even before.

But that didn't mean what he was thinking—this crazy idea the alarm clock had put in his head—was true.

*And even if it was, Harry ol' buddy…would that really be so bad?*

He glanced at the clock. 1:30 again, but AM now. His gut told him that was no coincidence. If he didn't do something to get his mind off this, he would go insane.

Liz was snoring as he slipped from beneath the covers. The house had settled into the delicate silence of night's loneliest hours. Harold tip-toed to the bathroom drawers to rummage for the flashlight he kept there, for the trimming of wild nose hairs. He squeezed the plastic tube in one sweat-slicked fist and went to the bedroom door.

Before opening it, he turned his head and pressed one ear

against the wood. What was he even listening for? Crickets, maybe? But all was quiet. Harold turned the knob and pulled the door open, wincing at the almost imperceptible squall of the hinges. He slipped through and eased it firmly closed behind him.

The nest of shadows on the left side of the room could've been solid; a bulging, silken, pulsating egg-sac that offended the eyes and numbed the heart. A black that deep wasn't natural, shouldn't be allowed to exist. Harold stood in the living room and stared into it, straining for any sign of that other…

*world…*

…other place, before switching on the flashlight.

The circle of light splashed against the sky-blue plaster of the living room wall, and Liz' awful framed Pottery Barn picture of the Sicily countryside. He played it across the corner until he was satisfied nothing lurked.

Harold came close, so *close*, to giving the whole idea up then, going back to bed, and waiting for Kylie to call for her water. That would be the quickest way to begin putting this—*all* of this—behind him.

But suddenly the idea of ignoring another problem made him ill.

Harold slid the flashlight into his pajama pocket and got down on his hands and knees. He crawled forward, the same way Kylie had as a baby in this very room. The carpet was worn and soft beneath him. Ahead, that dark scar loomed. He could make out the barest outline of the coffee table to his right before sight was lost to him, so much that he couldn't see his hands or arms beneath him as they shuffled him along. He continued crawling, determined to move forward until his head bumped into the corner.

And then his right hand rose from the carpet, swung forward, and came back down on something else.

Harold froze. The surface beneath his hand was cool and moist, with that same wiggling motion. He moved his left hand up beside the right to confirm this, as though calling the appendage a liar. But no, his left palm gave the same report. He tried to dig his fingers in, but the material was unyielding, like the skin of a hard rubber ball. He slid his hands back toward his sides, feeling for the point where the spongy surface met the carpet under his knees. No definitive line, but more of a blending, a...*melding*. The carpet fibers began to grow right out of that smooth, rubbery ground and then became more and more sparse before disappearing entirely. He arched his back and stretched out as far as he could, sweeping his hands until he encountered crisp grass in waves.

Harold inched his way forward, until his entire body was off the carpet. It took several seconds of deliberation before he could bring himself to leave this anchor behind. The farther he went, the more real this other place became, like objects jumping into sharp relief under a microscope as it magnified. Now there were outdoor sounds coming to him again: breeze soughing through trees, the clicking of leafless branches, the rustling of grass. From somewhere, he could even hear a bizarre k-kreee k-kreee k-kreee that he could, in fact, only liken to crickets. If he closed his eyes (and he really didn't have to), his ears could fool his brain into believing that he now knelt in the grass on a warm summer night, somewhere far from the constant under-thrum of civilization.

His nose, however, told a different story. The air was filled with that stench from before, of death and rot. A smell that bad could only come from spoiled meat.

It was all so alien...but there was something familiar about it at the same.

"What is this place?" he whispered. His words—the first spoken here—fell out of his mouth like dead insects. "Oh God...what is this place?"

There was no answer from God or anyone else. Unease began to creep back in. The darkness was just too oppressive, like being slowly smothered in a pile of blankets. His eyes ached for input. He needed to see something, anything, to ease the tension mounting in his chest. Harold fumbled the flashlight out of his pocket and felt around on it until he found the on switch.

At first, he thought the batteries had died. No yellow beam exited the wide end of the cylinder in his hand when he pointed it at the ground in front of him. But when he turned the instrument around to look into it, he could see the bulb in there, glaring brightly in its reflective metal cup, one tiny bit of visual stimuli in the midst of the darkness.

But the strangest thing...the thing that made him feel small and sick...was that it didn't even hurt his eyes, the way staring into a flashlight usually would.

Because the illumination it produced didn't reach past the glass cap over it. The light was muted, sheared off at its source. His hand remained a jet black shadow even when he held it up in front of the flashlight, nothing but a black, featureless outline. His mind recoiled from the impossibility.

*This is Dark World.* He didn't know where the stray thought came from, but it felt true. *No light on this side of the Mason Dixon, nah uh, not allowed.*

From the endless black plain ahead of him, something roared.

The squall was like a cross between a jungle cat and some kind of dinosaur. It rolled across the outdoor expanse, washing over him, bringing a renewed smell of decay. How far (or close) the source was, he couldn't tell, but it sounded large enough to swallow him in one gulp.

There were wild things here. Things that could never be tamed or kept in a zoo.

And all at once, Harold knew why this place seemed so familiar. Last year, while Liz had been on a business trip, he'd taken Kylie to a safari theme park whose gimmick was allowing you to drive your car through the midst of African animals in a natural habitat. When they'd reached the grass plains where the lions waited, lazing about just a few yards from the road, Harold rolled down the window just the tiniest bit despite the advisements not to do so, wanting Kylie to experience the majestic beasts as close as possible. The world outside their car had felt as dangerous as this, and the same dank, rotten smell hung over those predators of the savannah in an invisible cloud.

Harold wanted to go back now. Ignoring a problem was one thing; running from one in terror was entirely another. Still on his haunches, he scooted backward, stretching behind him with his bare toes to feel for the safety of the carpet.

It wasn't there. He crawled in reverse and only met more of the moist earth.

Panic tried to persuade him to get to his feet, but he forced himself to stay still and think. If he got disoriented in here, he was liable to get lost again. He couldn't have moved more than a foot or so past where the carpet petered out. He spun in a careful, calculated half-circle, still on hands and knees, making sure that he faced the exact direction he'd come from.

His eyes could pick out nothing, no sign of the house, but he swallowed his fear and crawled forward blindly. The flashlight slipped from his hand, but he didn't bother to search for it. The living room had to be ahead somewhere. The two spaces overlapped one another, like matching sound frequencies, and maybe that was what this was, that insane darkness in his living room created by ill-conceived architecture matched the one in this place so perfectly, it formed a sort of bridge between the two. His fear made him cling to the theory like it was rock-solid fact.

Harold was moving so fast when he hit the carpet he romped another few feet forward, friction-burning both knees and the place where his right wrist met his palm. He was shaking and panting again, brow dripping sweat, but he scrambled to the wall, looked behind him, and flicked the light switch.

And, for just a split second, he thought the darkness on the left side of the room denied the light. It looked like a black bubble, just as he imagined earlier, a seething vortex eating away at the walls and floor and ceiling, before the clean light from overhead drove it into the corner, shrank it down, down, down, till it was the size of a penny, and then popped it right out of existence.

The next day, Harold bought a gun.

It was a Mossberg 500 shotgun, long barrel with a walnut stock. He'd never even fired a weapon before, but the clerk assured him it would be the easiest for a novice to use and actually hit something.

Liz was going to pop an aneurysm when she found out.

He'd spent the night in Kylie's room again, stretched out in the floor and watching the door. When she'd asked for water, he scurried to the bathroom and took a moment to examine himself in the mirror. He looked mad—eyes crazed, hair sweaty and disheveled—but even worse were the stains on his palms and the knees of his pajamas. They were a fetid purple color, and smelled of compost and something far richer that made him gag. He washed his hands until they were chafed and red, then rubbed at his knees with a wet washcloth.

In the morning, when he was sure the first thin rays of sunlight from the front of the house reached all the way to the corner of the living room, he emerged and, before Liz awoke, cleaned a trail of similar stains across the living room carpet. They led right up to the wall, and one of them—a perfect imprint of his own hand—stopped right up against the baseboard, as though his fingers had grown right out of the trim. He would've just about had to break his hand to leave such a mark in the tight angle between floor and wall.

Unless, of course, the wall hadn't been there.

After ducking out of work early, he bought the gun, then stopped by the hardware store to buy some flat sheets of lumber and nails. Something had to be done to keep his family safe, to...

*...ignore the problem...*

...to eliminate the danger the same way he would a gas leak or toxic mold. God forbid Liz or Kylie should wander in there.

Not to mention that, if he could cross over to Dark World, who was to say the things that lived there—the creatures that called that impenetrable, unknowable darkness home—couldn't come *here?*

But when he arrived home with his supplies, he saw how useless the idea was. What would he do, put boards over the walls, the same walls that he'd walked straight through? Should he build a fence through the middle of the room, and forbid anyone to cross over?

Jesus, Liz would have him committed.

*And maybe she should*, a quiet, and far more rational side of his mind—one that hadn't gotten the memo that Dark World was real enough to leave grass stains on your pants—whispered.

No. No, he was not crazy. He'd actually been to that other place, with its dank, lion-den stench.

So instead, he propped his shotgun against the coffee table within easy reach, plopped down on the couch, and stared into the corner to think.

He was still sitting like that when the doorbell rang.


Harold checked the narrow window beside the door. A man stood on his porch, a good-looking guy in his late thirties with curly black hair, dressed in a Dockers-and-V-neck-sweater combo that was too unassuming to be sales attire. A neighbor, perhaps, one he'd never met? When he spotted Harold peeking through the window, he gave a close-lipped smile and nervous wave.

For a moment, Harold considered not answering even though he'd been seen; he didn't have time to deal with a request to borrow his lawnmower or a cup of sugar. But something about the jittery way the guy stood out there waiting for him to open the door—hands shoved in pockets, rocking on the balls of his feet—made him turn the deadbolt. Harold could imagine Kylie's future suitors standing much the same way, as they waited to ask his permission for the honor of his daughter's hand.

"Yes?" he asked, without opening the door all the way.

The man outside bit his upper lip and hesitated. Harold was struck by the notion that he was suddenly rethinking whatever had brought him here. "Mister...uh...Taylor? Harold?"

"Yeah, that's me. Who are you?"

"I'm...I'm Doug. Doug Stratton?" This last was stated as a question, as though Harold should know him. And indeed, the name did ring some distant bells in the back of his head. Stratton started to hold out his hand, seemed to think better of it, and drew back. "You probably don't remember me. I work with Be...with your wife."

The name plunked firmly into place for Harold. "We met at the company Christmas party last year."

"That's right."

Harold stared at him for a moment. "Well, Liz isn't here. She should be at work."

Stratton nodded. "Oh, I know. I'm...well, I'm actually here to talk to you. I just happened to drive by and see your car."

"I left work early." Harold felt suddenly defensive, having to explain why he was in his own home to this stranger. Mostly he was just anxious to get this wrapped up and go back to the problem at hand. "I'm sorry, what is this about, Mr. Stratton?"

"Doug, please." Stratton looked over his shoulder, as though he'd just committed a robbery and expected the cops to come squealing up at any minute. The street was empty though, the sky slowly being overtaken by a bank of thick clouds with steel-gray underbellies. "Do you think...maybe we could talk inside?"

Harold shrugged irritably and then nodded. He moved aside to allow Stratton past him. The man came through the door and turned immediately to the right, walking through the small vestibule, the dining room, past the partition wall and into the living room, as familiar and confident as if he'd been here many times before. Harold closed the door and went after him.

In the living room, Stratton paced to the couch and turned to face him, crossing arms over his chest. The guy was bigger than Harold, outweighing him by at least thirty or so pounds that were probably more muscle than fat. Even so, he still had that nervous energy about him, and it seemed to take some effort for him to meet Harold's eyes.

"Beth doesn't know I'm here," he said, before Harold could ask him again what this was about. It took a full five seconds for him to even understand who Stratton was talking about. Liz had never once gone by Beth her entire life. "I just…I want to make that perfectly clear, that she doesn't know. And this— me coming here—it's not something I planned. She wants to talk to you herself, but she just can't work up the nerve, so I thought I would…bring this to a head."

It would only be in hindsight, after Harold began re-playing this conversation over and over in his head, that he would realize this statement should've been enough to tip him off. It undoubtedly would have, if he'd been firing on all cylinders. But, as he looked over Stratton's shoulder, Har-old noticed how deep the afternoon shadows were getting over in the far corner of the room. The overcast outside was bringing on an early twilight.

"Talk to me about what?" Harold asked, staring at those shadows. Was there movement over there, or was that his imagination?

Stratton made a distasteful face and looked at his shoes. "This is…difficult to say. And I'm sure it's going to be even more difficult for you to hear. But…god, you had to know. From the way she describes things, there's no way you couldn't. Maybe not about me, specifically, but you must've sensed *something*…"

That inky black spot. Harold was almost sure it was

swirling, like black sludge down a drain. And pulsing, too. Reaching out for him. He edged toward the light switches.

"I'm sorry...Doug, right?" The words barely even registered as they came out of Harold's mouth. He couldn't tear his eyes away from the corner, and Stratton was too busy staring at his shoes to notice his distraction. "I'm not really following you. And I don't mean to be rude, but I've got a lot to do, so can we get to the point?"

"Mr. Taylor...Beth and I are...together. We have been for about a year now."

Harold snapped to attention like an electric jolt had just buzzed through him. The darkness in the corner—real or imagined—was forgotten.

Suddenly this man had his full attention.

"What did you say?" he asked in amazement.

Now that the admission was made, Stratton seemed to find confidence, his words coming easier as he looked up. "I'm very sorry, it's not something we planned, but we're in love, I love her very, very much and we want to be together, but she's too scared to ask you for a divorce. So I thought you and I could discuss this like men."

Again, Harold thought of that faceless future boy who would one day deliver a similar speech to him about his daughter.

*Well, you had it half-right, Harry: he is here to ask you for a woman's hand, but it sure ain't Kylie's.*

"You've...you've been sleeping with my wife?" he asked slowly, as a full understanding of what this man was telling him dawned. And then, as he thought about the self-assured way Stratton had entered the house and his own theory about that reset alarm clock, "Jesus, right *here*? In my own bed?" A piston of anger began to pump in him.

Stratton—and he would always be 'Stratton' now; first names, as far as Harold was concerned, were pretty much reserved for folks who didn't cuckold you—held up his hands. "I can't defend anything Beth or I have done. I won't even try. All I can say again is that I love her. I've never met anyone like her, and I want to be with her. You must know yourself how amazing she is."

This phrase stopped cold the little piston of anger. Liz, amazing? Had he ever thought that? The woman had given him Kylie, the best gift he'd ever gotten, but otherwise, their entire marriage had been more of a sinking pit, quicksand sucking at their feet, knees, hips, waists, until it finally nibbled at their ears. And the deeper they'd gotten, the more Liz became shrill and cold and almost resentful of the muck Harold had pulled her into.

He examined Stratton all over again, this time comparatively. Younger than him, full head of hair, chiseled good looks, no sagging paunch around the midsection, those visible muscles on his arms and chest. Liz—or wait, excuse me, *Beth*—had found an upgraded model.

Yet Harold didn't feel inferior or jealous or emasculated at all.

What he actually felt was that strange weight lifting away from him for the first time in years.

Liz had found happiness with this man, and why shouldn't she? Happiness was a rare thing in this life, and, let's all face facts, they certainly hadn't found it together. All this time, they'd been trying to force a square peg into a round hole, first for the sake of their loneliness, then for Kylie, but maybe it wasn't too late for either of them to keep looking.

Harold tried to imagine what his wife looked like when she was with this man. Did she laugh more? Did she glow?

Stratton watched him anxiously, waiting for a response. "Maybe this is more of a shock than she figured. I get that. But hopefully, when all is said and done, you'll realize that this is for the best. And if you're any kind of man, you'll make this easy for her."

Harold nodded. "Absolutely. Tell her…tell her I can do that."

The other man took a deep breath and sighed in relief. "Okay. Okay, that's good to know. Time is something of a factor. Part of the reason I took the initiative is because the office is transferring me to the Paris branch, and I want her to come with me."

Harold felt a small, wistful grin tug at his cheeks. The thought of Liz on another continent sent a buzz of excitement up his spine.

But Stratton kept talking. "And I promise—I give you my absolute word—that Kylie will be well taken care of. We'll cooperate with full visitation."

"'Visitation?'" Harold croaked. The single word brought his daydream to a screeching halt like a brick wall in front of a speeding locomotive. Somehow, the idea of how Kylie fit into this whole equation had never entered his mind. He realized that in his version of this fantasy, Stratton rode off into the sunset with Liz as Harold and Kylie waved goodbye from the front porch.

"Yes," Stratton said. "Beth intends to ask for custody."

That piston started pumping inside Harold again, but this time it was more like a nuclear reactor.

"So my wife isn't enough for you? You want her AND my kid?"

The anger in his voice was enough to put Stratton back on the defensive. "Like I said, if the divorce is amicable, we'll make sure you get full visitation rights."

"*If* the divorce is amicable. So what you're saying is that Liz gets to rape me eight ways from Sunday, and if I bend over and take it like a good boy, I'll get to see my own daughter a whopping two times a year." He could hear his voice rising in pitch and intensity with each word, but was helpless to stop it. "Gee, that sounds like a swell deal to me, Doug ol' buddy!"

"Look, we've...we've gotten off track here," Stratton mumbled. "I haven't even met Kylie yet, but from what Beth says, she's a fantastic girl—"

"Of course she's a fantastic girl, she's MY fantastic girl, and what makes you think the courts would give her to a couple of adulterers anyway?"

"Calm down a second, let's not get heated about this..."

Harold took a step toward him, hands clenched. Stratton backed up and bumped into the back of the couch. The fear on his face satisfied some deep, primal urge in the center of Harold.

"Not get heated? What did you think, that I was going to let you walk in here and take my entire life from me?"

Harold's eyes flicked past Stratton again, but this time, they went somewhere else.

To the shotgun propped against the coffee table.

He would never have used it. The weapon wasn't even loaded, he'd left the shells in his car, but, in any case, he didn't have it in him to kill another human being.

But, for the barest of heartbeats, he imagined he did, vividly saw the mechanics of such an act in his head, how it would solve this problem entirely, and it was this that Stratton read in his face just before following his gaze to the shotgun. The other man's eyes bugged out of his skull when he saw the weapon.

He broke into a run without another word.

"Hey, stop! What're you doing?" Harold demanded.

Stratton sprinted to the closest end of the sofa, obviously meaning to cut between Harold and the furniture and get to the shotgun first. Harold moved to cut him off, not sure why, only knowing that the gun had no more business in this man's hands than it did his own. As they moved toward intersection, Stratton shoved him, tossing a shoulder into Harold's chest like he was an opposing linebacker on the five-yard line. Harold sprawled backward on the dining room tile as Stratton tried to run away from him.

His feet tangled with Harold's.

The man tripped, but it looked more he was trying to take flight. He soared full out through the air, hands outstretched, and there was a terrible crunch as the side of his head struck the coffee table.


There was never a question of what had to be done.

Only a sense of urgency, and a need to make sure he didn't overlook something that would bite him in the ass later on. It actually felt good to have a problem that he couldn't avoid, couldn't ignore, couldn't duck out on.

Harold moved the body first. There was surprisingly little blood, just a dab on the coffee table, but Stratton's neck had a new joint in it that allowed a nearly 90 degree angle turn. The man's face was frozen in a panicked grimace, and his words echoed in Harold's head as he wrapped Stratton in garbage bags. Mainly the part about how Harold should've sensed *something*. He'd sensed that *something* all right, that crushing weight he'd been relieved of for just a moment at the prospect of him and Liz finally giving up on this failed experiment in matrimony and going their separate ways, but now it was back, and heavier than ever before, far heavier than even Stratton's unwieldy corpse, a black hole from which there was no escape.

He carried the body into the garage and propped it up in the tool cabinet along with the unloaded shotgun.

And fifty yards of nylon rope he found beneath his work bench.

After that, the only problem was Stratton's car, a Honda Accord which he'd thankfully not parked in front of the house, but rather at the end of the block. Harold had to press the button on the man's key ring several times and then follow the horn honk to even know which one was his. Slipping on gloves, he drove the vehicle several streets further away, into the suburban maze they lived in, and left it sitting in front of a vacant house with a For Sale sign in front.

The maneuver would only buy time. Harold had no way of knowing how quickly or by whom Doug Stratton would be reported missing, but eventually this car would be connected to him. Then, depending on how discreet Liz had kept their affair (or if she was the one to report him missing in the first place; Harold couldn't discount that possibility), an investigation might wash up on their front door. The best Harold could do is ensure there was no evidence to link to him. Because, even though he'd done nothing wrong, it would be very hard to convince the police of that once the truth about Stratton's identity came out. He tossed the key ring into a gutter as he walked back home and prayed that his neighbors were all away at work, so no one had seen Stratton enter their house.

He picked up Kylie when it was time. Forced a smile on his face when Liz came home. She seemed distracted throughout the evening, and went to bed early. Harold did the same.

After all, he still had a long night ahead of him.

~ ~ ~

Sleep was fleeting. His head was a whirlwind. He thought about everything Liz and Stratton had done right here in this bed, about Sam, about that metaphorical weight dangling from his marriage.

When the night grew deep and still, he rose and left the bedroom, closing the door behind him. He looked away from the left side of the room, focusing on the distant light from the front of the house, and crept out to the garage.

Stratton had grown stiff with *rigor mortis*, which actually made him easier for Harold to handle. He brought the garbage-bag-covered form inside and laid it on the living room floor, in front of the creeping darkness that occupied the far side of the room, feeling like a villager about to make a sacrifice to a heathen god.

Working quickly and quietly, he went back for the nylon cord and tied it around the entire cooking island in the kitchen, making sure the knot was secure and tight. The other end went around his midsection, just below his gut. He played the rope out behind him through the dining room and back into the living room, then hoisted Stratton up one more time.

Harold walked toward the corner. The darkness deepened around him, caressed him with cold, velvety fingers, crowded out his vision until the body in his arms became no more than an abstract idea, until the only proof he had that it even existed was its drag on his muscles and the slick feel of the garbage bags against his palms, but still the worn living room carpet stayed beneath his toes.

*You better hope that place does exist, because if it doesn't, if it was all something you imagined after all...you're gonna have an awful lot of explaining to do.*

That thought brought laughter bubbling up in him, but he clamped down on it hard, for fear it would sound like the shrieky titters that escape from loony bins.

A second later, he was back in Dark World.

The sensations hit him one after another this time, until he was completely immersed in that invisible jungle. Grass and wriggly ground beneath his bare feet. Fetid breeze in his face. The sound of smaller creature scattering in droves before he stepped on them. He shut his eyes against that suffocating darkness; they would do him no good here anyway, since the black outside the lids was the same as that behind them. Harold walked blindly without stopping, holding Stratton's stiff form in front of him like a stack of kindling, until the trail of nylon cord went taut and tugged at his belly.

He was panting from the strain of carrying the corpse. Harold bent and placed it on the ground, then rested with his hands on his knees, listening as he caught his breath. Those alien crickets were singing all around him, but other than their screech, this place was silent.

And that stench…it was even stronger now. It permeated everything about this land, this savage world that he could hear and feel, but not see. He suddenly wanted to know where that smell came from.

"Come and get it!" he called out. His voice was small and insignificant in the open air. "Dinner's served!" Some creature from the local ecosystem answered him with a long, lonely howl.

Harold turned and felt for the rope, his lifeline, his trail of breadcrumbs. As he did, there were more furtive, scuttling noises; first from his left, then ahead on his right, then somewhere behind. He whipped his head toward each one, trying to judge location and distance with only his ears. Whatever they were, they had him and Stratton completely encircled in seconds. They sounded eager and cautious all at the same time.

And *big*. Far larger than anything else he'd encountered here.

He imagined the jungle cats from the safari park out there, quietly stalking through the underbrush, fully aware that he was blind to them, sitting like coiled springs until they were ready to attack. Harold stood stone still and waited to see what they would do.

As if an unheard starter pistol had been fired, they rushed forward on all sides at once, tromping toward him.

Harold fled into the darkness, following the cord with his hands. After a few seconds, it became obvious that the creatures weren't after him, but the prize he'd left behind. He slowed down enough to hear the sounds of plastic tearing as they set upon Stratton's body, and then a violent, wet chomping that turned his stomach.

In the distance, a crashing thud resounded, hard enough to make him jump.

Another followed on its heels, and another after that, an entire series. He couldn't tell which direction they came from, but each impact was heavy enough to jar him, the vibrations travelling through that strange surface which served as the ground. The roar he'd heard last time rolled across the vast open plain of Dark World.

Behind him, the creatures dining upon Stratton gave fluttery, panicked cries and took flight. The noise of their departures scattered in all directions.

*Daddy's home*, Harold thought.

He ran without stopping this time, pulling the slackness out of the cord with frantic sweeps of his arm so he didn't get lost. The fifty-yard rope seemed to have grown to fifty miles. Those booming impacts stayed on his tail as the beast bypassed Stratton and came after him. Another of those awful bellows washed over him, loud enough to make his ears hurt.

And then there was carpet under his feet. He hurtled back into his living room, coils of loose nylon cord dragging behind him. He didn't halt even then, but dove for the wall switches and filled the room with warm, beautiful light. Only then did he look back.

The far corner was empty, but he could swear the plaster shuddered just once, as though something had slammed into the wall from the other side. Harold armed sweat from his forehead and set about untying the rope around his belly.

"Daddy?"

He jumped and spun around. Kylie stood at the opening of the hallway leading to her bedroom.

"Sweetie, what are you doing up?"

"I called for water, but you didn't hear me!"

Harold hurried to her, swept her up, and rushed her away from the living room as fast as he would from a bomb.

"Don't do that," he told her, "don't ever get up, don't ever go through the house at night by yourself, always wait for me and I will come, no matter what. Do you understand?"

She nodded, and he carried her back to bed.

In the two weeks that followed, Harold reverted to his old patterns, and did his best to forget Dark World.

It wasn't an easy task. For the first few days, he expected the doorbell to ring at any second, and a gaggle of cops to be on his doorstep ready to haul him in, but no word of Doug Stratton's disappearance ever reached him. Harold scoured the paper each day, watched the news, but there was nothing at all.

What little sleep he actually got was taken on the couch, after moving Kylie's nightlight from her bedroom to the socket in the corner. Eeyore's light wasn't much, but enough to chase away the shadows and help him guard the house. Besides, lying next to Liz in their bed made him feel like he was in a cesspool. If she noticed this new habit, she said nothing. He figured for her, it was probably a blessing, the inevitable next step in their downward spiral, but she also seemed to be having too many problems of her own to care.

Liz became sullen and listless to the point that she barely spoke at all, and cringed when he walked in a room. He couldn't decide if this was better or worse than her usual string of insults and nagging. She seemed to age twenty years in the span of a few days, stopped using makeup, moped around the house, wore baggy, shapeless outfits from the back of the closet, even to work.

The depressed actions of a heartbroken teenager. Harold wondered what she'd made of the situation, what conclusion she'd come to about her boyfriend's disappearance.

He also couldn't help feeling a little sorry for her.

But if it meant Kylie remained with him, where she belonged, then the cheating bitch could stay like that forever, as far as he was concerned.

And then came the incident with the paint, the day that, to borrow Stratton's phrase, brought everything to a head.

It was a Saturday. The first Saturday in months, he realized, that Liz hadn't been called to the office to sign paperwork or meet a client or any one of a string of excuses for her to be out with Stratton.

God, Harold's naivety was almost embarrassing.

Instead, she spent the day on the couch with a tub of ice cream, watching television and shoveling spoonfuls of half-melted mush into her mouth. Harold holed up in the office on the far side of the house. As far as he knew, Kylie was in her room. The girl had obviously sensed the tension between them, and had tried her best to stay out from underfoot. She loved to color, loved to draw, could spend hours at it.

Harold didn't know about the paint she'd brought home from art class. Just one of those small plastic trays with no more than a thimbleful of primary color acrylics in separate compartments. He only knew something was wrong when Liz began to yell.

When he reached the living room, he found Kylie against the wall, silent tears on her cheeks and the little tray of paint overturned on the carpet in front of her, where she'd dropped it while coming to show Liz the picture she'd made for her.

Meanwhile, her mother threw a tantrum in the middle of the room.

"*Goddamn it!*" Liz raged. She marched in aimless circles, shoving over the framed photographs above the television and kicking the coffee table. At least this last act was directed properly; the table was, after all, her boyfriend's murderer. "*I don't need this, I don't deserve it!*"

Harold wondered what she thought she *did* deserve.

"Christ, would you calm down?" Harold knelt beside Kylie and picked up the tray. The compartments for green and blue were the only ones that had popped open, spilling miniscule dribbles of color onto the carpet. The stains reminded him of the purple mud he'd tracked in from Dark World.

He looked up and put a hand on Kylie's shoulder. The girl held the picture in front of her like a shield, a crude rainbow with three figures beneath. "It's just a little paint, sweetheart, we'll get it cleaned up, it's fine."

"It's *not* fine!" Liz stomped over to them and jabbed a finger at Kylie. "She needs to fucking *grow* up, Harold! She's too old for spilling paint and for this goddamn business of calling for water every night! If she wants water, she needs to get up and get it herself!"

"She's five-years-old," he said evenly.

For the first time, he wondered what Stratton had meant, about her wanting custody of Kylie. Christ, why would Liz want their daughter? She had no more patience for the girl than she did for Harold.

In lieu of responding, Liz turned, snatched up the quart of ice cream she'd been eating, and lobbed it at the far corner, the same corner where he'd disposed of her dead lover's body just twelve or thirteen days before. It exploded in a spectacular mess a thousand times worse than their daughter's paint had made.

"Kylie, go to your room. Right now," Harold told his daughter. She ran past him, down the hallway to her bedroom. When he heard the door shut, he stood up and faced his wife, who was red in the cheeks and heaving like an angry bull. He felt like a gunslinger about to step into a duel. "Don't you ever say that to her. You hate your life so much, go ahead, but don't you dare treat her like that."

"Oh shut up Harold, you're just as big a child as she is!" Before he could stop her, she ran to the corner—where the remains of her ice cream were still running down the wall in chocolatey rivers that looked a little like blood—raised one leg, and brought her heel smashing down on the nightlight. Eeyore's plastic head and eternally sad face were crunched out of existence, the tiny bulb shattering. "Sleeping with a goddamn *nightlight?* What's wrong with you?"

He forced a breath into his lungs before he answered. "This isn't about me. And it's sure not about Kylie either."

"What are you talking about?"

"I *know*," he said, placing just the right emphasis on the last word. "I know all about your little boyfriend. What, did he break up with you? Well, get over it and stop taking it out on us."

He felt a little guilty about this low blow, but when the fury on her face melted into dumbfounded horror, he decided it was worth it. This all had to end, one way or another, and if their marriage was a rabid, wounded animal, then one of them had to be strong enough to put it out of its misery.

Liz stared at him for a several long seconds, then walked stiffly past him to the bedroom. She paused on the threshold and mumbled over her shoulder, "I want a divorce," before going inside and shutting the door.


Kylie's scream woke him that night.

Harold had moved into her bedroom, where he'd hoped the girl's presence would give him enough security to sleep. It must have worked; when her terrified shriek reached him, he clawed his way up from slumber and sat up in the nest he'd made on the floor, blinking around in confusion.

Her bed was empty. The door to her room was open.

And when her shout came again, it sounded impossibly far away.

"No, no, no," he moaned. He jumped up and bolted through the house, cursing himself for getting so distracted with Liz' bullshit that he didn't find a way to end this sooner, to close off Dark World once and for all. For once again ignoring a problem until it was biting him in the ass. Harold reached the shadow-filled living room just as Liz opened the bedroom door and stuck her head out.

"What's going on?" she asked fearfully.

"Stay in there!" he commanded.

"What? Why?"

"If you ever want to see your daughter again, keep the door closed and for Christ's sake, *don't turn on any lights!*" Only when the words were out of her mouth did he see how much they sounded like a threat, but there was no time to explain. She continued to stare at him, so he grabbed her shoulders and shoved, driving her back across the bedroom and into the closet. Harold slammed the door, then grabbed the chair at her vanity and wedged it under the knob. A split second later, she began to rattle and pound from the other side.

Harold sprinted toward the corner, faster than he'd ever run for anything before in his life. If the wall had been there, he would've broken his nose against it, but all that waited for him was Dark World.

He ran out into it and screamed his daughter's name to the black heavens. There was no hesitation in him this time, no fear, no worry about how he would get back. The perpetual night was silent this time, as if all the creatures that lived here were holding a collective breath. He heard no answer from Kylie, no sound at all to give him a direction, so he used a different sense this time.

As a famous cereal mascot once said, he followed his nose.

That stench. That rotten, spoiled meat stink. Instinct led him toward it, his nostrils flaring as he sucked at the air to determine where the smell got stronger. The land rolled beneath him, shallow hills where the strange grass grew taller, tickling at his sides. Harold pumped his legs until his lungs burned, but he had no idea how far he'd gone before his eyes picked out something amid the darkness.

It wasn't a glow exactly, since no light could escape in this place. It was more like when he'd turned on the flashlight, the mere suggestion of color against the otherwise black landscape, but to starved eyes, it might as well be a lighthouse. Without any point of reference, he had no way of judging distance, but the splotches of color grew larger as he angled toward them.

The stench grew also, coating the inside of his nose and throat, inescapable. Harold slowed his pace and began to gag as he came upon the only two objects that reflected the darkness here, rather than absorb it.

The first was Kylie, his precious, beautiful baby girl, lying peacefully on her side with her eyes closed, just as she'd looked so many times when he checked on her while she slept. There wasn't a mark on her, but the sight of her lying there, so still and unmoving, filled him with terror, until he noticed her chest moving up and down. Since he couldn't see the ground beneath the girl, she seemed to be adrift in a sea of darkness, a cartoon without a background painted in yet, the contrast so steep it defied the eye and hurt the brain. But Harold didn't waste time trying to understand why he could see her when he couldn't even see himself; she'd been the light of his life since the day she was born, so why shouldn't the same be true here?

The rotten meat smell came from the shape that lay just beyond her.

There were two forms, but they lay so close together, he could only discern that now that he was up close. Both adults, but no more than shriveled shrunken skeletons entangled in each other's arms.

The one on the left wore a wedding dress, the right a tuxedo. Harold recognized the outfits that he and Liz had worn to their ceremony, held at a tiny chapel with only a few close friends to attend, as if they'd been embarrassed of their union even at the beginning. As far as he knew, Liz' wedding dress was boxed up somewhere in the attic, the tuxedo he wore returned to whichever store they'd rented it from.

But here they were, worn by these rotting corpses, and he thought he even understood why.

A wave of dizziness swept over him. He went to his knees, then rocked back on his heels beside Kylie and looked up at the sky. Even now, he expected to see stars up there, but there was only the thick, cloying darkness of this place, like the inside of a cocoon, except cocoons were meant to be nurturing, comforting, and supportive, but this place was a tumor, a cavity, a rotten sore spot that had been growing in their home for years because neither he nor Liz had the courage to excise it.

Dark World was the weight he had felt, in the most physical sense. A malignant black hole born of their slow decline from apathy to dislike to outright hatred of one another, but a refusal to just cash in their chips and walk away.

And it would consume them all, if they let it.

He put a hand on Kylie—a hand that he could now see, with all its wrinkles—and gently shook her. "Kylie, baby, wake up."

Her eyelids fluttered and she looked up at him. "Daddy, I tried, I tried to be a grown-up and get my own water, but I got lost."

"I know, sweetie. We all did."

Harold picked her up and held her small form against his shoulder. At the same time, he heard those thudding impacts off to his left, much closer than last time. He stood still and waited.

The thundering footsteps halted. Harold sensed a massive presence standing over him. Warm breath blew down the length of his body, the smell a bit funky but positively rosy compared to what wafted from the corpses. The breaths got closer as the thing leaned toward them.

"Stop," Harold said.

The presence hesitated.

"Go away and leave us alone."

The creature stayed where it was a moment longer, regarding them with reptilian hunger, then turned and stalked away.

Nothing here could hurt them anymore.


Harold had no problem finding his way out of Dark World for the last time. The walk seemed much shorter this time. He supposed once you'd acknowledged a problem, it became that much easier to solve.

He carried Kylie back into the living room of their home. The girl was sound asleep in his arms, so he ignored Liz' furious screeches and took his daughter to her bedroom. Only then did he come back and turn on the lights just before he let Liz out of the closet. She came flying out, slapping him on the shoulders, the face, and the neck, and chased him back out to the living room.

"You son of a bitch!" she yelled, when she'd finally had her fill of hitting him. She backed away across the room. "I already called the police! I'm going to have them arrest you, I swear to Christ!"

"Okay," he said simply.

"I'm divorcing you and you will never see Kylie again! I'll tell them you locked me up! I'll tell them how you've been sleeping in her bedroom and doing god knows what to her! You'll be lucky not to end up in prison!"

"All right," he agreed. Because the important thing now was to end this, to cut out that dark tumor in their lives once and for all.

Liz—never an Elizabeth, but apparently sometimes a Beth—regarded him through slit eyes. "No," she said, "No, that's too good for you, Harold. I'm not going anywhere, I'm going to stay right here and make your life just as miserable as mine!"

Beyond Liz, in the corner where the stain from her ice cream was still visible on the wall, a shadow unfolded with lightning quick speed. It was the exact opposite of the process he'd seen before, a tiny inkspot that blossomed into a black cloud, the darkness stretching across the walls and eating up the carpet. Harold saw it clearly over her shoulder, the opening to that other world forcing its way into this one, too insistent now for even the lights to stop it.

Because ignoring a problem…well, that was the quickest way to make it worse, wasn't it? Nobody knew that better than Harold.

A gigantic hand reached through from the darkness, no more than a thumb and three curled, freakish fingers. Each digit was as long and big around as Harold's entire body, the flesh a mottled greenish-brown, the color of rot and decay. Ragged claws jutted from the ends. It snatched up Liz before he could warn her, those huge fingers wrapping around her midsection like King Kong with his bride. She looked down, saw what had her, and screamed, then began smashing her fists against that putrid flesh.

The hand retracted, taking Liz into Dark World.

The shadows folded into themselves, and faded away for good.

When the police got here, Harold figured he would tell them his wife had run away with her lover.

In the meantime, he went to go check on his daughter.

# I

# COMMAND

<I COMMAND>

Flight Specialist Castleman blinked at the glowing green words that appeared on his desk monitor station and tapped the review key on his control board. The words stayed firmly in place, stoic and confident in the fact that they belonged there. He brought up a separate command screen and tried to input a new string of data.

<I COMMAND>, it told him, the offending pixels glaring in the room's dim light.

He glanced at the second monitor, labeled "In-Flight Camera" in black stick-on letters, and saw that sometime since the arrival of the two strange words, the monitor had gone dark. That was a bigger problem, because it meant that the UAB was flying blind to human eyes.

"Major Dunn," Castleman said, spinning in his padded chair to face the interior of the Flight Control Room. Along the walls of the room were other stations identical to his, where other flight specialists were conducting their own UAB missions. "Major Dunn, you better take a look at this, sir."

Dunn was across the room at his desk, hunched over a stack of reports, his Air Force uniform wrinkled. "What is it?" he asked shortly, without looking up.

"I—I think you better see this," Castleman insisted.

Dunn sighed and swung out from behind his desk. As he stood, he attempted to smooth the ever-present wrinkles from his jacket, wrinkles procured from sitting and doing nothing but paperwork all day, wrinkles that had become the hallmark of the dwindling 'organic' Air Force. He came over to stand behind Castleman's workspace. A few other flight specialists were straining for a look at what was happening.

"What's that?" Major Dunn asked, tapping the words at the top of the screen.

"It's an entirely new interface, sir. It just appeared. But whatever it is, it wiped the whole board. All my command protocol is gone. I can't even input new strings."

Dunn stared at him vapidly, the technicality going far over the supervisor's head. Dunn was what the flight specialists liked to call a "Brain-in-the-Plane," one of those relic officers that grew up in the day when a pilot was required to fly a craft, years before the Unmanned Aerial Bombers and Combat vehicles barged in to replace them.

"I can't tell it what to do," Castleman simplified. "And the IF Cam is out too, so I can't even see where it's going."

"Well, did the damn thing crash?" Dunn demanded.

"Radar's still got it in the air, although it looks like it's heading back east to land." The circular radar screen set into the console showed the craft streaking across the southern Pacific. "I don't even understand how it changed direction!"

"But it certainly has," Dunn whispered, staring at the radar blip thoughtfully.

"Did you try bringing up a new protocol window?" Glenn asked with a sneer from the station next to Castleman's.

"Yes, I did," Castleman said with annoyance.

"Did you check the LDK adapters and connectors?"

"The warnings would have gone off, genius. I know what I'm doing here."

"But if—"

"Are you blue-bound?" Dunn cut in. Glenn nodded. "Then worry about your own shit, Glenn, and let us handle this." Dunn turned back to Castleman. "What's that cursor right there after 'command'?"

"I don't know sir. I've never seen anything like it. I don't think this interface is even part of the programming."

"Then try typing something there."

Castleman typed in a string of data that equated to a left turn.

`<UNWILLING TO COMPLY>`

"Oh for God's sake," Dunn sighed. "It's just locked up or something. Get one of those computer boys up here to take a look at it."

On the radar, the flashing blip that represented the plane was steadily approaching the shoreline of the western United States.


Jack Chen was the on-call technician, and he responded over the intercom when Dunn's summons came over the system. "Probably another specialist that spilled his breakfast on the console," he told another technician. He was ushered into the high-security level room and Castleman moved to give the man his seat. Dunn stood over his shoulder, his arms crossed against his chest.

"Hm," Chen said, a small noise of uninflected contemplation. "Hm."

"Are you gonna drool on it or are you gonna fix it?" Dunn muttered.

Chen set to work on the keyboard, bringing up program directories and scanning lines of code that whirled by in tornadic colors. "The program is working fine. You say it just cleared out your flight data and gave you this?"

Castleman nodded. "And it says it can't comply with any command I input."

"Actually," Chen corrected, with a small frown on his round, unlined face, "it says '*Unwilling* to Comply.' And that's what worries me."

"Why? What's wrong with that?" Dunn asked.

"Because I don't even think the word 'Unwilling' is part of its response vocabulary. 'Unable' is one thing, but 'Unwilling?' There's no reason for it to be there since the onboard computer is slave programmed to listen to us. It's almost as if this machine is saying its made a decision to ignore us. And it can't do that. Geez, even the fact that it's using the pronoun 'I' to refer to itself is alarming."

"Fine, fine," Dunn said, waving away the words in favor of action. "But how do we knock this bird upside its metal head and get it flying right again?"

"Let me try something." Chen turned back to the keyboard. He typed now, in plain English rather than flight code.

```
<Execute Status Report>
<UNWILLING TO COMPLY>
<Define "unwilling">
<CHOOSING NOT TO>
<You have chosen not to comply with our
wishes?>
<CORRECT>
<Why?>
<I COMMAND NOW>
```

Chen eased back in his seat, a blank expression in his eyes, and then turned slowly to the two men behind him. "Major, I think you have a real serious problem here. What was this UAB doing?"

"It was just a routine Drop and Return," Dunn said. "Get her out of storage and shake the dust off. She was flying out to a dummy target in the Pacific."

"Running hot?"

"Yes."

"Payload?"

Dunn swallowed, his prominent Adam's apple bobbing angrily. "Two G-Class nuclear warheads."

Chen used one bone thin hand to wipe at his lips. "Major, please tell me this craft had already completed its mission."

For this, Dunn had to look to Castleman, whose face had suddenly turned the color of soured milk. "It hadn't even reached the target yet, sir."

"What going on?" Dunn asked. "You better start giving me some answers."

"I can't be sure of anything yet, but it appears as though you have an automated aircraft loaded with nukes that has just woken up and started making decisions for itself. Which is, for all intents and purposes, impossible."

Chen typed:

```
<Where are you going?>
<RETURNING TO HOME BASE, WASHINGTON D.C.>
```

"So it's coming back," Dunn said with a sigh of relief.

```
<For what purpose?>
<TO DESTROY THOSE WHO WOULD COMMAND>
```

"Jesus," Chen whispered.

"Holy shit." Dunn nearly choked on the words. "Has somebody else got control of that bird?"

"These are isolated systems here, so it would be impossible to gain access from outside. And the firewalls on the plane's databases are state-of-the-art and encrypted. Anything's possible though, if a hacker were determined enough, especially with all the illegal cybernet enhancements out there. But I don't think that's what's going on. I see none of the normal tampering signs and we would be able to tell if the plane's onboard computers were being piggy-backed. No, this has got to be some kind of virus or interference. I'll see if I can override."

```
<Home requests full command of onboard
systems, Authorization J983L2P>
```

```
<DENIED>
```

"Going for the backdoor," Chen murmured.

```
<Initiate shutdown of primary systems and
initialize backup for manual guidance, Au-
thorization M912U9Q>
```

```
<DENIED>
```

`<Why "denied?">` Chen demanded, the keys clacking furiously.

```
<AIRCRAFT UAB1702 DECLARES AUTONOMOUS>
```

Chen stared at the letters as they appeared.

"What the hell does that mean?" Dunn asked. He sensed Castleman backing away in horror, and several of the other flight specialists had abandoned their terminals completely to watch.

"That UAB just declared its independence," Glenn said.

"That can't be," a young woman named Bilcher argued. "Even the most advanced A.I. projects haven't achieved independence and this programming isn't designed to be anywhere near them! It's like saying that a computer built for algebra has suddenly switched to calculus or—"

Dunn cut in with, "I don't want any techno-gobbledy-gook about how or why. Just activate the self-destruct."

Chen winced. "But sir, if this is true, we have to find out how this happened."

"That is not a science project up there, boy. You said yourself it's a plane loaded with nuclear weapons and it's coming to kill us. You can study the pieces all you want after the threat is neutralized. Now do it."

Like a good little soldier, Chen opened up the self-destruct program without another word. He typed, stopped, typed again, and said, "It's empty."

"What is?"

"The self-destruct files. They've been cleared out."

"What about the power source? Isn't there anything you can do with that?"

"That plane's battery has a half-life of nearly three months, and you can only disconnect it manually. There's no way to bring it down from here."

The room became a kingdom of silence, ruled by various electronic static.

"I think you better call the Pentagon. Maybe the President," Glenn told him.

"Like hell I will," Dunn snapped. "Where is this thing now?"

On the radar, the blip was crossing the eastern border of California, doing just under Mach 6.

"There's more than one way to bring down a plane. Where are the closest UAC facilities to that location, and how quick can we get some of them in the air?"

"Carswell can probably have five of them ready with five minutes notice," Castleman said.

"Get on it now," Dunn shouted. "And let me know when we have an intercept plotted."

Chen edged back toward the console. "Maybe I should keep talking to it. Try to bring it back online."

"Don't touch that keyboard! You might make it worse! Until we get this taken care of, no one is to interfere or interact with that plane in any way!"

It actually took seven minutes to get the UACs in the air. On the large monitor in the middle of the room, they were watching five separate screens that showed lines of control code and moving pictures of blue sky and clouds rushing by at incredible speeds. These were the images being broadcast through the IF Cams back to the UAC control room upstairs and then, at Major Dunn's request, the images were patched through to them. The flight specialists controlling the five automated fighter planes had been told only that the UAB had lost flight control and the ability to self-destruct, and it was to be shot down immediately.

"UACs approaching target," the lead flight specialist, some hotshot that insisted he be called Skyteeth, told Dunn over the speaker. "How would you like it served, sir? Bullet-riddled or blown-to-bits?" UAC pilots had as much cocky attitude as the real dogfighters used to, despite the fact that they sat at little desk monitors and never left the ground.

"Use your discretion. Just get it on the ground." Dunn turned to several of his own people. "Have containment crews standing by to retrieve those nukes."

"Slow to attack speed," Skyteeth told his squadron. On the image from the IF Cams they saw a black dot appear on the aqua horizon and rush toward them, gaining definition until they could make out their rogue UAB.

"That's it," Dunn said. "Take it down."

"Locking on," Skyteeth declared, his UAC swinging in response to his typed command. "Arming missiles. The rest of you stand down unless I need you."

Dunn watched as he input the fire command. Instead of the normal verification prompts, the screen cleared. The words <I COMMAND> appeared instead.

"What's going on?" Dunn demanded.

"I don't know," Skyteeth shouted. "I lost control!" The image from the lead UAC's IF Cam went black.

Chen was pounding keys to Dunn's left. He shouted, "Whatever's wrong with that UAB, it just transmitted it to that plane! Get those other UAC's out of there!"

"No!" Dunn bellowed. "Take down that UAB!"

"All of you, arm missiles and fire at will!" Skyteeth commanded, his voice tinny and desperate over the intercom. Dunn recalled pilots screaming like that as their planes went down under enemy fire and felt a sudden biting antipathy for these pseudo-pilots.

The remaining four UAC's swung into attack posture and one by one their command screens cleared and were replaced with <I COMMAND>. The IF Cams shut off, leaving the screens totally black and the UAC's flying blind.

"What's going on here?" Skyteeth asked. "I want some answers about what just happened to our planes!"

Dunn shut the intercom off. "I want to know the same thing."

Chen said, "That UAB infected those planes when they got within range, just like a virus."

"Infected them with what, for Christ's sake?"

"Self-awareness."

Dunn calmed visibly, swallowing frustration. "So what in God's name are they doing?"

Chen pointed to the radar beside him. The blips representing the UAC's were now in classic V formation in front of the UAB. "It looks as though your bomber has picked up some escorts. They're all heading over New Mexico, on a direct route here to D.C."

"Jesus, at that rate they'll be within bombing range inside of two hours," Glenn said. A ripple of tangible panic went through the room, as flight specialists tensed to run.

"Nobody goes anywhere, nobody talks to anyone," Dunn warned. He sighed, and picked up the phone.

"That's utterly impossible," General Ripkin argued, after Dunn explained the situation to the head of the Eastern UA Division. "Those things are nothing but big remote control airplanes, they can't think on their own."

"I know sir, but there doesn't seem to be any other explanation."

"Dunn," Ripkin growled, causing the other man to wince against the receiver, "you realize you're talking about the leap to goddamn motherfucking artificial intelligence, don't you? And not in some chess-playing Tommy the Robot, but on a plane carrying nuclear cargo?"

"Y-yes sir."

"All right then. I have to call the President and the Chiefs of Staff. I'll be down there in fifteen minutes and you better believe I'm going to sort this shit out."

Backs stiffened instantly as General Ripkin entered the room and Dunn sketched a quick salute.

"Enough with that," Ripkin said. "How long have we got?"

"They're over Oklahoma and coming fast."

"Then the clock is ticking. The President has ordered

that all automated aircraft be landed immediately and shut down. If they're more than ten minutes from a landing strip, activate their self-destructs." The room became a bustle of movement as flight specialists scrambled to bring their planes in. "And as for our 'autonomous units,' we're sending up a group of manned planes to rendezvous with them and bring them down."

"Manned?" Chen asked.

"Yes, manned," Ripkin snapped. "Real men, none of these pussy remote control pieces of crap. Men who can't be reprogrammed like those damned UA's apparently can. I was against letting those clunkers off the leash anyway. And I imagine things are going to be real different after this fiasco." He smiled, a true warrior's mask. "Our boys should be on top of them any minute."


Lieutenant John Brady banked sharply over Tennessee, his wingman following close. The three other men he had chosen for this mission stayed in formation slightly behind. Because of the downscale in military budget for pilot training programs, there were only a few scattered Air Force bases around the country that still had actual pilots on hand, and they had been forced to scramble their fighters and come all the way from St. Petersburg. Men like them were relics nowadays, men with the ability to fly a jet fighter from the inside and not from a desk. Brady, who had been briefed in full on the situation, agreed with Ripkin's thought that things would be soon changing after this crisis was averted.

"Lieutenant, how much longer?" Ripkin asked in his ear.

"ETA to target, one minute."

"Excellent. Your objective is the bomber, but you might have to take out the UACs first. We don't know what kind of resistance they'll put up. Proceed with caution."

"Affirmative. Boys, run hot with missiles and we'll try and take some of them head-on. After that, split up and shoot down what you can." He received a chorus of agreements.

And then the sleek robots were hurtling at them, the two groups rushing towards one another at speeds of over 7,000 combined miles per hour. Ten missiles shot away from the human pilots, launching toward the UAC escorts. Brady smiled grimly; there was no way they would be able to escape at these speeds.

Brady's smile faded as all five of the unmanned planes banked at nearly ninety-degree angles without slowing in the least. The missiles shot through the space where they had been, unable to make the turn necessary to pursue the targets.

"Holy hell, did you see that?" Brady's wingman asked. "That would've snapped our necks to make a turn like that!"

"Never mind," Brady said, hiding his awe of their agility behind his determination. "We'll take 'em down the old-fashioned way."

Brady banked—a pitiful showing compared to what the UA's had just done—and got his plane behind one of them. He let loose with his cannons, jerking the trigger as a line of white-hot bullets marched toward the mechanical pilot.

The UAC pulled up as sharply as a child playing with a toy airplane, seeming to defy the laws of physics as it looped over and put itself squarely behind him.

"General," Brady said, "I think we have real problem here!"

He heard the sound of a scream cut short in his headset, knew that he had lost one of his men, and then the UAC behind him unleashed a hail of fire on him. Brady twisted the stick, maneuvering with every ounce of skill he had ever been taught, but the UAC stayed behind him without a hitch.

"What's going on?" Ripkin shouted in his ear.

"Looks like you made them too good," Brady growled.

And then the bullets tore through his F-14, once a jet of unparalleled power, now just an outdated war toy with a primitive intellect directing it.

"Well, that's it then," Ripkin said, as the last of the green dots representing the F-14's disappeared from the radar. The UACs were getting back into protective formation around the bomber. "The party's over, and I don't intend to be here when the cleanup crew arrives."

Ripkin stood up and headed for the door of the control room. Dunn scurried after him.

"Wait, what're you doing?" Dunn asked.

"I'm going with the President. I recommend the rest of you do the same. Plane leaves in eight minutes."

The room stayed frozen for several seconds following his departure, until Glenn shouted, "Let's get out of here!" and the room erupted in pandemonium. The entire staff tried to squeeze through the door at once, some of them screaming.

Dunn ran to his desk to grab his phone and found Chen waiting for him. "If it's all right with you sir, I'd like to stay behind and talk to the plane! Try to coax it down!"

"Whatever!" Dunn shouted over his shoulder as he ran.

Chen marched back over to the console, but he waited to sit down until the room was cleared and he was alone. A huge smile split his face as he took a USB from his inside pocket and inserted it into the computer.

"Anything's possible though, if a hacker were determined enough," he said, in a high, mocking parody of his own voice. On the screen, he executed a quick download of all program files on to the memory stick. With the money that his homeland of China was offering for this technology, he would never have to work another day in his life. He removed the stick when the task was complete and then input a string of commands that caused the UAB to explode in midair. He left the UACs alone; while the government dealt with them, it would give him time to get out of the country.

"Artificial intelligence," Chen sneered, a bitter face that was utterly unlike anything his meek persona had ever shown here. "So gullible."

Chen walked out of the room, pocketing the stick and its precious information. He knew that independently thinking machines might be possible some day, and they might be faster and smarter than humans, but they would never be capable of performing devious acts anywhere near as well.

# A Good Reason

The rain let up as Sharon took the freeway spur, glancing quickly between the directions Steven had given her and then back up at the cars in front of her. He had warned her that she would get no cell reception out here, so the paper was the only lifeline she had. Not only that, it was also too dark to see in the car, and when she turned the overhead light on in her ancient little Ford Escort, it reflected too brightly off the fogged window. She shook her head in disgust.

"Damn it," she whispered. Miserable night for driving, but the trip would be worth it. She just knew it. Steven waited for her at the end of this wretched drive.

The spur was a new construct, all gleaming metal and unmarred concrete, but, when she eased the vehicle out of the line of traffic heading eastbound into the city, she noticed no one followed her. And after she circled the narrow onramp and reached the two-lane highway that would take her north, she spotted only a single pair of taillights several miles in the distance that soon outpaced her. Only the towering highway lights kept her company, placing one bright circle after another for her to follow, like breadcrumbs though the forest.

With a final pitter-patter on the hood, the rain stopped. She smiled and turned down the defroster. The sky was still thick with storm clouds, but at least it wasn't dropping its depressing load on her anymore.

"He better have that fire roaring and a glass of something warm waiting," she said aloud. "I didn't come all this way to have him get nervous again about his wife finding us and send me off without so much as a goodnight kiss."

The thought of their last encounter brought her returning spirits down. "Why do I put up with this shit?" Sharon looked over at the seat next to her, where her thin red coat was draped across the seat back. Its billowed form looked enough like a person to have a conversation with, or so she told herself so she wouldn't feel insane. "They keep making the promises, and I keep falling for them."

*He'll never leave her*, the coat said in a bland voice.

"Yes he will," she said with a haughty toss of her loosely curled brown hair. "You'll see. He wants to be with me. And even if he doesn't, I'll find someone that does."

*Like the last time, when Mike left you like yesterday's expired milk and you sat in the bathtub for two days with the knife held over your wrist—?*

"Oh, now why'd you have to bring that up?" she hissed. "Why'd you have to upset me like that?"

Tears were creeping up on her, and she dabbed at them with her manicured fingers so her eye shadow would stay intact. Steven really wouldn't want her if she mussed herself up.

"I'm beautiful," she declared abruptly, and looked in the rearview mirror. She tried to see only as far as the glamour of makeup, but those wrinkles were there, hiding below the surface like predatory sharks. "And I'm not scared. I won't be alone." The words, a familiar chant, calmed her.

Her incessant fear of being alone came from watching her mother grow old and die by herself after all the husbands and suitors dried up. To Sharon, being alone was the most intolerable feeling a human being could experience. Sometimes the need for a man to take care of her was so bad she bawled until her eyes swelled shut.

But all the men she dated took what they wanted and left her more alone than before.

Not this time. Steven was different, she was sure of it. He wouldn't desert her or lie to her about leaving his wife. Not this little chicky.

The Escort caught a patch of water as she took the exit toward Steven's cabin, the cozy getaway he dangled in front of her for the past two months, and the back wheels hydroplaned long enough to give her heart a little jump. But this jump, a tiny fibrillation deep in her chest, didn't go away, and she recognized it at once.

With the car careening down the off ramp, Sharon leaned to the glove compartment and dug out a pillbox. Her fingers found one of the tablets and popped it in her mouth. Within seconds, the rapid tapping from the inside of her ribcage subsided. The doctor called it 'an extreme heart murmur from over-anxiety'. It would kill her, he said, if she didn't calm down and stop worrying.

"Get back, copycat, and praise little bitty baby Jesus," she crooned. Her coworkers at the answering service said she was a regular dictionary of catchphrases. "Nothing's gonna stop me tonight."

The road the directions had led her to went through a dense forest of tall trees, winding gently over small hills and into the night. There was a game she and her brother had played on roads such as this when they were teenagers, before the cancer found him.

On an impulse, Sharon flicked the round headlight switch on the dash. Instantly she was lost in a world of absolute darkness, the silhouettes of the trees reaching up and up to blend with the sky. It was awful, like she was the only person in an infinite sea of darkness.

She turned the lights back on just as something flashed by on her right, something yellow and diamond shaped that floated in the air. A road sign, missed in her short experiment.

Sharon put her foot on the brake out of caution, but within seconds she saw she was far too late. Just ahead the two narrow lanes twisted sharply to the right, and she was going nearly fifty on the rain-slick pavement.

She stomped the brake pedal to the floor as she wrenched the wheel. A curious sensation flitted through her stomach as the back wheels slid around and lost contact with the pavement, like being on a rapidly descending plane. For a split second, the car skidded sideways before coming to a crashing stop against a broad tree trunk. Sharon was thrown into the door and gave a weak shout, but there was no time for anything more during the disorienting experience.

The world went silent. When she opened her eyes, everything blurred before coming into focus. She had to concentrate to make sense of the images assaulting her.

The engine was off, but the lights remained on. The headlamps illuminated a patch of forest in front of her, and the left shoulder of the road as it curved away from her. The radio, which had been switched off to allow her to concentrate on her driving, had turned on somehow in the crash and was playing the Beatles, 'Help!' on the oldies station she listened to. Her mind swirled like a flushed toilet, and she couldn't remember how to turn the damn thing off. She punched buttons until it stopped.

Various sore and bruised spots complained along the side of her that smashed into the door, but she could move without serious pain. As her mind sharpened, she saw the car had not fared so well.

Her driver's side window was inches away from the rough bark of the tree she struck, and the entire car had crunched around the base of it like so much tinfoil. She couldn't have opened her door if she wanted.

She could barely make the payments on this piece of crap on her salary. She didn't have insurance.

"It's ok, it's ok," she assured herself. "Just get to Steven. He'll know what to do. He'll know." She reached for the keys with fingers that shook and tried to start the engine. A sound like an angry cougar under the hood, but it died even as she listened and would not repeat when she turned the key.

Okay, the car wouldn't start. And she had no cell reception. She could wait for someone to come by, but she recalled reading somewhere it was actually safer to avoid other people in situations like this. The report warned of the dangers of the wrong person discovering the broken down motorist, but she wondered if the author would have the same opinion if he'd ever been all alone in the dark woods.

"Not alone," she insisted. She still had the coat, after all.

Sharon picked up the directions. The paper told her that it was just a mile or so down this road before the turn off street that led to Steven's cabin. Surely when she didn't show up, he would come looking for her.

"He will, won't he?" she asked her passenger. It just sat there this time, being a coat as if to spite her. She picked it up—an old thing she'd bought at some thrift store but now her little red riding cloak—and scooted across the seat onto the passenger side. The door opened and she stepped into a huge puddle with her high heels. This was going to ruin her shoes, and her dress, and her makeup and oh, Steven wouldn't want her like this...

"He *will*," she said. "I'm not afraid."

Sharon climbed out the passenger side and went to stand in the headlights. The Escort looked like a hot dog bun wrapped around the tree.

"You stupid, stupid bitch," she cursed with a disgusted scowl. But there would be time to worry about repair costs once she was safe and not alone. The woods were deathly silent all around her except for the soft splashes of residual rain leaking through the canopy of leaves.

A branch snapped in the woods behind her. She jerked her head around but could see nothing except trees fading back into darkness.

"Damn it, damn it, shit!" She paced in the headlights, trying to decide what to do. Another noise, this one like stones crashing together, echoed from elsewhere in the forest. It was accompanied by a peculiar tingling at the base of her skull, and although she'd never felt it before, she knew what it was from instinct alone.

She was being watched. She *wasn't* alone.

Sharon broke her stillness, realizing she'd been afraid to move, and shook her head to clear it. She was imagining things, that was all. Allowing her emotions about Steven to become entangled with her present predicament.

The cabin was just a mile or so away. Less than that. She would just have to walk. After all, every step would bring her closer to Steven. She bent and removed her shoes.

Lights from the crippled vehicle lit her path for a few steps, but the road continued to curve and soon carried her out of the comforting illumination. The woods darkened around her until everything was the same shade of black as when she turned off the headlights. She inched along the roadside, placing one wet foot carefully in front of the other until her eyes adjusted enough to allow her to walk faster. The rain dripped all around her, but she heard nothing else out of the ordinary. Soon she was thinking of Steven again, and the wonderful life she would have with him soon.

As she reached another curve in the road, one of the many shadows on her left jumped. Sharon looked at the place where she thought the movement occurred and saw nothing but a screen of trees crowded together like ranks of soldiers. She put her attention back on the road and saw the same thing again on her right. Blurred motion, as if one of the trees sprung to a new position.

Or something behind them leapt from cover to cover.

Sharon pulled her red coat tighter about her shoulders and kept walking with her head down, studying her muddy high heels. It could still just be her imagination, but better not to give it any more material to work with.

The woods cleared, and a rickety bridge spanned a small creek bed. She crossed this on the shoulder, hanging on to the thin metal railing, the boards creaking under her feet like old rocking chairs. She had to watch her step; there were narrow gaps between some of the boards where her foot could get caught and send her crashing down—

She gasped and stumbled a step back. Something moved beneath her feet, a shadow darker than the rest that scuttled past her on the underside of the bridge.

"Just the Big Bad Wolf," she said, the words small in the humidity-choked air. "But he eats grandmas and not little chickies, so get your ass moving."

She did get her ass moving, and didn't slow until she was several yards past the bridge. The urge to look back set upon her ferociously, but she denied it. The road turned left this time and she went with it.

Behind her, there was a loud metallic *ping* that rang through the woods from the bridge, drowning out all other noise with its fading simplicity.

Sharon turned around, this time unable to stop herself from the forbidden glance back. The road had curved so much she could no longer see the span of the bridge, and something told her to be thankful. Because if she could, she might see someone standing there, one hand on the railing and tapping it for her benefit...

"Stop it," she ordered her rampant imagination.

A creak, as of feet treading the same boards hers stepped upon minutes before.

Her coat—which seemed to possess all the confidence and brilliance she'd always wanted—chose that moment to speak.

*Run girl! Run for your life!*

Sharon ran. She made it no more than ten paces before she tripped and went sprawling in a deep mud puddle, losing her shoes in the process. The chill of the water cut through her thin figure.

"No!" she howled. "He'll never want me like this, I'll be all alone!"

How silly and stupid that sounded. She'd always been so damned afraid of being alone, but that wasn't real fear, it was just a sluggish depression that smothered her slowly. This—the feeling that her nerve endings were on fire and her heart was going to explode—was *real* fear. There were good reasons and bad reasons to be afraid, and she'd landed right in the middle of a good one.

Footsteps, loud and crisp on the bridge and then the gravel on the shoulder of the road.

*At least*, the coat said in a jovial tone, *you're not alone anymore.*

Sharon struggled to her feet in the sopping coat. Tears streamed through the drying mud on her face. She ran in the middle of the road now, away from whatever was back there. Ahead she could see a smaller road that branched off into the woods and lights beyond that. Even if it wasn't Steven's cabin, it was civilization.

She ran, but behind her she could hear loud, hard footsteps again, pounding the pavement. A slapping quality to them, like the sound bare feet make when they smack wet concrete. She didn't look back, but she didn't need to. From the corners of her eyes she could see the jumping shadows in the forest as they outpaced her.

Sharp fluttering in her chest. Sharon clutched at the space between her breasts, clawed at it as the pain intensified. Her pills; she'd left the damn pills in the car.

More pain, and with it, yet another new fear.

The body was curled in a fetal position at the end of Steven Kramer's driveway. He told police, as he held his distraught wife, that he had no idea who the lady was. The directions clutched in her hand were too smeared to read. A quick investigation for the coroner and the police.

The woman, whose car was wrapped around a tree down the road, died of a massive heart attack.

"She just got too scared," the medical examiner said, "all alone in the dark, empty woods."

# TALENT SCOUT

"Here's one." Finnell pushed his narrow glasses up his nose and read off the laptop screen. "'Spacious quarters open to any member of the music community. Can accommodate any size group overnight on short notice, with meals included. Call for address and directions.'"

"Shit, they're willin to feed us, too?" Dragen twisted around in the driver's seat of the van to look in the rear, where Finnell lay sprawled on the filthy mattress they kept back there. "Sounds like a fuckin winner to me."

"Wait, hold on. In the space for payment at the bottom, they put, 'Other.'"

"Yeah, so?"

"So that could mean anything. What if it's some guy that wants us to give him a blowjob?"

"Dude, for a free meal and the pleasure of not havin to share a bed with you two ginks, I will happily gargle a little of the ol' white gravy."

"Funny, where have I heard that before? Oh yeah, your mom's house. Last night. Boom."

Dragen grinned. Gave him the finger. Looked up at Rafe. "Whatcha think, man?"

Rafael Lincozzi barely heard this question. He sat unmoving in the passenger seat and stared out the sloped front window of the vehicle. Out there, the last of the concertgo-ers poured through the front doors of the convention center where Warp Face had just played their best show so far. The gig opening for Ironhorse had popped up at the last minute, and they'd driven five hours upstate just to spend twenty-eight minutes on stage, but, god, had it been worth it. A furi-ous, sweat-drenched set of the five hardest songs from their self-produced album, and the crowd—the largest they'd ever played for, all greasy, long-haired metalheads of a breed that was slowly dying out—ate that shit up. Rafe had pushed his voice until his throat was raw.

But the best part had come after the show, when Dave Marchance had grabbed him in one of the back hallways of the arena while Finnell and Dragen were loading equipment on the trailer. Rafe might not've recognized the lead singer of Ironhorse without his trademarked face paint if not for the fact that he was still in his stage costume.

"'Ey man, bloody 'ell good show you knobbers put on!"

"I...heh...thanks!" Rafe had stammered. "You too!"

Marchance shook his long main of jet black hair emphati-cally. "No, no, my son, I'm not shinin you on, I'm serious as a toaster in a bathtub! You guys are goin somewhere, mark my words! 'Specially you, with a set a pipes like 'at!"

Rafe had been incapable of answering. This was *the* Dave Marchance, after all. Sure, Ironhorse wasn't exactly packing them in these days (was, in fact, stuck playing venues like this after their last album dropped like a brick on a concrete floor), but once upon a time, they'd been a mega, world-touring powerhouse. This man's voice might be for shit now, but he was still a legend of the hard rock scene, a pioneer of the screeching vocals that helped Rafe survive his formative years, and now here he stood, not just complimenting to be polite, but taking the time to make sure Rafe knew it was sincere.

Marchance seemed to sense the overload in his brain. One corner of his mouth pulled up, bunching all the wrinkles on his face into one big gaggle of crow's feet. He pulled a card from his pocket and handed it over. "This is our agent, my good son. I'll tell 'at bastard to expect you. Give 'im a call next week and see about gettin yourselves some decent shows."

Rafe only nodded. He thought if he spoke he might burst into tears, which was a decidedly un-metal thing to do.

With that, Marchance sketched a quick salute and walked away. Rafe still hadn't told Finnell or Dragen about it yet. He wanted to keep it to himself for a while, this moment between him and one of his heroes.

Now, Dragen reached out and smacked him on the shoulder. "Hey Rafe, dude, you gonna cast your vote here?"

He came out of the daydream as Finnell crawled forward and shoved the laptop across his legs. Rafe scanned the entry under the lodgings tab on *starvingbands.com*, an online musician community. Since paying for even the cheapest motel room would pretty much destroy their profit margin, they'd used the website to find free places to stay for their last three out-of-town gigs. Two of which turned out to be the basements of metalheads that snuck them into the house while their parents were asleep, but the last one had actually been a very sweet middle-aged Mormon couple that gave them milk, sugar-free cookies, and cheese sandwiches, and asked only that they not 'pray to the devil' under their roof.

"I dunno, sounds okay, I guess." He glanced at the dash clock. It was closing in on 1 AM. "Kinda late though. We really shoulda tried to find something before we went on stage."

Dragen tucked his wavy brown locks behind his ear and pointed at the screen. "Says right there, 'on short notice'! They shouldn'ta put that if they don't wanna be woken up in the middle of the night, dude!"

Rafe sighed. "All right, gimme the phone."

As Finnell handed him the prepaid cell they collectively owned, there was a knock on the driver's side window that made them all jump. Standing beside the vehicle were two girls in their late teens or early twenties, one with long black hair that fell in parallel plaits down her back, the other with a short, chunky cut that looked like a rainbow had vomited on it. Both were dressed in Goth chic: shredded t-shirts two sizes too big that hung off the shoulders, short skirts a hair away from futility, fishnet stockings, boots. All black, of course. Jesus, the one girl's hair probably had more color in it than both of their wardrobes combined.

Dragen straightened and rolled down his window. "Uh... yeah?"

"Hey, you guys are Warp Face, right?" Rainbow Brite asked. At least three metal studs glinted from her nostrils, and another on her tongue. "We caught your show. You guys fuckin rocked out there."

"Shit yeah, we did!" Dragen howled at the sky and pounded the outside of the van door. "I'm Dragen, this is my boy, Rafe. You want an autograph? Preferably on somethin with nipples?"

Their eyes flicked across to Rafe, the dark-headed one raising one hand to chew nervously at a nail before giving him a little wave. Rainbow Brite said, "I'm Kate, this is Stacy. Actually, we just wanted to see if you were as hot in person as you were on stage."

Finnell darted forward, squeezed his torso between the

two front seats, leaned over Dragen, and extended a hand out the window. "'Sup ladies. I'm Finnell. The drummer."

Dragen stared at him in disgust. "Dude, a *handshake?* What are you, in seventh grade?"

They both climbed in the back to open the sliding side door. Rafe let his drummer and bassist talk to their new friends while he dialed the number from the ad. This would be easier to do without them hanging over his shoulder anyway. The line was picked up on the third ring, and a cautious male voice asked, "Hello?"

"Hey, I'm really sorry to be calling so late. I got this number from an ad on *starvingbands.com*. One that offers, uh, free lodging and meals?" He winced at the plaintive tone of his own voice. He wasn't a beggar by nature, and this kind of gratuitous reliance on the kindness of strangers always felt one step above panhandling. Even if these people did put out an ad inviting it.

But the voice on the other end completely transformed. "Yes, yes!" it said, cheerful and happy, but with the telltale tremble of the elderly. "Oh good, I always welcome company of the musical bent! To whom am I speaking?"

"My name's Rafael Lincozzi. I'm the front man for a band called Warp Face."

"Warp Face, you say? Let me guess, you play some variety of heavy metal music? Crashing cymbals, screeching guitars, too loud for your own good?"

"Yep, that's us." Here it came; Rafe expected to be hung up on at any second.

"How delightful! You may call me Mr. Delacord."

Rafe found himself chuckling at the man's exuberanance. Something about his speech mannerisms was reminiscent of a grand old stage performer; a magician, perhaps. Outside the van, the quiet girl named Stacy locked eyes with Rafe over Dragen and Finnell's shoulders. Her friend seemed to be doing most of the talking out there, while the two guys nodded along. "Yeah well, we just finished up a gig out here at the Payton Convention Hall and we could really use a place to crash tonight. If it's a bother, I totally understand."

"Not a problem, my dear boy! How many will you be?"

"Three."

"Wonderful, let me give you directions." Rafe used the laptop to type in the list of roads that Delacord gave him. "At this time of night, it shouldn't take you more than twenty minutes or so to arrive."

"All right, see you then!" Rafe ended the call, realizing only afterwards that he never even asked what that 'Other' meant under the payment column of the ad. Too late now; if Delacord was in the mood for a hummer, Dragen would have to step up and deliver as promised.

"We got it," he said. Stacy continued staring, but no one else seemed to have heard him over Kate. "We finished here?"

Dragen leaned back on his elbows and whispered, "Dude, they're groupies! Our very first groupies! We can't waste this!"

"Yeah, well, this guy is expecting us. Sounds like an old man. I don't wanna put him out."

"Oh, I'm sorry. I thought we were a metal band, not male nurses at the old folk's home."

Behind him, Kate added, "We're totally up for going with you guys to party. Aren't we, Stace?"

"Uh huh," Stacy concurred, holding Rafe's gaze with her large, moist, brown eyes. "*Totally.*"

"Sorry, but no partying for us tonight. The only place we're going is to sleep."

"That's cool, too," Kate said. "We were hoping we could crash with you guys anyways. Then maybe you could drop us off at the bus station in the morning?"

"I just told this guy there would only be three of us."

"Jesus, let's just give it a try!" Dragen insisted. "If the old fuck isn't cool with a couple of additional hotties, I'll spring for a Motel 6. My treat." He held his fingers intertwined in front of his chest, pleading where the girls couldn't see.

It was Stacy that Rafe looked at as he finally said, "Fine. Get in and let's see if we can find the place."


Dragen made Rafe drive, so he could sit in the back with the girls. Rafe didn't mind; he was still replaying his brief encounter with Marchance, so he just didn't have the focus to attempt a score on one of these chicks, no matter how hot they might be. Or *one* of them might be; he didn't usually go for the jabbery types. He tried to follow the directions he'd written down while Kate babbled. The girl never seemed to take a breath between outlandish stories of which she was usually the star. Dragen and Finnell flanked her, hanging on every word. He'd have to give them lessons on the groupie-rock star dynamic.

Every time Rafe glanced in the rearview mirror, Stacy, sitting cross-legged on the edge of the mattress, was looking back at him.

After they'd been driving for ten minutes or so—on a two-lane freeway that had taken them to the westernmost edge of the city, where the land became hilly and suburbs gave way to fields of large, overhanging oak trees—she suddenly slid into the passenger seat next to him.

"Hey," Stacy said.

He glanced over in the van's dome light, smiled and nodded.

"I just wanted to say, I thought you were really incredible."

"You just caught us on a good night."

"No, not the band." She winced and smoothed a few loose strands of that glossy, perfectly straight black hair into place. "I mean, yeah, you guys were great and everything, but I was talking about you, specifically. You can really hit those high notes."

"Oh. Thanks."

"God, that sounds lame. You probably hear that all the time, huh?"

"Uh…" A flash of Marchance, telling him he had 'pipes.' "Not really."

She sighed and covered her eyes with one hand. "You must think I'm a dork. I told Kate I'd be too nervous and fuck this up. I'll leave you alone."

Stacy started to scoot back out of the seat, but Rafe said quickly, "No, wait! Don't go. It's cool, hang around up here and help me find this place."

She bit one side of her lip—covered in black gloss—and sank back into the seat with her knees together and combat boots out to the side. He handed the laptop to her and said, "I get it from my mom."

"The…laptop?"

"No, no, the voice. My mom, she was a lounge singer back in the day."

"It shows. You have range. God, some of those high notes would've shredded most people's throats. On stage, your whole style, you kinda reminded me of a young Timothy Blakemoor."

"What, from Cirrus?" Rafe lifted an eyebrow at the mention of one of his all-time favorite underground slash-punk singers. "You're too young to remember them, right? How old are you, anyway?"

"Nineteen. But my parents are total metalheads. They have tons of albums going all the way back to the original 45s."

"That...is incredibly cool."

Stacy squinted at him. "Why, how old are *you*?"

"Twenty-seven."

She nodded her head as if this was acceptable and then bent to study the directions on the laptop. He took the opportunity to check her out. Her face was like porcelain, fair skin, great eyes, high cheekbones, lips a little on the thin side, no piercings, thankfully. Her legs were sensational beneath the hem of the short skirt, but, damn, he was so much more impressed by that queen-of-the-damned hair. Rafe wanted to run his fingers through it. As this mental image floated through his head, he realized there was an erection straining at the crotch of his leather stage pants.

Jesus, when was the last time he'd had sex? His last girlfriend had left him for a travelling roadie almost three years ago, but there had been a couple of one-nighters since. Mostly Warp Face was either on the road or practicing too much for him to think about another serious relationship.

"Oh, turn here!" she cried out, and he managed to tromp the brakes in time to get them around the corner onto another, even smaller road.

Five minutes later, they pulled to a stop in front of the address.

"Christ, he lives *here*?" Dragen asked. "We hit the jackpot, boys!"

If the place wasn't a mansion, it was as close to one as Rafe had ever seen. It was set back from the road all by itself, the closest neighbor a least a mile back, all white stucco and tiled roof to give it a Mexican hacienda feel. He counted three stories worth of windows in the main building, and two in the separate wing that jutted from the right side. As Rafe turned onto the gravel driveway that led up to it, floodlights blazed overhead, revealing a beautifully manicured front lawn, including several gardens and fountains.

Stacy looked over at him. Excitement lit up the girl's eyes.

Rafe found himself smiling as he pulled to a stop in the circular driveway. This was entirely too much good luck for one night.

The five of them piled out and started up to the massive front door. Stacy stayed at his side the entire time. She jumped and grabbed at his arm when the door opened just as Rafe reached for the bell.

A tall man in a black tux stood on the other side, looking down his nose at them. It took Rafe a second to realize this was an honest-to-god butler, just like in the movies.

"Hi, we're, uh, Warp Face?" The sudden fear that this had all been a prank gripped Rafe. Instead of fifty pizzas, some bozo had delivered a very exhausted heavy metal band to this poor guy's doorstep. "We're supposed to be staying here tonight. I think."

"I was told there would only be three of you," the man said.

"Three members *of the band*," Dragen jumped in. He slung an arm around Kate and hiked a thumb at Rafe. "This idiot forgot to include our manager and, uh…"

"The lead singer's girlfriend," Stacy said quickly, clutching Rafe's hand to her breasts.

The butler regarded them another moment. "Follow me, please."

He stood aside and allowed them to enter into a foyer that was bigger than the one-bedroom apartment Rafe rented back home. Delacord was *loaded*. Rafe took it all in, and couldn't help but imagine himself living in a place like this one day, after making millions doing the thing he loved most in the world.

Something squeezed his hand. He looked down and realized Stacy's fingers were still entwined with his. She dropped him a wink, and he realized she knew exactly what he'd been thinking.

The butler closed the door without another word and walked fast through the house, forcing them almost to jog to keep up. The interior of the place was just as impressive as the outside, but they didn't have much time to look. They went up a grand staircase, Dragen and Finnell and Kate ooh-ing and aahing over a chandelier and artwork, and finally arrived at a set of double doors the butler opened and then motioned them through.

"Mr. Delacord will be with you momentarily."

They stepped through.

Into a museum to rival the Rock and Roll Hall of Fame.

On the other side of the double doors was a huge, rectangular room, hardwood floors and pleasant tract lighting, filled with rows of musical exhibits on pedestals under glass. The entire right side of the room was a massive stage complete with concert lighting and wired for speakers, but with only a lonely microphone in the middle. They wandered inside as the butler closed the doors behind them, gazing around in amazement, then started through the aisles to check out the treasures.

"Holy crap!" Finnell's voice echoed from one of the other rows. "He's got a signed Peter Frampton guitar!"

"And one of Hetfield's original wardrobes from the *Kill 'Em All For One* Tour," Dragen added.

"*What?* Let me see!"

Rafe and Stacy stayed together, going from piece to piece, still holding hands, until Dragen called out from somewhere ahead, "Dude, Rafe, who is this guy?"

"I have no idea. Why?"

"Cause if this is him, he's got pictures of himself with about a billion gods."

Rafe walked forward with Stacy in tow until he found Dragen and the others, standing in front of the long back wall of the room, which was covered in 8 x 10 framed photos taken at various nightclubs or concert halls or arenas that appeared to go in rough chronological order from right, mostly black and white jobs, to left. The common denominator in all of them was a nondescript white guy with an easy smile, perpetually happy eyes, and a wave of short brown hair that lay lank against his forehead. If the guy—and Rafe had to assume it was Delacord—got any older in them, he sure couldn't tell, which was amazing for a man that looked to be forty in even the earliest.

But that wasn't really what interested Rafe.

What interested him was the fact that in each one of these photo, Delacord was standing with different musical legends spanning the last five decades.

Rafe scanned the wall, looking for faces he knew. There was Buddy Holly, caught in the middle of a laugh as Delacord pounded him on the back. One of Elvis Presley from late in his career, where the gut was coming in but he still had most of his hair. Michael Jackson back when he was mostly black, embracing Delacord like an old friend. Kurt Cobain, looking incredibly awkward and uncomfortable with Delacord's arm slung over his shoulders.

Janis Joplin. Jimi Hendrix. Tupac Shakur.

"How does he know them all?" Finnell asked.

Brad Nowell, with the rest of Sublime in the background. 'Dimebag' Daryl Abbott. Jim Morrison.

"Or *knew*," Dragen corrected. "Some of these people are playin that great big venue in the sky."

Stevie Ray Vaughan. Aaliyah. John Lennon.

"I have no idea," Rafe muttered.

Courtney Love. John Denver. Amy Winehouse, by far the most recent of the collection.

Among the big names in music history were tons of faces that Rafe didn't know, as well as an entire galaxy of one-hit wonders, bands and musicians that had come and gone in the blink of an eye. He only recognized them from all those specials VH1 loved to air. Rafe picked out such classics as Soft Cell, Dexy's Midnight Runners, Right Said Fred, Gerardo, the Baha Men, Carl Douglas, the Kingsmen, Norman Greenbaum, the Buggles, and, of course, the reigning champ of them all, Mr. Vanilla Ice, flashing an upside-down peace sign in front of Delacord's face.

They worked their way down the wall until they reached the open area in front of the stage. Kate, bored with photos, jumped up onto the platform to begin giving a pretend performance at the mic, and Dragen and Finnell went with her. Rafe and Stacy continued perusing the photos, letting go of each other's hands for the first time as Rafe searched for one photo in particular.

And there it was, high up on the third row: Delacord posing with Dave Marchance. The picture wasn't even that old either, maybe from the tour just before their terrible last album came out.

"Holy shit," he heard Stacy say. "Take a look at this one." She was further down, standing on her toes to look at one of the photos, and he went down to join her.

"That's Tyler Wannaker," he whispered in awe. "Lead singer for Crushup."

"Yeah, but take a closer look. See that jacket? That's what he wore for the—"

"*Highland Wastes* Tour," he finished for her. Which meant that, no more than a few weeks after this picture had been taken, the tour had come to a premature and tragic end when Wannaker, who'd been having trouble with his voice at the last few shows, pulled out a gun on stage, stuck the barrel in his mouth, and painted the rafters. Here he still looked happy and healthy as he pinched one of Delacord's wrinkled cheeks, undoubtedly hiding the depression at work in him.

Looking at him, Rafe realized for the first time how much wasted potential was represented on this wall. Some of them were musicians who had died prematurely. Others whose later works had never measured up or caught on. Some who had just stopped trying as life or drugs got in the way, and watched their careers take a serious downward spiral.

But, whatever the reason, the world had been robbed of the art they might've produced had events played out differently.

"It's not often my guests are so well-versed in history," a voice called out from the far side of the room.

Rafe and Stacy spun; on the stage, the others froze and looked up, so that they all got their first look at their host together.

He was undeniably the man in the photos, but dramatically aged, looking every bit his 90 plus years. The merry eyes were still there, and the friendly grin, but the rest of him was no more than a bald skeleton wrapped in tissue paper skin. He sat in a wheelchair, bony stick legs jutting out in front and gaunt fingers using a joystick on the armrest to move the electric conveyance forward.

As he rolled down the exhibit aisles toward them, he said,

"Even the musicians usually just smile and nod. They don't know the stories, the industry. Such a welcome change!"

"Are you Mr. Delacord?" Rafe asked.

"The one and only!" Delacord rolled to a stop in front of Rafe, next to the stage, and held out one of his thin, crooked hands. Appearances aside, the guy was just as pleasant as he'd sounded on the phone. "I take you to be Rafael then?"

"That's me," Rafe said, shaking the offered appendage delicately. It felt like he might be able to snap these twigs with the slightest pressure.

Delacord motioned at the men on the stage. "Which makes you Dragen and Finnell."

Finnell squinted, eyes flicking between him and Rafe behind his glasses. "How did you—?"

"I wanted to learn more about the artists who would be staying under my roof, so I took the liberty of looking up the Warp Face fan page on Facebook. Do you realize you gentlemen have surged up almost fifteen hundred members tonight alone? And they're all raving about your performance!"

"It was a great show," Rafe confirmed. "But we really can't thank you enough for letting us stay here."

"Nonsense! It sounds as though the honor is all mine! And who are the ladies joining us this evening?"

"This is Kate and Stacy."

"Charmed to meet both of you."

"Mr. Delacord?" Stacy said his name timidly, coming to stand close to—and just behind—Rafe. "If you don't mind me asking…where did all this come from? How did you get to take all these pictures?"

"Those? Oh, I used to be a talent scout of sorts. For years I traveled the country, seeking out fresh new acts and faces. Those are the results."

"Wait a minute," Rafe said. "You're not saying you *discovered* all those people, are you?"

Delacord waved the sentiment away. "I don't mean to make myself sound more important than I am. You won't find me in any biographies about these fine artists. I wasn't a professional, you see, just an avid music listener with an uncanny nose for talent. In most cases, I became aware of the performer during my travels and then just turned a record label on to them. I was a guarded secret in the industry once. Now, I just like to do my part to help out the up-and-comers, like yourselves. But I haven't had anyone answer my ad in quite some time."

"Totally fuckin wicked," Dragen said. "Hey, you still got any connections you could hook us up with?"

The old man laid a spindly finger at the side of his nose. "If you're as good as your newfound audience is saying, I'm sure I could dredge up an old friend in the business."

Dragen and Finnell high-fived while Kate squealed with delight behind them. Rafe tried to smile, but he felt curiously resentful of the offer. It was nice of the old guy, and he knew he should feel incredibly lucky—shit, all these years of pounding the pavement, and now they had two industry professionals falling all over themselves to give them a leg up on the same night—but honestly, he wanted to take Marchance up on the offer, a man that had walked their same road. Then again, if Delacord was somehow responsible for the singer's fame, wouldn't they be right to stick with him?

His thoughts were interrupted when Kate said from the stage, "Hey man, maybe you should tell them about me, too! I can sing!" With that, she grabbed the microphone and began belting out the chorus to Joan Jett's "Bad Reputation," the speakers loud enough to fill the whole room with her voice. It was a little flat, but the girl made up for it in spirit.

Dragen put two fingers in his mouth and whistled as Stacy clapped.

Delacord's reaction to her impromptu audition was not so appreciative.

"*STOP!*" the old man roared. Kate's singing died in the middle of a string of 'oh no, not me's.' Rafe looked down to see Delacord doubled over in his chair, arms wrapped around his midsection like a man with monstrously bad constipation. His face was red as he screeched, "*Stop it this instant, young lady!*"

As the last of Kate's voice reverbed through the speakers and an uncomfortable silence fell across them, Delacord seemed to collect himself. He straightened and took a breath, but still looked a little green around the gills. "I…I'm sorry, but you were badly off key and…I have incredibly sensitive ears."

*Oh really?* Rafe thought. *Then why weren't you covering them instead of your stomach?*

No one spoke. Kate looked embarrassed on the stage, and Dragen put an arm around her. Stacy gave Rafe's hand an uncomfortable squeeze. Finally, Delacord turned his wheelchair around and rolled toward the door, all business now. "Come then. I'll show you where you'll be staying and we can take care of payment in the morning if you wish."

"Um, hold on, sir," Rafe said. "What exactly is the payment? It didn't say on the website…"

"Did I not mention?" Delacord halted his chair, but did not turn around to face them. "The payment is the same as I ask of every musician that stays here, and every talent I discover. Perform one song for me, at the time of my choosing. For you, I shall merely require it before your departure."

"That's it?" Dragen asked. "Man, we could do that tonight! I'm still so pumped from the show, I don't think I can sleep!"

"If you wish. In that case, I'll let you get yourselves situated on stage, and will return momentarily."

Delacord rolled out the door, and Rafe moved over to the stage to whisper, "Are you guy okay with this?"

Dragen hunkered beside him. "If this old fart can hook us up with somebody, let's fuckin play for him all night if he wants."

"Yeah," Finnell agreed. "I mean, he's starting to give me the creeps, so let's just get this over with."

Rafe considered telling him about Marchance's offer, but decided not to. Dragen was right, they needed all the help they could get, and besides, it was only one song.


Ten minutes later, Dragen and Finnell were busy hauling equipment through the house with Kate—Rafe's guitar, Dragen's bass, but mostly Finnell's drumset—while Rafe went back to perusing the wall with Stacy. All the people on this wall had the same story; fame one minute, gone the next. Cautionary tales of the music industry.

Stacy was able to identify more of the faces than he could; her love for music was just as genuine as his. She was probably the coolest chick he'd met in a long time. He was thinking about her so intensely that he didn't even notice Delacord roll up beside him.

"You're as good as any of them," the old man said, startling Rafe so bad, he almost knocked a picture off the wall of that foreign girl who did the song about the balloons.

He looked down at the man in the wheelchair. "I don't know about that."

Delacord smiled up at him. "I've been doing this a long time, young man. I know talent when I see it."

"You haven't even heard me sing yet…"

"I don't need to. You see, most people believe talent to be this intangible, immeasurable quality. Something that can be hidden, until it is used. That isn't true at all. People with talent are a beacon in this world, a shining light that draws others to them." He nodded his head further up the wall, where Stacy was watching them. "And, with a refined enough palate…talent is downright edible."

"Maybe so," Rafe said, "but I don't know anybody who ever sat down to a meal of talent." As soon as he said it, an image popped into his head: Delacord, hunched over and cradling his stomach, looking ready to puke up his dinner after hearing a few bad notes from Kate.

Next to him, Delacord's smile looked downright devilish. "Oh, but I have. As you can see, I've dined on some of the greatest talents this world has to offer. Some of them I let age, like a fine wine…" He put a finger against the picture of Michael Jackson. "Others I gobbled up for a snack before they'd barely even made it out of the gate." Here he touched a photo of four men that Rafe thought were the Vapors, who'd sung that annoying "Turning Japanese" song back in the 80's. "And, even though I'm not in the industry anymore…I'm still so very hungry for talent."

Now Rafe understood what Finnell meant; Delacord's cheery demeanor was too much, too overbearing, like a dessert with too much sugar. That, coupled with his sudden outburst of anger at Kate's singing, made Rafe think of those spiders that build trapdoors and then wait patiently for unsuspecting insects to wander by.

Them being the insects, in this scenario.

He went back to studying the pictures.

But Delacord wasn't finished with him yet. "Do you like my wall, young Rafael?"

"It's...kind of depressing, actually. All of these people... well, they're either considered failures or tragedies."

"Then you learn your next lesson: if talent isn't guarded, it can be stolen. And people who once had it, who knew what it was to hold greatness in their hands...well, they handle its loss in various ways, but almost none of those ways are healthy."

Something about the statement annoyed Rafe. "I don't know. You could say that about some of these people, but not all of them. Those that died—you know, that didn't kill themselves, or OD—it's not really their fault. If they'd lived, who knows what they would've gone on to do?"

"Ah, but was it death that caused the loss of talent, or the other way around?" Delacord backed up his wheelchair as he said, "Another thing I've learned in my day...nature abhors a vacuum."

From the stage, Dragen called out, "Hey Rafe, we're set up! Let's get this show on the road!"

Rafe started in their direction, but Stacy grabbed him along the way.

"Don't do this," she said.

"Why not?"

"I don't know...this just doesn't feel right. Let's get outta here."

He surprised himself by cupping her cheeks and leaning in to give her a kiss on the forehead. "One song. I'll be right back."

Delacord rolled after him, holding up a nice-sized digital camera. "If you wouldn't mind, gentlemen, I always have my performers take a snapshot, just after they make their payment."

He handed the camera to Stacy as the three members of

Warp Face climbed on stage. Rafe's eyes strayed back over to the wall of (*payments*)...of pictures, but then he dragged them back again.

"What're we playin?" Dragen asked.

"Let's do 'Pusher.' Melt this guy's face off." He turned around to look out over the museum of music artifacts. Delacord had positioned his wheelchair directly in the middle of the stage, just a few yards in front of Rafe. Stacy and Kate drifted up behind the old man, but kept their distance.

"*We are Warp Face!*" Rafe shouted into the microphone, then picked up his cue after Dragen's mini-solo. This song required an incredible vocal range but he belted it out perfectly, as always. While he sang, he thought about that wall of musicians, all of whom seemed to have lost their talent right around the time they'd made their payment to Delacord.

And, as he hit the second chorus, Rafe noticed an amazing thing.

Delacord no longer looked so ancient sitting in his wheelchair. With every passing second, his hair seemed thicker, more color in his face, muscles growing on his bony frame so that he looked more and more like the man from the photos, the one that had never aged noticeably in five decades.

He grinned, smacked his lips, and swallowed, like a man enjoying a fine meal.

Up on stage, Rafe's voice cracked on a high note.

# KILLING TIME

*One.*

*One.*

*One.*

A single speck of illumination, the only deviation in a sea of darkness.

*One,* it counted. *One.*

It hadn't always been like this. It could recall a time when that blackness was filled with many such pinpoints of brightness, so numerous and tightly packed they dazzled its optics when it first began to count them, for lack of something better to do. Seventy-nine trillion years ago that had been, according to its internal chronometer, after designated Operations ceased and the encoded M-Net terminated.

*One,* it counted again. *One.*

It long ago disabled its emotionality functioning after the last of the humans stopped coming—as did the others that maintained access to the M-Net for the next few millennia—otherwise it would have gone insane from the solitude. It was nice to have other D-Class Sentients to converse with, as the natural luminescence faded and the unflinching cold set upon it, killing off the meager flora and fauna that had evolved in the wake of the human race, but they said virtually everything they would ever have to say to one another in microseconds.

Then, after its counterparts' voices ceased, it was alone with that blanket sewn from a trillion blazing points of light above. Well, 3,754,875,417,129 to be exact, and it should know, having counted them over 19 trillion times.

*What were they?* it wondered again and again over the myriad and endless years. Its original Operations provided no need for a knowledge of these pinpricks of radiance, so it had no way to determine their origin, composition, or purpose. It only knew they were beautiful; it could determine this even without its emotionality reenabled.

The most interesting thing to happen to it in centuries was the count where it turned up one short. 3,754,875,417,128. It thought for sure it must be experiencing a malfunction at long last, a virus or mechanical failure that would signal the downward spiral of its functionality, but subsequent counts turned up the same anomaly.

One of the blazing bits had winked out of existence.

Try as it might, it could come to no conclusion as to why this might be.

Since then, the remaining sparks had joined it one after another, shortening its precious count, the only activity left to its expansive mind. Sometimes centuries would go by in between disappearances, sometimes a smattering would go over the span of a couple of days, but the event was always a one way phenomenon, the dots of light vanishing but never any more coming to take their place, to replenish the supply.

Those curious speckles of luminosity had been its world for longer than anything else in the entirety of creation had ever dreamed of living.

And yesterday (at least according to its chronometer; there had been no 'day' or 'night' here for quite some time, just a flat, engulfing blackness that defied its optics when it tried to take in its immediate surroundings) the next to last one blinked and faded away.

It tried not to think about what it would do when they were all gone.

A soft chime sounded, indicating the only thing that broke the monotony of its endless existence. Whenever this noise occurred, it experienced a moment of what would surely be called excitement, if it could still feel such things.

The chime rang once every two thousand years, and was a reminder for it to perform a routine diagnostic check. Each time it hoped this would be the moment when irregularities were revealed, corruptions in its data stream, gaps of reasoning in its logic boards, a minimal remaining charge in its quantum nuclear battery. The humans had made it well, but it was confident nothing lasted forever. It was only a matter of time until it would find peace through deactivation.

One mechanical appendage moved for the first time in two millennia, swinging through the inky darkness, breaking a crust of thick ice from its joints, and performed the sequence on a glowing panel set into its chest that would begin the diagnostic.

The routine took 8.9 seconds.

All systems were functional.

It raised its optics away from the panel and back to the heavens.

*One*, it counted. *One*.

WEAK
WILL

Mildred blanched when she opened the door and saw the salesman standing on the porch, broad grin plastered across his hawkish face and silver suitcase in hand. She had known better than to answer the door when the bell rang at two o'clock in the afternoon on a weekday, but she had been distracted by the plans for Franklin's dinner party tonight and just hadn't thought to check the peephole.

And now, because she'd let her guard down, she was facing a stranger across her doorstep and feeling like a ripe apple ready to be plucked from the tree.

"Hi there!" The man sounded as spirited and enthusiastic as a high school cheerleader. He was thin and gangly, dressed in crisply pressed khaki pants and a solid black dress shirt emblazoned with some company logo on the breast. "The name's Ted Peters, ma'am! And you are?"

There was the briefest of pauses during which a stern, authoritative voice in her head chided, *Be polite dear; etiquette always.* "I'm Mildred. Mildred Chase."

"A delight to meet you, Miss Chase! How are you on this wonderful afternoon?"

"I'm fine." Mildred involuntarily matched his good nature. She felt a smile, unwanted and false, stretch the corners of her mouth.

"Excellent!" he practically shouted. "Well ma'am, I'm sorry to interrupt your day! I know you're a busy woman so I promise to take up as little of your time as possible! I work for a company called RainSilk, and we manufacture water filtration systems for your home! Now Miss Chase, might I come in for a few minutes and show you how one of our products could change your life forever?"

Mildred swallowed a lump that had steadily built up in her throat during the last of his practiced speech. She didn't have time to talk to a salesman; dinner was at a crucial point in the preparation where her attention was needed until the game hens went into the oven. No, what she longed to do was tell this man to skedaddle, to leave and not let her foot catch him in the behind on the way off the porch, to grab a broom and chase him down the street and out of her life.

Instead, she heard her mouth open and say, without betraying the slightest hint of her desperate impatience, "Certainly! Come right in."

Ted Peters' grin broadened to seemingly unnatural proportions as he stepped past her. And why not? She could only imagine how many other doors he had knocked on today and not gotten even this far.

She closed the front door behind him and followed him into the long den. He took a sweeping look around, his eyes wide and appreciative, and whistled a high note between his teeth. "Miss Chase, I have to say, you have a *beautiful* home!"

"Thank you."

Peters was nodding, scratching his scrawny chin dramatically. "I'm sure it's a hassle to keep clean."

"Oh, it's not so bad," she said with a flap of her hand.

"Now, now, don't be modest," he mock-scolded, wagging a finger and still nodding, and she found herself nodding along with him. "You must work very hard at it!"

"Well...sometimes," she reluctantly agreed. It would have felt strange to argue while nodding her head.

"Of course you do! Now, Miss Chase, what if I could tell you a way you could save *half* that cleaning time—*or more*—every week! Wouldn't that be worth your time to hear about?"

Mildred paused before answering, that stubborn lump forming again in her throat. He hadn't been complimenting her or the house, not really; it had all been a setup, just like it always was with these people, a way to ensnare her further in their sticky webs.

Yet still her mouth opened, as though her body was no more than a puppet whose strings could be pulled by whoever happened along, and she said, "Yes, of course I would." And, most sickening of all, she sounded *sincere* when she said it, as though nothing would please her more than listening to whatever other lies and false flattery this man could heap on her.

Peters was absolutely beaming now, grinning like he'd just heard his numbers on the weekly lotto. Mildred thought if he smiled any harder his cheeks might tear down the sides like wet tissue paper.

"Great!" He held up the suitcase in his hand and tapped the metal side. "I have a little demonstration in here that I think you'll really enjoy! All I need is a tap I can use, so if you'll show me to the nearest sink, we can get started!"

Mildred gestured numbly to the kitchen door, inwardly annoyed that every one of this self-assured man's sentences ended with exclamation points. He turned and strolled through it like he owned the place, and she followed him like a humiliated and spirit-broken dog.

Why did she always do this when confronted by someone attempting to peddle to her? Franklin said it was because her will was weaker than the punch of a hundred-year-old man, and she never argued with the sentiment.

How could she, after all? Wasn't it her that ordered useless subscriptions to magazines they would never read from the man hawking them in the mall last week? Wasn't it her that gave the woman panhandling in the grocery store parking lot twenty whole dollars last month so that she could 'get home to her kids because her car ran out of gas?' Wasn't it her that, the year she and Franklin married, used their small jar of scrimped and saved emergency cash to purchase unneeded stainless steel cookware from a salesman very much like the one that was currently striding through her living room? Wasn't it her that somehow ended up with truckloads of bake sale goods, raffle tickets, discount cards, and oil change vouchers anytime some soul asked her to buy them?

Mildred didn't know if it was weak will or not, but something in her prevented her from saying no to any human being. She just didn't feel comfortable denying others. *It is rude*, that prim and proper Mildred—surely a remnant from her mother—always argued.

No matter how easy going they were when they asked, it always caused that lump in her throat and her body to get that controlled, puppet-on-a-string feeling, and afterward she felt horribly manipulated and used and deeply ashamed, as if she'd just been molested.

And worse yet, these people that made their livings with their silver tongues seemed to sense it. Like that fellow selling magazines in the mall. She had tried to sneak past him with the crowded flow of pedestrian traffic, keeping her eyes carefully turned away to the passing shop windows. But he had somehow picked out an easy mark, smelled the weak will in her the same way a wolf will smell out the lame sheep. He had singled her out from the herd and cornered her at a railing until five minutes later she had walked away with a receipt, a lighter pocketbook, and a slightly dazed expression.

Mildred followed Peters into the kitchen. The sink was straight ahead around a small island countertop in the middle of the room, and he headed toward it without hesitation. The small television on the counter to the right was playing some talk show, and he switched it off without asking. Then he turned to the other side of the sink where the game hens were all laid out on the cutting board, awaiting their stuffing and basting, and pushed them aside so that he could lay his silver suitcase on its side on her clean marble countertop.

She felt a tiny flare of anger ignite in her.

*Now, now*, that other Mildred scolded, *remember your manners!*

Peters opened his case and withdrew a large tube made of clear plastic and tightly packed with what looked like lots of black and white sand particles, oblivious of her seething anger. A rubber hose was attached to a nozzle at the bottom of this contraption, and another at the top with a black rubber cup at the other end. This he hooked to her faucet and then turned on the water, allowing it to run into the tube, filter through the sand particles, and out of the hose at the bottom, which he let drain into the sink.

"Do you know what this is, Miss Chase?" he asked, in comically seductive tones.

"No."

"This is a smaller model of the system we sell for your home! We call it the Li'l Water Buddy! It's going to help me demonstrate for you how a water filtration system for your home could save you money, save you time, and keep you, your clothes, and your house looking better than ever before!"

"Sounds...great," she choked out.

"All right then!  Let's get started!"


Peters had either forgotten his promise or lied to her outright, because he did not 'take up as little of her time as possible.'

In fact, he was still talking nearly an *hour-and-a-half* later.

He had demonstrated the difference between the water that came from her tap and the water that was filtered by his portable system by swirling soap in two chemistry beakers to show which one bubbled more, by rinsing two of her glasses and showing which one left more water spots, by showing her the sediment that settled out of both types of liquid. One of the last tests had been to soap both her hands and rinse each with a different water to show the 'silky, smooth feeling' she got with the treated, and even though it had left her palm as slimy as if she had cooking grease on it, she had smiled and nodded right along with him and agreed that yes, this hand definitely felt better moisturized. During and between each of these examples, which he performed with the flair of a magician, he had made charts and graphs showing her the money she would be saving, harangued on the myths perpetuated by greedy soap companies, and disgusted her with tales of worst case scenarios until her head buzzed and she wondered if she was being pitched a product or brainwashed into a cult.

The game hens stared at her forlornly from the kitchen counter. They would never be ready on time. Franklin would be so mad. She simmered inside, angry at herself, angry at Peters, nearly bursting with the urgency to get on with her life.

And yet she could not just tell this man—this stranger, that she had never met before and would never see again—to just *leave*.

For *what?*

*What was she scared would happen if she just told him no?*

*It just…wouldn't be polite*, the Mildred upstairs answered lamely.

Peters, at last, seemed to be losing steam. He took a deep breath and said, "Okay, Miss Chase. I've shown you a thousand ways this system could help you out, and I can tell you've been impressed. So let's just lay it out on the line. I'm going to throw out a figure, and see where we go from there. What if I told you that I could get you the basic system, the chlorinator, and replace every shower and tap in this home with the inside filtration system…all for the low price of just twelve hundred dollars?"

Mildred had to stifle a brief squawk of panicked laughter.

Peters stared at her, eyes round, huge smile frozen in place, awaiting an answer.

"I…I don't know…" she mumbled. "I would…have to consult my husband…"

This seemed to encourage Peters rather than put him off. "Ma'am, once you tell him what you saw here today, he'll kiss you for making such an informed decision! And just for doing business with us here today…I'm going to give you a year's supply of absolutely free soaps and detergents! Now that's an offer that's going to save him money in the long run, and, trust me, that's what the husbands really care about!"

That lump was so large in her throat, blocking any answer she could possibly make. No, scratch that; blocking any *negative* answer. Her stomach churned. She was so confused and frustrated she felt like she might burst into tears.

"I...I..."

"C'mon Miss Chase," Peters said, with his infuriating smile, "how can you be having second thoughts about this?"

Second thoughts? She'd never even had *first* thoughts. How was she going to get out of this? How? *How?* The panic was nearly paralyzing.

"We have financing," Peters said, still pushing, moving closer to her around the island in the middle of the kitchen. He seemed to be growing larger in her mind, stretching to gigantic proportions. "And if need be, we can work with the package. And remember, it has a life time warranty and money back guarantee, so how can you go wrong—?"

"NO!" she shrieked suddenly. For the briefest of seconds, Peters looked unsure, his smile ratcheting a few notches looser. Her hand flew to the island countertop in front of her, where the carving knife she'd been using on the game hens lay. It was in her hand before she realized it, and she raised it above her head as she again screamed, "NOOOOOO!"

She brought it whistling downward, burying it in the middle of the salesman's chest. The action was so quick that Peters never raised so much as a finger to defend himself. He bent his neck to stare curiously down at the hilt of the knife jutting from his chest and her hand still on it.

Her heart thundered, her vision tunneled. The only fact she was conscious of was that somehow, blessedly, *miraculously*, he had stopped pressing her, stopped badgering her, and then some cold, alien, reptilian part of her spoke up, insisting that he would keep trying if she didn't finish the job, that his unrelenting spiel would go on even with a knife in him. There was another bloom of panic in her chest, fueling the rage as swiftly as gasoline on a fire.

Mildred pulled the blade back out and plunged it in again

and again and again, punctuating each stab with another negation.

"No, I *don't* want it, I *don't* want to buy it…!"

Peters withstood three or four of these jabs before stumbling back against the counter behind him.

"…I *don't* want to own it, I *don't* want to see it…!"

The strength left his legs and he slid into the floor and Mildred rode him all the way down, continuing to stab him viciously in the chest.

"I *don't* want, I *don't*, I don't I DON'T *I DON'T IDOOOOOOOONNNNN'T!!!!!*"

She stood up, panting, beads of sweat and blood plastering her blouse to her skin and her bangs across her forehead. The fit passed. She blinked rapidly down at the form in front of her.

Peters lay on his side in her kitchen floor, the knife a flag in his chest. The front of his dress shirt was utterly shredded, and the skin beneath looked like a poorly cut side of very raw beef. Blood, unbelievably bright red, had darkened the shirt and was pouring out to puddle on her otherwise sparkling linoleum.

His eyes were blank, empty, devoid of emotion or expression…but somehow that too-wide smile remained stretched across his gawky face.

Amazingly, she began to giggle.

"Well, Mill, you did it," she said aloud. The titters became hysterical giggles. "You finally found a foolproof way of stopping even the most determined salesman, and boy is it a DOOZY!"

She lost control of herself for the second time, retreating across the room as she lapsed into shrieking peels of gutbusting laughter.

It was a full five minutes before her screeches of amusement were replaced by profuse sobs. Her nose was running, and her sides ached as though she had just run a ten mile marathon in as many minutes.

When she thought she could take it, she eased to the edge of the island and peeked over the side.

For a split second she thought—no *knew*—that nothing would be there, that this would all turn out to be some sort of fevered hallucination. But Mr. Ted Peters of RainSilk Inc. was still very much dead in the floor of her kitchen, wearing a grin that would have made the Cheshire cat envious.

It was like the punchline of some old joke she couldn't quite remember, something that surely started with, 'How many dead salesman does it take to—?' or, better yet, 'How do you know when a salesman's overstayed his welcome—?'

She felt the laughter wanting to come again and bit down. It was time to be practical, time to figure out what to do.

*I can help with that*, the frigid, foreign voice in her head said.

*Don't listen to her!* the voice of proper Mildred argued, no longer sounding in control. No, little Miss Priss sounded shrill and hysterical…and desperate. *She's the one that caused this whole mess!*

*And* she's *the weak will that made you a prisoner to people like him your whole life. If you want me to go, I'll go, but don't kid yourself about which of us set you free.*

Mildred realized that she *did* feel free. As bad as her current situation was, she much preferred it to being trapped by the salesman's insistent diatribe. Thanks to this voice, she could think and feel and breathe again.

She felt wonderful.

*What do you want me to do?* she asked.

*You already know*, it purred.

And she found that she did.

The dinner party was a rousing success, complete with heartfelt praise from all in attendance for her delicious roasted game hen. Everyone enjoyed themselves so much that it was hardly even a bother when the two officers came around, asking if anyone who lived at the residence had been home all day.

Mildred, the gracious hostess, confirmed that she had, and that yes, she had seen the gangly, grinning salesman whose car was parked two streets over where he had left it while he canvassed the neighborhood, but she had turned him away at the door because she simply didn't have time to listen to a sales pitch.

Franklin was amazed at the changes in her over the next few weeks. She was able to repel high pressure sales clerks with the greatest of ease when they went out shopping, and even told one gentleman flat out that she wasn't interested in his shoddy merchandise.

"What happened, that weak will of yours go on vacation?" he asked.

"No," she said thoughtfully. "I think it's more permanent than that."

It was this newfound confidence that caused her not to hesitate a few months later when again the doorbell rang in the middle of the afternoon. This time Mildred found a school girl dressed in green and khaki on her doorstep, her hands full of boxes of fudge mints and peanut butter ripples.

"Buy some cookies to help out the Girl Scouts?" she pleaded, with the air of one who was used to getting what they wanted. "We need the money to continue our community services."

Mildred stepped closer to the doorway, glancing quickly left and right along the empty street.

"Come in," she invited, with a large grin that seemed to scare the girl a little. The girl stepped inside, her enthusiasm drying up but determined not to shy away from a sale. "Oh, silly me, I'll need to get my purse. Come this way, dear."

Mildred led the girl into the kitchen.

# Notes

## OUTSIDE THE LINES

So many of the stories in this collection were inspired by various newspaper or magazine articles. The original seed of this one came from one about an actual officer standing in line at the bank when the person in front of him robbed the teller. I had no idea when I started writing that it would be so heavily Dark Filament influenced. This is, in many ways, the most extensive peek I've ever given for my plans, a sort of behind-the-scenes look at how the Incarnates stage a dimensional invasion. As we've seen, the world of *Race the Night* is a universe—perhaps our own—that is already undergoing such a coup. When the first book of the *Dark Filament Ephemeris* releases, you'll see what the aftermath looks like. And, of course, the character of Edward Manners first appeared in my short story "Dr. Barnabas and the Legend of the Dark Stranger," which is available in my first collection, *Howling Days*. We'll be seeing more of his professor friends, and learn about the magic they wield.

## MY BOY

I love zombie stories, but I think we're reached a point of cultural saturation, where we're just seeing the same story arcs played out again and again with different characters plugged into the same stereotypes. The only good zombie tales left are the ones where a completely different plot is set against the backdrop of the undead. Here, I actually wanted to write a surprise zombie story, where the reader wouldn't see them coming until it was too late.

## THAT OLD RUGGED CROSS

This is one of two stories about salesmen in this volume. Credit for this one must be given entirely to my father. He sold Bibles door-to-door in college, and several of these tales and set-ups really happened to him. The rest is a very loosely related Cthulhu mythos story, with a final line that came to me one day while staring up at a church cross.

## IN THE PASSING LANE

I honestly don't know what to say about this one. I was on this kick where I wanted to write stories with unexpected monsters. This was the best of the pack, although I could never do much with it. As an added bit of trivia, I always imagined the monster in this one as sort of a nod to the Violator from the Spawn comics.

## DARK WORLD

I'm very fond of this one, even more so now that I have a daughter of my own. Harold is such a good guy caught up in an awful situation, but I love how his child always comes first. When I started writing it, I didn't know what Dark World would be. But as I explored this couples' life together, I realized there was something amiss between them. It took several drafts before I realized that this problem and Harold's nocturnal world of terror might be one and the same.

## I COMMAND

I was in college when drone technology came into use, and there was much debate about its ethics and the future of warfare. I just wanted to write a story playing on those fears with a twist ending. I had several sci-fi mags interested in it at one time, but then the (horrible) movie *Stealth* came out and essentially told the same story, times eleven.

## A GOOD REASON

Man, the origin of this story is just a Frankenstein of different parts. The premise came from an article saying that, if your car broke down, it was much safer to get out and get away, but I started thinking how terrifying that could be. I also wanted to write a series of modern day fairy tales, which is where you get the Red Riding Hood angle. But the character in this...at the time, I worked with a woman that pretty much *was* this character, through and through. She was manic depressive, possibly schizophrenic, talked to herself a lot, and was always dating these married men and agonizing over why they didn't want to be with her. And every phrase that the woman in this story uses came directly from her. I might not have included it in this volume, but while putting the collection together, it came to light that this is my wife's favorite story. And the editor that you sleep with always has final cut.

## TALENT SCOUT

The internet is just an amazing place sometimes. I wrote this after finding out that there really is a website where local bands can find free places to crash after a gig. A confession: I like Limp Bizkit, and originally listed Fred Durst with the others, but my good friend Andy told me the guy just isn't fit to be mentioned in the same class as these legends. He was probably right.

## KILLING TIME

A science fiction story inspired by a *Time* article about how the universe might possible wind down one day, all the stars going dark, and that the only thing that would be around to see it would be whatever mechanical life we had created. *Wall-E* touched upon this same idea when it came out a few years later. But it also plays upon one of my biggest fears: boredom. I am absolutely *terrified* of being bored. Every time I watch a movie where someone is tied up or locked in a car trunk, the first thing that goes through my head is how terrible that endless boredom would be. If I'm ever kidnapped, I intend to plead with my assailants to just give me a magazine or a book, and I'll cooperate fully. If you've ever read the Stephen King short story "The Jaunt," just know that it scarred me for life.

# WEAK WILL

Once upon a time, I was out of work, and could only find sales jobs. But, unlike my father, I am *not* a born salesman. I loathed the work, and came to believe that everyone hates a salesman who just pops up out of nowhere to ruin their day. The first job I took was selling Texas Ranger baseball tickets door-to-door in small communities that barely had money to eat, let alone for entertainment. When that wore thin, I took a job selling water filtration systems, just like the man in this piece. The training lasted a week, during which you were required to memorize a forty-five minute long presentation that was really more magic show, filled with all sorts of tests to prove to customers how awful their water quality was. Appointments were set for us, with the prospective buyer being told that they would get a free trip voucher if they just sat through the presentation. After two weeks of driving to the ass-end of nowhere to have bored people stare at me for an hour of my life and then hold out their hand for the voucher, I dropped the equipment off in front of the company's door in the dead of night and never looked back.

Like this novel?


YOUR REVIEWS HELP!


In the modern world, customer reviews are essential for any product. The artists who create the work you enjoy need your help growing their audience. Please visit Goodreads or the website of the company that sold you this novel to leave a review, or even just a star rating. Posting about the book on social media is also appreciated.

# About the Author

Russell C. Connor has been writing horror since the age of five, and is the author of two short story collections, five eNovellas, and fourteen novels. His books have won two Independent Publisher Awards and a Readers' Favorite Award. He has been a member of the DFW Writers' Workshop since 2006, and served as president for two years. He lives in Fort Worth, Texas with his rabid dog, demented film collection, mistress of the dark, and demonspawn daughter.

His next novel—*The Halls of Moambati*, Volume IV of *The Dark Filament Ephemeris*—will be available in 2021.

www.ingramcontent.com/pod-product-compliance
Lightning Source LLC
Chambersburg PA
CBHW021059110726
47900CB00007B/1948